MW01135146

The Ruins 4

A Dystopian Society in a Post-Apocalyptic World

Book 4 of The Ruins Series
By
T.W. Piperbrook

T.W. Piperbrook

www.twpiperbrook.com
www.facebook.com/twpiperbrook

Cover Design and Layout

Alex Saskalidis, a.k.a. 187designz

Editing & Proofreading

Cathy Moeschet

Print Formatting

Streetlight Graphics

Technical Consultants

John Cummings

Charles A.

Preface

Welcome to the last installment of THE RUINS.

You've reached the end—the culmination of 300,000 words, and four books that are some of the most enjoyable I've written. Thank you so much for sticking with the series.

Watching Bray, Kirby, and William grow and bond has been just as fun as creating new worlds for them to explore.

Bray has come a long way from the lone, demon-slaying Warden outside of Brighton. Kirby has pulled us neck-deep into her struggle between past and future, and William has grown from a young, scared boy in Brighton into an endearing, capable individual.

Sometimes the best meetings come from chance. Although these three characters met by "accident" in THE LAST SURVIVORS, I am happy they did, if only so they could bring us along for the ride.

As I mention in the Afterword, I have several projects I'm excited to write next. Hopefully, you will consider joining me.

But first: the final book of THE RUINS.

Trapped in a tower under the oppressive rule of The Gifted, William fears for his friends' lives. Bray and Kirby cope with the loss of Cullen, amidst the uncaring fists of the guards.

What is the price of freedom? And will anyone get out of New City alive?

We will find out.

-Tyler Piperbrook

January 2018

THE RUINS Background: Pertinent Recap of The Last Survivors

Three hundred years after the fall of society, the last fragments of civilization are clinging to life, living in the ruins of the ancient cities in nearly-medieval conditions. Technology has been reduced to legend, monsters roam the forests, and fear reigns supreme. Wind-borne spores disfigure men unlucky enough to be infected, twisting their minds and turning them into creatures to be feared. The survivors have different names for these creatures, but some call them the demons, or twisted men.

After accidentally killing the mother of an infected boy, a Warden named Bray—a hunter of demons—vows to keep the motherless boy safe. He loses track of the boy, William, in the Ancient City, only to watch as the boy takes up with a band of demons, succumbing to the spore's madness. Before Bray can rescue William, a violent army captures the boy.

While tracking William, Bray encounters a woman named Kirby from a strange settlement, who carries several pieces of Tech Magic he's never seen—guns.

Telling some clever lies, Bray gets Kirby to join him, under the guise that William is his son.

They track the army to Brighton.

After surviving a bloody battle, in which Bray is shot and wounded, Kirby reveals to Bray that she is also infected. She also reveals that she has figured out some of Bray's lies, but she respects his bravery and his allegiance to William.

Eventually, they rescue an emotionally battered William, who has taken revenge on the worst of his abductors by commanding a pack of demons to kill them.

William swears off his demon brothers, and the three make a pact to leave Brighton for good, in the hopes of discovering what lies in the ruins.

THE RUINS Book 1 Recap

Bray, Kirby, and William return to Kirby's settlement, New Hope, in hopes of securing the rest of Kirby's stash of guns, only to find the settlement raided. After an altercation with two men with strange markings, Kirby rescues a survivor named Flora, who is from a settlement she has never seen. Flora explains that the pillaging men are from an enemy tribe called Halifax. She does not tell them that she was supposed to bring back the scalp of a Halifax man to her people, in order to be considered for marriage.

After William takes ill, Flora lures them back to her settlement — a pair of islands in a wide river, accessed by a single, sloping road leading down from the bridge — in the hopes that she can exchange the guns, and information about William's power, to make up for her failed quest.

Bray, Kirby, and William are welcomed into The Arches, where Jonathan and Bartholomew, the bridge commanders, set them up with a place to rest. Bartholomew and Jonathan say they will introduce them to the islands' ruler, Deacon, when he returns from a hunt.

Bray meets a neighbor named Jaydra, who makes him suspicious about the islands. She explains that the oldest islanders — The Important Ones — are protected on the second island. She also mentions that everyone is expected to work and provide for the community.

Bray, Kirby, and William meet Deacon.

On the surface, Deacon appears helpful, though he is obviously interested in their guns. Deacon devises a plan to watch over Kirby, Bray, and William so he can decide how to access Kirby's guns, and William's power over the demons. He discusses the possibility of an impending war with Halifax with a man named Jonas, one of his closest advisors. Jonas, a man with an affinity for ancient devices, and an even greater affinity for creating devices of torture, uses these devices on several Halifax men he and Deacon have captured.

Flora, hoping to make up for her failed quest and preserve her life, offers Bray's scalp to Deacon, if Deacon deems him a hindrance to the use of the god weapons, and accessing William's power. She also agrees to keep a close watch on Bray, Kirby, and William.

Bray decides to go hunting with several of the islanders, to earn his keep and provide food for Kirby and a sick William. While on the hunt, he proves his worth as a hunter and fighter, but fails to kill a deer, which Wardens believe is bad luck, but which angers the island hunters.

Back on the island, William grows sicker while Kirby worries. Flora and Jaydra talk to Bartholomew, who agrees to house William on the second island. While riding to the island, Kirby and William are surprised by a group of soldiers.

Bray returns from the hunt to find a strange ceremony occurring on the bridge in the middle of a fog. Deacon presides over an excited crowd as a woman is thrown to her death off the bridge—a woman that Bray fears is Kirby.

THE RUINS Book 2 Recap

Suspecting Kirby has been thrown from the bridge at The Arches, Bray causes a small scene. The hunters calm him, assuring him that Kirby and William are all right. Bray hunts for his friends on the first island. While searching, he is attacked by a group of guards, led by Bartholomew and Jonathan, and left for dead in the river. Bartholomew sends Flora to bring Bray's scalp back to Deacon.

On the second island, Kirby looks after a sick William. She encounters the strange man named Jonas, who uses a ploy to separate her from William. Deacon kidnaps William while Kirby is distracted. Deacon, Jonas, and some guards confront Kirby, demanding more guns in exchange for William's life. Kirby tells them there may be more weapons in her settlement. Deacon forces her to return to New Hope with a small party consisting of Jonas, Ruben, and Heinrich, with the intention of meeting with a larger group, in order to obtain guns and exchange them for William's life.

At the Halifax settlement, the Halifax people gain experience with firearms.

Bray climbs from the river, beaten and bruised. He fears Kirby and William are dead. Before he can make a decision to rescue them, Flora tracks him down and attacks. A bloody battle ensues as she tries to get his scalp. The altercation ends when Halifax soldiers surround them with guns, forcing them to march back to Halifax.

While traveling to New Hope, Kirby, Jonas, Ruben, and Heinrich discover the larger party of islanders with whom they were supposed to meet, dead at the hands of Halifax soldiers. A survivor of that massacre reaches The Arches, warning Deacon of the escalating violence. Fearing war, Deacon sends scouts to Halifax to find out what is going on.

William, trapped on the second island, tries to escape his squalid prison.

Bray meets Enoch, the leader of Halifax, who shares a mutual hatred for the people of The Arches. According to Enoch, the people of The Arches stole their land and have practiced cruelty for generations. The Halifax people interrogate Flora without success. Convincing Enoch to let him speak with her, Bray makes some headway, discovering Flora's anger toward Deacon due to the death of her father. He convinces Flora to work with them, and tries convincing Enoch they can work together to defeat the islanders. Enoch is not certain.

In the wild, more Halifax soldiers attack Kirby, Jonas, Heinrich, and Ruben. They kill Heinrich and Ruben, and severely wound Jonas. Kirby and Jonas hole up in a small building, staving off the Halifax men with Kirby's grenades.

Back in Halifax, Enoch and Bray receive word of a strange, trapped woman with incredible weapons. They march out to discover Kirby. Bray and Kirby reunite, returning to Halifax with Enoch. They finally convince Enoch to go to battle, after Enoch hears tales from Jonas about the torture he has committed against the people of Halifax. In a bloody ceremony, the Halifax people take retribution on Jonas.

Deacon's scouts, hiding close to Halifax, hear the ceremony and make the educated guess that war is coming. They inform Deacon so he can prepare.

Bray, Kirby, Flora, and three hundred Halifax soldiers return to The Arches, engaging in a savage battle. By the battle's end, Flora, Deacon, and Enoch are killed, while the remaining Halifax people—under the direction of the Halifax soldier Samron—reclaim the islands. William escapes his prison and reunites with Bray and Kirby.

Bray, Kirby, and William ride south on their horses, on the slim hope they will find a place where the Ancient's Tech Magic has been preserved, a place where they will be safe.

THE RUINS Book 3 Recap

After months of travel, Bray, Kirby, and William arrive in a hot southern region. Since leaving The Arches, William's warts have spread to the side of his head, making Bray and Kirby suspect — or at least hope — that he might be like one of the smart demons they encountered near Brighton: Jingo. Meanwhile, Bray and Kirby have developed a physical and emotional relationship.

Reaching a new ruined city, Bray, Kirby, and William discover a lone, dirty man named Cullen, hiding in some underground tunnels that Kirby explains are called subways. Together, they escape a pack of savage men they call The Clickers, but not before Bray is wounded by an arrow. Cullen tells them that The Clickers killed his brothers and left him alone and hiding.

Heading for safety, the group arrives at a strange, fascinating place with windmills and a large tower, situated at the forefront of a city with walls coming out from the building's sides, surrounding the city. Rows of rich crops lie in front of it. As the group gets close, demons surround them. Several strange, robed men appear on a balcony on the building, removing their hoods and revealing that they are smart demons, like Jingo. They are fascinated by William's similar appearance. Thinking of a clever lie to go along with the smart demons' inquiries, Bray says he and his friends are emissaries coming to trade. The smart demons — who call themselves The Gifted — invite Bray, Kirby, William, and Cullen in.

The Clickers continue tracking Bray and his friends.

Bray, Kirby, William, and Cullen meet a Gifted man named Rudyard, who instructs them to leave their weapons at the door. Rudyard takes them upstairs and introduces them to The Gifted's leader — a man named Tolstoy — as well as a woman named Amelia, and seven other robed men. The Gifted not only have rudimentary electricity, but also other devices of Tech Magic, as well as incredible knowledge. The Gifted tell the story of "The Collapse" three hundred years earlier, caused by a mutated spore. Most of the infected became demons, but a rare few turn into people like The Gifted, who are smarter, and cannot die from age. The Gifted believe William might be one of them. Gesturing out the window, Tolstoy shows Bray, Kirby, William, and Cullen a city filled with uninfected humans — a place they call New City.

While staying in the tower, Kirby and Bray wake up one morning to discover The Clickers outside the tower window, engaging in a trade with Rudyard for a tattered man. Kirby makes the astute guess that the people in New City are human slaves. Before they can escape, The Gifted see through Bray's earlier lie, enslave Bray, Kirby, and Cullen, and force William into the tower as their protégé.

Bray, Kirby, and Cullen are beaten and thrown into cells by Head Guards — uninfected humans who help control the city, led by two guards named Ollie and Avery. A man named Drew, a slave in New City who is from Kirby's former settlement of New Hope, speaks to her through the cell wall. He tells her that he and some others are planning an escape.

Meanwhile, William decides to play along with The Gifted, in hopes that he can save his friends. The female Gifted — Amelia — starts teaching him to read and write.

After being released, Bray, Kirby, and Cullen are put to work as Field Hands and assigned houses. Bray meets his roommate Teddy, while Kirby meets Esmeralda and her daughter Fiona. They learn that Rudyard and the Head Guards control the demon army, which are fed in a Feeding Pen inside New City. They also learn that The Gifteds' machines produce items for trade, and sustain the population. Cullen struggles to perform his duties, while the brutish guard named Ollie targets Kirby.

In the tower, Tolstoy and Amelia meet to ensure William is cooperating. Acting out a plan, William steals a hairpin from Amelia, giving him access to the tower. He sneaks out at night, down to a floor he knows is empty — the third floor — watching the demons and the city from a balcony. Unable to concoct an immediate way to help his friends, he returns to his room.

While lining up with the other Field Hands in the cornfields, Cullen sees The Clickers trading with Rudyard. Traumatized and mentally unstable, he makes the unwise decision to flee. Bray tries to pull him back into line, but guards catch them. Bray and Cullen are assigned to clean the Feeding Pen as a punishment.

In the tower, Amelia shows William an ancient relic — an old, empty gun called an 1860 Model Colt Army — that William thinks might be a warning. Soon after, he receives a surprise visit in his room from Amelia, who takes him to the third-floor balcony, where Tolstoy and the rest of The Gifted wait. They force him to watch the guards beat Bray and Cullen in the Feeding Pen in the city. The guards drag Bray out into the courtyard, but Cullen is left inside the pen, where he is consumed by demons.

Tolstoy warns William to cooperate, or his other friends are next.

Chapter 1: Bray

"What's going on?"

Commotion ripped Bray's attention from the door of his small house and into the courtyard of New City.

A swell of noise greater than he was used to hearing swept through the air as slaves emerged from houses and alleys, moving quickly toward the wide, dirt area with the bonfires, talking in animated tones, speaking more loudly than they would have dared in the fields, the Shucking Rooms, or in the shops on the city's eastern side. Bray stared out the threshold, peering out into a morning that was already sweltering from the heat. He couldn't see past the torrent of moving people. Teddy held a look of nervous confusion on his face as he abandoned his breakfast and went to Bray's side.

"I would stay here," Teddy warned, in the same cautious tone he always held when something bad was about to take place. "We're probably better off not knowing."

Bray watched people pour past, creating a wall of bodies in the middle of the courtyard. Most glanced over their shoulders toward one of the paths, chatting nervously. An irrepressible fear took hold of Bray as he looked for Kirby. She had been safe this morning.

But that didn't mean she was safe now.

Weeks after losing Cullen to the mob of bloodthirsty demons, Bray could still hear his friend's cries. Cullen's horrified screams had invaded every squalid home, striking fear in the heart of every slave, even those who hadn't lived close to the Feeding Pen. Cullen's corpse had barely resembled a human's when the guards pulled it through the gate. Bits of flesh clung to his tattered, gnawed bones. Cullen's face was gone.

The Head Guards had paraded his corpse through the streets in a wagon, making sure every slave in every open doorway saw him as they wheeled him to one of the Glass Houses, where he was hastily cremated. No one was allowed to say goodbye — certainly not Bray or Kirby.

That corpse was a warning to any who dared defying the Head Guards, or The Gifted.

Bray stretched his stiff limbs. The wounds he received that day had mostly healed, but each yellow and purple blemish on his skin reminded him of the death he'd escaped.

Was Kirby next?

Unable to suppress a growing fear, Bray told Teddy, "I'll be back."

Teddy shouted out another warning, but Bray had already left the threshold, stepping away from the house and joining the growing crowd in the courtyard. Looking right and left, he noticed guards on the edges of the pathways, prodding some of the slower, gawking people. The slaves were anxious, but the guards were strangely eager. Bray followed the moving crowd until he'd reached the back row of what was quickly becoming a circle. Catching the eye of a dirty, skinny man, he asked, "What's happening?"

Wiping the remains of some breakfast from his face, the man said, "I'm not sure. They told us to gather around the bonfires. That's all I know."

Some cries drew Bray's attention to one of the alleys.

His pulse quickened.

Two Head Guards appeared down the pathway, tugging a shaggy-haired, kicking man. Behind them, more guards manhandled a taller, male slave. Bray tensed as he recognized two of the men from the fields, near whom he'd worked a few times. A few children raced away from the commotion, heeding their parents' warnings.

Reaching the edge of the circle, the guards pulled the men through the parting crowd and into the center of the courtyard.

Bray pushed into a crowd several layers deep. A few slaves grunted angrily. One or two gave him scared looks, afraid to cause a scene. Breaking through the mob, Bray took up between a freckled woman and a gaunt man, neither of who looked at him. Ollie and Avery stood in the middle of the open area in the courtyard, brandishing long knives as the guards dragged the wriggling men near them.

Seeing the weapon in Ollie's hands, the men whimpered.

Some children who had not run clung to their mother's skirts, or hid behind the men's legs as they waited for a pronouncement, or a scene they wouldn't soon forget. Bray's pulse pounded.

Ensuring he had the eye of every man, woman, and child around the courtyard, Ollie jabbed a fat, dirty finger at the captive slaves. "Thieves!" he shouted.

The captive men quivered.

"These men were caught stealing a loaf of bread from one of our guards, Roberto," Avery hollered, turning to the circling crowd. "They were brought here for punishment."

The shaggy-haired man wailed, "Let us go! Please!"

The audience shifted uncomfortably.

No one helped.

Of course, they couldn't.

Cocking his fat head to the side, Ollie said, "We all know thievery isn't tolerated in New City."

The other guards looked on in stern silence.

"Please!" the shaggy-haired man cried. "We didn't do anything wrong!"

Ollie's face creased in anger.

"Roberto saw you thieving," Avery cut in. "Do not lie."

Regret crossed the shaggy-haired man's face as he silenced. Ollie crept closer, holding his knife up to the scared man's throat.

With an obstinate bark, Ollie said, "Lie again, and I will cut your throat."

The shaggy-haired man's eyes grew wide.

Looking from the slaves to the crowd, Ollie projected his voice. "Roberto, why don't you tell the crowd what you saw, so everyone can learn the same lesson?"

Speaking loudly enough that even those in the back rows could hear, one of the bearded guards, evidently Roberto, stepped from the edges of the crowd and held up a loaf of bread. "My family was out back, doing laundry. When I returned from my duties, I found the tall slave guarding our doorway, while the other pulled our bread from inside. They waited until our door was unlocked to rob us."

The shaggy-haired man shook his head in denial as he saw and heard the damming evidence.

"I chased them through the alleys and tackled one of them," Roberto said. "Freddy and Ryan got the other." He motioned to a few other guards, who nodded sternly.

"You would risk your lives over some bread?" Avery asked.

A silence fell over the courtyard as everyone waited for an answer. Feeling the weight of the accusation, the tall man cleared his throat and spoke up. "We were hungry. We only received half our rations last week." He looked between Ollie, Avery, and the other Head Guards, avoiding Roberto's eyes. "When we asked Roberto, he said we wouldn't get any more until next week."

"A shortage," Roberto grunted, with a firm nod.

A few guards chuckled. None in the crowd laughed. Sensing no good would come from an argument, the tall man quieted.

Growing impatient, Roberto pointed at the tall slave and his shaggy-haired friend. "They are obviously thieves. Let's gut them."

"We're not going to gut them," Ollie told him.

"Throw them in the Feeding Pen, then," Roberto argued. "It will save us a few ears of corn."

"Ollie and I have another idea," Avery said, stepping forward and exchanging a knowing glance with Ollie. "We talked about it on the way. Perhaps a different sort of punishment is in order."

"What kind of punishment?" Roberto asked, growing impatient.

Avery said, "If they are as hungry as they say, we will allow them to prove it."

Recapturing the attention of the entire crowd, Ollie said, "They can have their bread. But they will have to fight for it."

"Fight?" Terror sparked in the shaggy-haired man's eyes and the tall man's mouth fell open.

A smile crossed Roberto's face as he caught the gist of the idea. "I like that. It might even be worth my loaf of bread."

Avery nodded, proud of his idea. Stepping forward, capturing the attention of the entire audience, he announced, "The only way out of this circle is through each other's blood. The two thieves will fight each other to the death for the food they stole. If either one tries escaping, they're feed for The Plagued Ones."

Stepping next to Avery, Ollie warned, "Anyone who tries helping them will join the loser in death."

Gasps filled the crowd. Children buried themselves further in their mother's skirts.

Returning his attention to the two men, Avery said, "When we release you, you will fight. Neither of you will leave until one of you dies."

Roberto dangled the bread higher, showing the crowd,

and then tossed it onto the ground near the captive slaves' feet. The bread rolled to a stop, covered in dirt. Horror crossed the slave's faces as they realized the finality of their sentence.

Forcing defiance through his fear, the tall man stuck out his chin and said, "I will not fight. You will have to feed me to The Plagued Ones first."

Avery's eyes narrowed in anger as he heard a retort he wasn't used to. "You will fight him, or we will torture you both. He will die first, so you can watch."

The tall man opened and closed his mouth, stuck between horrific choices. "I will allow him to win, then."

"If I sense either of you are not fighting, Roberto will gut you both," Avery said, making a show of turning the long knife in his hand. "And then no man will keep his life."

"Neither matters much to us," Ollie grunted. "In fact, we'd enjoy it if you didn't cooperate."

Tears rolled down the shaggy-haired man's face as he said, "Give us some other punishment. Anything. I will clean the Feeding Pen. I will forfeit my rations."

"Your families will already forfeit your rations for a week," Avery said, to the moans of a few scared, scraggly women who broke through the crowd, wailing their pleas.

"Let them go!" one of the women cried, reaching for the captive men in the middle.

"Shut up!" Ollie barked, forcing her to be silent.

"Please!" the shaggy-haired man cried. "Punish us, but not our families!"

"If you are strong enough to beg, you are strong enough to fight," Avery said matter-of-factly.

Without another word, Ollie and Avery walked to the edge of the circle, as if they were officials in a sack race, or a hay game. They signaled the guards, who let go of the prisoners. Slowly, the guards backed to where the nervous spectators watched.

Left alone, the two slaves stared at each other a moment. Neither traded angry words. Why would they? They were clearly friends who had conspired in a transgression. The shaggy-haired man smeared tears from his eyes.

Trembling, he told the tall man, "I will not fight you."

"Nor I you." The tall man looked from his unwilling opponent to the guards who had released him. Of course, their pleas were pointless.

Bray clenched his fists hopelessly, as if he might help. But everyone in the crowd heard the guards' warnings. They would die if they assisted. The wailing women pleaded to the guards, but the guards threatened them into silence.

A few of the slaves on the edge of the circle stepped forward, waiting expectantly, shifting from foot to foot.

The combatants stared at each other, not moving, not fighting.

"Give us a show, forest-dwellers!" yelled Roberto. "Spill each other's blood!"

"Fight!" yelled another guard.

A few women held their hands over their mouths. Reluctantly, the two slaves raised their fists.

"Get on with it!" a third guard yelled, losing his patience.

Ollie and Avery watched the petrified men in amusement.

Feeling the pressure of a horrific death, the tall man took a step toward his friend. He raised a fist.

"I'm sorry, Gabe," he said.

"I understand, Jonah," the other said. "We will do what we have to. The gods will know the truth."

The slaves on the edges of the circle looked on with growing anticipation.

One of them, an elderly man with long hair, was unable to control his nerves any longer. He took a risk and yelled to the tall man, "He is much smaller than you! Kill him and be done with it, so he doesn't suffer!"

A wrinkled crone, inspired by the first man's words, yelled, "Do it quickly!"

"*Fight, fight!*" the guards shouted, encouraging the crowd to participate.

The old man and the crone joined the chant. Bray looked around as a few more chimed in. A stringy-haired woman pumped her fist in the air. A middle-aged man cupped his mouth and shouted. Perhaps they yearned for an escape to the monotony of their lives. Or perhaps they wanted an end to the bloody spectacle that would plague their nightmares.

Among the chanters, Bray saw a few with twisted, bloodthirsty expressions.

The chant strengthened as all of the guards raised their voices, staring at the crowd and encouraging more participation.

"*Fight, fight!*"

Slowly, the chant rolled from the tongues of the guards to more slaves, until most in the front rows screamed along, driven by the shouts of their neighbors.

Bray swallowed as the chant grew louder and louder, echoing off the walls of the courtyard and the small houses.

The tall man—Jonah—swallowed a lump in his throat. He cocked back his fist, regret in his eyes.

"Kill him, you weak son of a bitch!" Roberto shrieked above everyone else, taking a taunting step.

Hearing those words, Jonah's face changed.

He turned.

He ran toward Roberto.

Roberto's mouth dropped as his taunt backfired and became a fight for his life. Jonah crossed the courtyard, threw his weight into a tackle, and knocked the surprised guard to the ground before he could draw his knife. Cocking back a fist, he punched Roberto. Blood sprayed from Roberto's face as Jonah broke his nose. More Head Guards ran to help, but Jonah had the advantage of pent-up rage, and surprise. He flung back his arms, cracking several of the other guards in the face, sending them flying before they could control him. Blood dripped from his swinging fists and he shrieked in rage.

The crowd's response grew louder.

Some cheered. Some hissed.

More than one cheered for Jonah.

People stepped forward as they saw a crack in the system that had contained them.

But that crack wouldn't last long.

"Pull him off!" Ollie shouted, anger taking over his face as he raced toward the spectacle, his blubbery stomach shaking.

More guards caught hold of Jonah's arms, flinging him off and stomping him. Jonah's hands flew up to protect his ribs and stomach, but a well-placed kick knocked one of his teeth from his mouth in a bloody spray. The guards gave him a few more stomps and kicks before Ollie intervened.

"Enough!" Ollie screamed. "Let him go!"

The Head Guards looked up in surprise. Roberto got to his feet, wiping stringy drool from his face.

"I want him dead," Roberto hissed, through a mouthful of blood as he pointed.

"And he will be," Ollie said confidently. "But I will gut his friend first."

The shaggy-haired man—Gabe—stood fearfully across the courtyard. His face paled. A merciless grin crossed Ollie's face as he took a menacing step.

"You will be tortured, because of what your friend has done," Ollie announced, making sure all in the crowd could hear, as he raised his knife. "Those are the rules. Your friend has opted not to fight."

"Please," Gabe said quietly, his voice quivering as he backed up against the crowd.

Ollie took another lumbering step.

"Give me another chance," Gabe pleaded.

"Jonah has made his choice for both of you. The fight is over," Ollie said.

"No, it's not."

With a primal scream, Gabe darted past Ollie and toward Jonah. Catching on to what was happening, the guards stepped back.

Still on the ground, Jonah flung up his arms, but not in time to deflect Gabe's vicious pounce. Gabe landed on top of Jonah, punching again and again, knocking through Jonah's defensive arms and striking his face.

Gabe's war cry grew louder.

He wasn't doing what the guards asked.

He was fighting for his life.

The crowd's chant resumed and more people stepped forward.

"Fight! Fight!"

The elderly man pumped his fist. The wrinkled crone clenched her hands. The bloodthirsty few cried louder than the rest, creating a wall of noise.

The guard's smirks grew wider.

Madness took over Gabe's face. It seemed as if the fight had cracked the last of his sanity. The wails of two hysterical, pleading women were lost underneath the chanting crowd as bones cracked and blood flew. With horror, Bray saw tears pouring down Gabe's face as he punched and punched, and Jonah's pleas turned to gurgles.

The gurgles ceased.

The crowd in the courtyard fell silent.

Gabe's flying fists stopped.

Looking around at the crowd and the guards, he found enough sanity to scream, "Is this what you wanted? You wanted him to die?"

Ollie looked from Avery to Roberto.

"I have done what you asked!" Gabe continued, weeping.

Ollie grunted. "So be it. You have earned your life."

Avery said, "Roberto, give him a beating to compensate for the bread he stole. Then send him to the cell."

Chapter 2: Bray

The crowd dispersed in a tangled, disorganized rush. Women herded children back through the alleyways. Sturdy men and women helped some of the elderly, who walked with their heads down, mumbling. Bray could see their remorse in their sagged shoulders, or in their eyes, as they scurried back to breakfasts they wouldn't eat. Most had stayed only long enough to watch Gabe dragged to the cell, but only because the guards ordered them. A few people— the men and women with bloodlust in their eyes — scurried away quicker than the others, ashamed of what they'd done. Long after the chants had faded, the majority of the slaves realized what the guards had known all along—the slaves were in no better position than Jonah, or Gabe. They lived their lives in slightly bigger cells than the one to which Gabe was dragged, waiting for the day they were pulled to the Glass Houses, like Jonah's body would be.

Bray had no interest in any of it.

He needed to find Kirby.

Moving against the flow of the crowd, he scanned the clustered, dirty faces. Seeing the battle made him desperate to verify that she was all right. For all he knew, she was in some hidden danger he couldn't see.

A few guards lingered at the mouth of the alleys, herding the slaves back to their homes. Some of them held the long, sharp knives they usually carried at their sides. Bray wanted to pull those knives from their hands and ram them into their bellies.

Hopefully someday soon.

Skirting around several groups of people who talked quietly as they walked, he found a scraggly, thin woman with long, dark hair. Bray opened his mouth and came toward her, before realizing it wasn't Kirby. The woman muttered something and went past. His nerves were almost unbearable when he spotted a person with a familiar gait, heading up of one of the pathways.

"Kirby!" he hissed, as loud as he dared.

"Bray!"

Kirby's face was skinnier than he remembered. Several weeks of enslavement had burned through what little fat they'd had. Bray couldn't remember the last time he had gotten a good look at her, when they didn't fear the guards. He had hoped things might get better.

Of course, they hadn't.

They suffered through rations that were never enough, sweated in fields that never got cooler, and worked for guards that had no sympathy. Their endless toil continued, as the summer approached its hottest days.

Kirby approached him with the same, sallow look that marked most of the slaves' faces. A wave of emotion he rarely allowed himself to feel rushed through him as they risked an embrace.

"Savages," Kirby whispered, wiping angry tears from her eyes. "Cruel, vicious savages."

Bray nodded, feeling a surge of hate that had never left since they'd been captured, cornered, and thrown into this life.

"We should walk and talk," Bray said quietly.

They turned and headed up the pathway, mixing with some other slaves. A few people spoke quietly, their faces downcast as they processed another loss of life. Others walked quickly with their heads down. From a distant alley,

Bray heard the long, mournful wails of the dead man's relatives. They passed a few guards before speaking more.

"Those men were killed for the sin of being hungry," Kirby spat. Anger and sadness blazed in her moist eyes. "I have watched too many die at the hands of one another, for the sake of another's pleasure."

Bray nodded. Kirby didn't need to speak of the atrocities she'd endured in her homeland for him to remember her stories. Kirby's days fighting in the arena still haunted her nights. More than once, she had awoken from some vivid nightmare, speaking names he didn't recognize.

"I do not know how much more I can take," Kirby said with a crack in her voice.

Bray looked over at her, recalling the talk they'd shared through the walls of the cell, when they'd first been dragged to New City. He'd promised her they would find a way out.

All they'd found was suffering and pain.

His promise to her felt as empty as the one he'd made William. Looking over his shoulder, he glanced at the shimmering building that rose high above New City. He hadn't seen William since that day Cullen had died, when William had screamed from the balcony. A part of Bray wondered if William had been a hallucination—a product of haze and pain. But William's desperate cries were unmistakable. William might not be toiling in a hot field, or working until his fingers ached, but he was living his own nightmare. He had escaped the battle of Brighton and the war at The Arches, only to be captured and enslaved regardless. William had witnessed Cullen's dying in even greater detail from his horrific perch.

For all he knew, William had seen this bloody fight, too.

Bray scanned up and down the building, but the balcony was empty, and the tinted glass prevented a better view.

Kirby forced composure through her anger. Somewhere

in the distance, another long, slow wail echoed through the crowded streets.

"We will make it out of this life," Bray promised. "I swear by the gods."

Chapter 3: William

William awoke with a start.

Long, resounding moans reached his ears.

Sweat trickled down the bumpy warts on his forehead as he sat up. For a moment, he thought he was still hearing his dream, but the noise came from outside his window. Wiping the perspiration away, he crossed the room — his fifteenth-floor prison — and pressed his face against the glass. It was hard to hear more than noises from up so high, and he certainly couldn't hear words.

But the commotion was real.

He scoured the small square buildings that filled New City. People moved in every direction, dispersing from something.

Whatever had happened was over.

Tangles of men, women, and children moved up the paths and into the dwellings. He couldn't tell guards from slaves.

A stabbing, nervous fear hit his stomach — the same feeling he had every time he thought of Bray and Kirby, rotting away in their cramped, dirty houses. Each time he looked at the dwellings below, he imagined cruel horrors behind every doorway — demons gnashing their filthy teeth, guards pummeling the slaves with merciless fists.

He wished he could verify that Bray and Kirby were all right.

He doubted he would ever have that security again.

Ever since Cullen's death, William had lived with a

lump in his throat, eating, learning, studying, and sleeping. He adhered to The Gifted's role, certain that another misstep would harm his friends. He cried when he was alone, underneath the covers, and in the dark. Even then, it felt like The Gifted watched him, monsters that ate, breathed, and studied without emotion. Their intelligence was a curse dragging them into madness.

Every time Amelia asked how he was feeling, William assured her he was fine, hoping she didn't see the truth behind his answer. He smiled when it was appropriate, laughed when he was supposed to, and nodded too often. Emotions were private, dangerous things.

He still wasn't sure what had given him away on that awful day, when Cullen had died.

Glancing over his shoulder, he stared at the dresser, underneath which was the hairpin. At one time, he was positive that Cullen had paid the price for his sneaky outing. But as more days passed, with no one coming to search his room, or reclaim the small piece of stolen metal, he had changed his theory. The Gifted must have seen through his placating conversations. They must have determined he was playing a role.

Perhaps they had no reason at all.

The Gifted were cruel, perverse beings, worse than the demon army they controlled, worse than any violent leader in Brighton. They might have intellect beyond any human, but they lived without conscience or remorse. William was nothing like them, and never wanted to be. They were the ancient evil that haunted his nightmares, lurked in every dark corner, and stalked him when he wasn't reading or studying among them. He'd never forget their emotionless, stern faces as they'd watched the demons chew Cullen's flesh. None had turned a sympathetic eye toward William, as he screamed for them to stop, and certainly not Cullen.

Even Amelia watched with a smug satisfaction.

One thing was certain; William wouldn't give them another excuse for their barbarity. He hadn't used the pin since his first outing, and he didn't plan on using it again.

Looking out the window, he envisioned his friends far below, living out the rest of their days. Perhaps the best hope he had for them was a protected life in New City, where they would always have food, if not enough. Perhaps the walls that barricaded the city sheltered them from the savage tribes that roamed the forests.

Perhaps in order to save them, he had to let them go.

Smearing a tear away from his eye, he looked out the window, watching the moving masses of people prepare for another day of unrelenting toil.

Chapter 4: Kirby

Kirby watched the men and women returning to their homes out the window of her small room. Only a handful spoke with one another. They hurried back to breakfasts most wouldn't be able to stomach, but they would eat, because they needed strength for the fields.

"Too many cruelties," Esmeralda said, spoon-feeding Fiona some cornmeal.

Kirby nodded, unable to put her emotion into words.

"With so many things happening each day, it is easy to forget some of them," Esmeralda said. "But this game was worse than many others. The guards are getting crueler as time goes on."

Kirby nodded as she forced down a bite. Too many things had become routine: sleeping, working, eating, and suffering. Seeing the fight this afternoon had brought some of the grisly details of her homeland back to her memory — things she tried to forget.

She couldn't dismiss the smell of blood, the rabid cries of the crowd, and the fueling screams of the guards. She recalled Gabe's face as he spun to face the guards, his cheeks smeared with his friend's blood and his tears. All of those things were horrible reminders of the arena, back in her homeland. Too many times, Kirby had been that winner, facing a crowd who would just as soon cheer for her blood as her opponent's.

"Some of the people regret their part in what happened,"

Esmeralda said, as she watched some quiet people pass. "But it will not bring back the man who died."

"And it will not stop it from happening again," Kirby said, bitterly.

"You talk as if that is a certainty," Esmeralda said.

"I have been here long enough to know that it is," Kirby said. "Some people will mourn, while others will justify their part in the horrid spectacle. Soon, they will move on, when some fresh, new atrocity occurs."

Esmeralda nodded sympathetically. "It sounds as if it wasn't any better where you are from."

Keeping to the same story she had told The Gifted, pretending she was from Brighton, Kirby said, "They weren't any better."

Esmeralda sighed as she scraped the last of the cornmeal from the bowl. "We hear whispers of cities and townships in the forests." She looked past Kirby and to the doorway, keeping her voice low. "They are pleasant to dream about, but it sounds as if they are fool's legends."

"I sometimes forget you have never been outside New City," Kirby remembered.

"The guards tell us the trees are a place of danger." Esmeralda shrugged. "They say we wouldn't last a day there."

Kirby furrowed her brow. "Have you ever been among the trees?"

"No," Esmeralda said, a wistful look crossing her face. "The closest I have been is the crop fields."

Kirby's reflection became an angry sadness as she realized she might never set foot in the trees again. "The forests can be dangerous," she said, "but they can be beautiful, too."

"A lot of our people were born here, as you know," Esmeralda said. "Some come from the forests, like you, but they do not speak of them. Speaking of such things is dangerous."

Kirby nodded. She had learned. She avoided conversation and did her work. She avoided death, barely.

"I used to dream about the forests, and the creatures I have not seen," Esmeralda said. "I dreamt of places where you could fill your stomach without rationing every bite. I dreamt of better places for Fiona."

Watching a guard walk by, Kirby carefully said, "Even in the forest, you have to work for your food."

Spooning Fiona another bite of cornmeal, Esmeralda said, "At least what happened this morning is done, and we are alive."

Kirby nodded. That was true, but the day was just beginning.

**

Kirby walked with the line of slaves out of the courtyard, through the gates leading to the crop fields, and past Rudyard. After a few weeks in New City, he'd given up his gloating. Now, he treated her as another slave, chastising her when it suited him, or ignoring her when he wanted. She was no different than any of the other humans: a child's plaything, here to do his bidding and his work. Avery had lost interest, as well.

Not so with Ollie.

Every so often, something would spark in Ollie's eyes as he watched Kirby work. He often lingered at the end of her row, staring at her as she pulled the corn from the stalks, mostly when the sun was hot enough to dampen her shirt. Hoping to sway his attention, she focused on her work until he went away.

Passing Ollie today, she felt his salacious gaze. Kirby would like to poke his eyes out with the sharp end of a corn cob. But that was as likely to happen as escape.

Not until she was past the guards did she risk a glance

behind her, finding Bray. He was farther back in the line, veering off with his wagon.

Kirby chose a row, pulling her wagon over the bumpy soil. A few mutants skittered away, weaving through the stalks after a small animal. Quelling the nervousness she always felt around the ugly beasts, she picked a spot free of other workers or mutants.

Kirby set down her wagon handle, reaching for an ear of corn.

She pulled it from the stalk and tossed it in her receptacle.

In the distance, the guards boisterously relived the fight.

After a while, she noticed a figure in the next row of stalks, watching her. Kirby tensed as the person shifted, trying to get a better view of her. It seemed as if they were getting closer. Every so often, the person adjusted their wagon, coming down the row of corn, until they were level with her on the other side.

Kirby leaned forward, catching a glimpse of a gaunt, dirty man to whom she hadn't been close in a while.

Drew.

Drew's face looked even more sunken, after only a few more weeks. His eyes flashed to hers as he gave her a barely perceptible nod.

"You're still alive," he said, as if the words were a miracle to both of them.

If they were anywhere other than a dirty prison, Kirby might've smiled. Instead, she gave a knowing nod.

"I'm sorry about your friend," he said, lowering his eyes.

"Thanks," Kirby said. She wondered how many times they'd traded the same words, and how many times they might trade them later.

"I would've given my condolences sooner, if I thought it was safe to do so," Drew said regretfully.

Kirby nodded. "There is no need to apologize."

Looking up and down the row, ensuring no one was near, Drew said, "I wanted to make sure nothing has changed from when we spoke last. I wanted to make sure we still share the same goals."

She stared at him intently. They'd both suffered equal atrocities in their homeland, and in the arena, when equally cruel masters owned them. Sharing his gaze, she could see the same obstinate spark of fire they'd had when they sailed those ships across the ocean, all those years ago.

Resolutely, Kirby said, "Nothing has changed."

"Good," Drew said. "We will meet tonight."

Chapter 5: William

William tensed as someone knocked at his door. No matter how much time passed, he couldn't get past his fear.

"Who is it?" he asked.

"Amelia." Her voice was gentle.

But then, it always was.

With nothing else to do, William had played along as she instructed him. He couldn't read fluently, but each day, he picked up more words, and every so often, he fumbled his way through a simpler sentence. If he wasn't captive in a cruel place, he might've been proud of his knowledge. Now he felt as if he was learning skills that he wouldn't be able to use, once The Gifted decided it was his turn to die.

He crossed the room. Every interaction felt like a test.

Sucking in a nervous breath, William reached the door and waited for her to open it.

Amelia stood at the threshold.

"Did I wake you?"

"No," William said, hoping he hadn't spoken too quickly.

"Tolstoy would like to see you," she said.

William smiled to disguise his pounding heart. "What does he want?" he asked.

"He didn't tell me," Amelia said, with the same smile she'd used when she watched Cullen die.

He joined her on the other side of the doorway, and she shut the door behind them. She started down the stairs.

Knowing he couldn't disobey, William followed.

His dread deepened with each step as he realized they weren't going up to The Library Room.

He looked out the windows as they descended, watching the slaves work in the fields. A few demons skittered through the corn stalks.

Stopping at the twelfth floor, Amelia knocked four times. The raps hung in the air as she waited. William studied Tolstoy's door, which looked even more solid and imposing than the others. He had never been inside Tolstoy's room, though he had learned where a few of The Gifted lived.

Footsteps echoed from inside the room.

William braced himself for whatever new spectacle of horror he faced. Maybe his friends were on the other side, bound, tortured, or dead. Or maybe he'd made another tragic mistake he didn't realize.

The door opened, revealing Tolstoy, alone.

"William," Tolstoy said, a smile creasing his wart-covered face.

Hiding his fearful swallow, William managed, "Hello."

He looked past Tolstoy, expecting to see his friends in peril; instead, he was faced with a magnificent room, much more extraordinary than his own. A bed the size and height of two of those in William's quarters sat against a wall. White, pristine blankets adorned its surface. Farther back, strange pictures and drawings lined the walls, preceding a grand desk, with a shelf full of books affixed to its back. The electric lights were dim, as they always were in the daylight hours.

"Come in," Tolstoy invited.

William looked for a threat he couldn't see, but he saw nothing other than furniture and adornments.

He entered the room with Amelia.

"I won't keep you long," Tolstoy said. "I know you are hungry. We will have breakfast after we talk."

"It's okay," William said. He made a show of looking over at the books. "You have even more books here."

"I do," Tolstoy said, looking pleased that he'd noticed.

"William has taken books in the evenings, after our daily studying," Amelia interrupted. "He has made great strides with his letters."

"So I hear," Tolstoy said. "Your hard work is showing rewards, William. Perhaps when you have progressed further, I will let you borrow some of my collection."

Tolstoy beckoned for William and Amelia to follow. They walked past the bed on the left and some strange pictures on the walls on the right. Glancing at them, William saw diagrams that reminded him of the blueprints he'd seen all those weeks ago, but these were different. Most showed human bodies, their arms held level at their sides, their legs in strange poses. Others showed infected people like The Gifted, with rounded or ridged warts on their heads, knees, or elbows. He couldn't decipher their purpose.

Noticing William's attention, Tolstoy explained, "Some of the things I have studied. Perhaps later, I will explain."

Tolstoy stopped at his desk, which was littered with books and supplies, and reached for a drawer. For a moment, William was certain he would reveal some cruel, Tech Magic device to incinerate him. But it wasn't Tech Magic.

Pulling out a piece of dark fabric, Tolstoy said, "This is for you, William."

"For…me?" William asked, confused.

Taking the cloth, William discovered a long, flowing robe. William stared up and down the clothing's smooth contour, as if the garment might sprout teeth and bite him. But the robe was soft and clean, absent of the holes or dirt stains that marred the clothing he'd worn for too long. It was about his size.

It looked just like Tolstoy's, like Amelia's.

Like The Gifteds'.

"I don't know what to say," William mumbled as he turned the object over in his hands.

"A thank you is all that is required," Amelia said with a smile.

"Thank you," William parroted.

"Why don't you try it on?" Tolstoy suggested. "It might be a little tight over your clothing, but we can get an idea of how it fits. Barron can size it, if you need."

"Okay." William nodded.

Tolstoy and Amelia waited expectantly as he held it in his shaky hands.

Swallowing, William unfolded the robe, shoved his arms through the holes, and slipped it over his head.

Chapter 6: Bray

Bray sat on his bedroll, looking out through the doorway and into the courtyard, which was mostly empty. From the houses around him, he heard the clink of dishes and the hushed whispers of children. Far in the distance, the wails of the dead slave's family bled through the streets. Wiping the remnants of some leftover soup from his mouth, he looked at Teddy, who sat across from him on his bedroll.

"The man's relatives will cry for a while, but eventually, the guards will silence them, too," Teddy said.

"Unfortunately true," Bray said, grunting, "They won't even be given enough time to grieve."

"The guards always find new ways to abuse their powers." Teddy sighed. "Perhaps it is a product of too much free time."

Bray nodded. He had seen too many similar men, abusing their powers in the towns and villages from where he came.

"In some ways, it is easier to have no family to worry about," Teddy said, looking down at his boots. "I miss mine, though."

"Your mother," Bray said, recalling one of Teddy's earlier stories. "She was your only relative. You said she died of sickness."

Teddy shifted on his bedroll, clearly reliving some distant pain. "I had a family, too. I didn't tell you about them."

"A family?"

Teddy sighed. "I had a wife and a child, when I was younger in New City. I didn't speak of them, because it is too painful. I met my wife here, and my child was born within the walls."

Sensing the man's somber mood, Bray didn't push him.

After a long moment, Teddy continued. "I wish I could've saved them, but of course I couldn't." Teddy wrung his hands, recalling a painful memory. Sorrow filling his eyes, he said, "My wife and I both worked in the fields then, as you do now. Most of the time, we worked separately."

"You were Field Hands?" Bray asked, recalling that the man worked in the sewing rooms now.

"Yes. For many years. More than I can count. One hot summer day, I heard screams. I couldn't see what was happening, but when I saw a guard coming for me, I had a guess. I knew Rosalyn was involved."

"What happened?"

"She collapsed in the heat. I don't know if the work was too hard, or the sun was too much, but she fell and never got up. I remember the Head Guard's face as he told me about her death. It was as if a piece of corn had fallen from a wagon. He told me I had to finish my shift before I could see her body. I will never forget his thoughtless expression. I begged, but he wouldn't relent. And so I abided his rule, picking my corn as the sun rose higher in the sky, thinking about the guard's uncaring face."

"I don't even remember when, but something snapped. One moment I was doing my duties, the next, I had my hands wrapped around the guard's throat. I remember his choked screams as he tried breaking free. He beat his fists against my head, trying to get away, but I wouldn't relent. It was as if the guard had killed Rosalyn by his own hands. Or at least, it felt that way."

"Other guards pulled me off him before I killed him. I barely understood what I'd done. All I could think about was Rosalyn. They burned her body the next afternoon, while I was in a cell. I never said goodbye." Teddy wiped a tear from his eye.

"I am sorry," Bray said, but the words felt as hollow and empty as they always did.

"My daughter Tabatha was only four years old when this happened. I was confined to a cell. During the day, they allowed her to stay with the woman who normally watched her, but at night, they made her stay alone in our house while I was imprisoned. Perhaps that is why they kept me alive, knowing they could inflict more pain on me through my daughter."

Bray felt an empathetic outrage.

"Tabatha slept for almost a week with no parents, in a house by herself, crying herself to sleep." Teddy coughed through a lump in his throat. "She was hardly old enough to feed herself, and certainly not old enough to be left alone. One night, she wandered off. I think she was searching for me. No one knows for sure, because we never got to ask her. She got too close to the wall. A handful of Plagued Ones on the other side heard a rattle, and they came running. A few got over. They ate her, like they ate your friend." Teddy's eyes grew distant, as he stared at the house's small hearth. "When I was released, I found out she was dead. Perhaps that is why they kept me alive. They knew my memories would haunt me forever."

"Too many deaths," Bray said grimly.

"If I seem cold, that is the reason. Do not take it as an insult."

Bray nodded. In a way, Teddy resembled Bray, during his days as a Warden outside of Brighton, with only his sword, his bag, and his scalps to keep his company.

But things were different now, with Kirby and William to worry about.

Reading the expression on his face, Teddy said, "Having

those you care about can be a risk, in a place such as this. Seeing your friend killed a few weeks ago reminded me of that. That is why I caution you often about being careful. Living in this city only causes pain."

Bray nodded. He thought of Kirby, eating lunch in that distant, dirty house, and to William, stowed away in that shimmering tower. He would do anything to keep both of them safe. "I understand," he said.

Chapter 7: William

William adjusted his robe as he sat at the small desk in the corner of The Library Room. The robe was itchy. In several places, it was too loose, and it scratched his skin. He wanted to pull the garment over his head and fling it off. He wanted to burn it, but he knew better. Instead, he stared at the words in the book in front of him, pretending to silently study. His eyes drifted off the page and to his left, where Herman and some other Gifted sat at their small desks. Herman let out a thin groan and shifted, reaching down to rub his lumpy knee. The Gifted were always readjusting, stretching their stiff limbs where the warts and lumps afflicted them. Their pain was a reminder of the pain that awaited William, if he lived as long as them.

He suspected their pain was the reason they retired to their quarters every afternoon, where they could spend time studying, or resting. Occasionally, he heard them moving up and down the stairs, heading to different floors. Amelia told him they exercised that way.

William's gaze drifted to the windows on the south side of the building.

Noticing his eyes off the page, Amelia walked over. William turned his attention back to the book he was reading.

"Is the robe too big for you?" Amelia asked.

"It is fine," William answered, adjusting some bunches in the fabric that hung over the sides of the chair.

"Barron can alter it."

Hearing his name, Barron looked across the room at William, smiling. He gave a cordial wave. Each time William looked at Barron, he recalled the man's wart-covered arm locked on him, forcing him to watch the death of his friend.

"Perhaps later," William said, returning the man's polite wave. "I will let you know."

Barron nodded and refocused on his studies.

"I am going to take a break to stretch my legs," Amelia said. "Would you like to join me?"

"Sure." William set down his book, grateful for the distraction. Around him, a few of The Gifted made noises in their throats as they turned pages, or swiveled in their chairs. One or two chatted quietly. He followed Amelia through the doorway next to the bookcases, to the room where the glass cases were kept.

"Tolstoy must be proud of you," Amelia said, as William adjusted his long sleeves. "You are the first outside of our group to receive a robe in a hundred and fifty years."

"It is a nice gift," William said, thinking how much he hated it. Hoping to hide his disgust, he said, "Tolstoy's room is magnificent. He has a desk larger than any I've seen."

"He spends much time there, as you've noticed," Amelia explained. "In fact, he rarely leaves."

William nodded. He barely saw the man, other than meals, and the occasional visit to The Library Room. "What does he study?"

"He is trying to decipher the reason for our existence, and the reasons for the spore's mutation," Amelia said.

William recalled something. "Is that why he has those drawings in his room?"

She nodded. "Tolstoy is always looking for patterns in the physical mutations of the spores. He wants to discover what separates us from The Plagued Ones, or from the humans. He wants to find a pattern, so he can understand why we turned more intelligent. Perhaps one day, we will understand our existence better."

"Does he have any guesses as to why we are different?"

"Most of the tests he's performed have yielded inconclusive results," Amelia said, with a shrug.

"What tests?"

Amelia glanced at the windows on one side of the room, and back at William. "Remember when I told you about the glass windows?"

"Yes." William swallowed as he recalled that conversation. He remembered the fright he'd felt when he heard the humans that died were part of them. Parroting what Amelia would want him to remember, he said, "You told me the windows were special, because the humans' ashes live on as part of them, after they are cremated in the Glass Houses."

"That is true," Amelia said. "But the humans live on in other ways, as well, through the knowledge they give us. Many years ago, we tried to find more intelligent ones, like us."

"How did you do that?"

"We thought if we could watch some of the infected people turn, we might see patterns in how they developed. So we separated the infected humans, observing them in special conditions where we could record their progress." Amelia's tone grew reflective. "Unfortunately, none of the people turned into anything other than The Plagued Ones."

William nodded. He knew that was true, most of the time.

Amelia said, "So we tried other things."

"Like what?"

Amelia chewed her lip. "We tried to recreate the spore's mutation."

The idea didn't make sense to William. "Recreate it?"

"Many out in the wild think that the spore is the will of the gods, but we knew better. So, we collected the spore when it went on the wind, and put it into the rooms with some uninfected humans."

Fear struck William's heart. "You turned men into monsters?"

"Unfortunately, that was the end result," Amelia said. "None of those we tested turned into The Gifted, like us. Almost all turned into savages. Unfortunately, the slaves who were the next to be tested didn't realize the importance of what we were trying to do. They resisted our efforts." Amelia sighed. "And so, they died."

William couldn't stop himself from asking the question, even though he didn't want to hear the answer. "How?"

"They killed themselves trying to escape, William," Amelia said plainly, as she looked at him. "They would rather perish than participate in a study for the greater good. But that is the way of most humans. They have selfish tendencies." She tucked her hair behind her ears. "They think only of themselves. Perhaps it is better they did not become The Gifted. We have abandoned that study in the years since."

William's stomach churned as he watched Amelia's emotionless eyes, her cold face. Looking down at the robe hanging over his small frame, he wanted to tear it from his body and fling it at her.

He knew exactly how those poor, abused people had felt.

He never wanted to be one of The Gifted.

Chapter 8: Kirby

"What's wrong?" Kirby asked.

She entered her house to find Esmeralda pacing, holding Fiona, who shrieked as she rejected her mother's soothing arms.

"She's in a mood," Esmeralda said over the crying, wriggling child. Worry painted her eyes as she looked at her daughter.

"Is she sick?"

"I think she's just colicky," Esmeralda said. "I hope she does not make too much noise tonight. The guards are not patient."

A few nosy people walked by the house, giving sympathetic or annoyed looks inside. Tears filled Esmeralda's eyes. It looked as if she was drowning in a river, looking for a saving branch.

Kirby felt as if she should help, but she didn't know how. She'd never had children of her own, but she knew the hardships could sometimes feel as potent as the joys.

"Do you think she would take some cornmeal?" Kirby asked.

"She rejected if before, but I'd try anything about now."

"Let me make a fresh batch. Give me a few moments," Kirby said, rising and walking to the hearth.

"Thank you." Esmeralda seemed grateful.

Kirby gathered the ingredients. Thankfully, she had enough water to boil. She started the cornmeal, cooked it, and brought it over. Fiona continued to cry and squirm until

Kirby held up a spoonful of food. Fiona puckered her lips, but with some coaxing, she took the cornmeal and stopped crying. The calm was welcome, after so many moments of disquiet.

"That's a good girl, Fiona," Esmeralda cooed. To Kirby, she said, "Thank you for your help."

"Don't mention it," Kirby said, spooning out a few portions of the meal so they could have lunch. "Perhaps the food will keep her calm."

With a moment of peace, Esmeralda sat on the bedroll. The bags under her eyes spoke of too many nights with no rest. The baby kept Kirby awake, too, but she didn't have a mother's degree of sleeplessness.

"I was hoping she would rest through the night at her age, as some of the others have," Esmeralda said, as she shifted Fiona on her lap. "I was hoping the gods would be kind."

"Soon, she will settle into a routine," Kirby assured her.

"I don't know how much longer I can take it. It is just so hard." Esmeralda sunk her head and cried. "I'm sorry. I didn't mean to ruin your lunch."

Sitting on the bedroll beside her, Kirby patted her arm to console her. "You are brave to raise a child here."

"I have no choice," Esmeralda said. Looking down at Fiona, her tears continued flowing. "I did not mean to have her. It was not a decision."

Kirby nodded. She had suspected as much. She knew too many women in similar situations — attacked, or abandoned when they became pregnant. "Do you know who the father is?"

Esmeralda nodded through her tears. "It is Ollie."

"The Head Guard?" Kirby looked around, as if saying the guard's name might have put them both in danger.

Seeing the expression on Kirby's face, Esmeralda clarified, "I am only speaking what everyone knows. I am not the first to have one of his children, or the child of another guard. He attacked me after work one day, and I became pregnant with his child. It is not a secret. Even his wife knows."

Kirby felt rage swell up inside her as she watched Esmeralda's red cheeks, puffy with the weight of her tears.

"It is the story of too many women here," Esmeralda said, as if that made it any better. "I was never married, and now I probably will never be. No man would share a home with me, now."

Tamping her rage, Kirby said, "Things will get easier."

"Fiona will get older, and some things will change, but not all of them. Most of the guard's wives stay in and raise their children, like Ollie's wife does. But not me. I was only given a certain number of months. These months will not ease the responsibility, or the hardship. Soon, I will be forced back to work, and things will be even harder. I will miss Fiona while the caretakers watch her."

"The caretakers?"

Esmeralda nodded. "The slaves tasked to keep watch over the young ones."

"There is always hope for a better life," Kirby said, wishing she could give a better answer.

Esmeralda sighed. Cleaning the last of her tears, she comforted Fiona, who was eager for another bite of food. "I do not mean to burden you with my story, Kirby. But I will tell you this: be careful where you go. Keep others around you. It will not eliminate the danger, but it might help."

Chapter 9: Kirby

Kirby peeled back the husks on her ear of corn, while the other workers in the Shucking Room chatted quietly around her. She couldn't forget Esmeralda's story. Watching the guards preen and pat each other's backs as they walked past the sweating, stinking room full of workers, she couldn't stop thinking of revenge—for Esmeralda, for *all* of them. Her anger was a roiling kettle in her stomach, ready to spill over and scald someone with her rage.

She wished she could say she was surprised by the guard's attacks. Of course, she wasn't. She had seen too many similar stories in her homeland.

Next to her, Jack performed his duty with mechanical, practiced hands. Over the course of weeks, he seemed to have developed a quiet kinship with Kirby. They spoke infrequently, mostly keeping out of trouble, updating each other quietly on the news.

"What happened this morning in the courtyard was a shame," he said reservedly.

Kirby looked over to find his face etched with sadness. For a moment, she thought he was speaking of Esmeralda, but of course he wasn't. He was speaking of the battle in the courtyard.

"It is a tragedy," Kirby said bitterly, glancing at the guards who walked by outside the building.

"They say the Head Guards beat Gabe so badly he

couldn't walk," Jack said. "You probably saw him dragged to the cell, after Avery gave the order."

"Everyone did." Kirby nodded gravely.

"He will be let out, as soon as he can work. I'm not sure when that will be."

Kirby nodded. She had heard the same thing.

"Perhaps he would be better off in the cell." Jack tossed a piece of corn into the bin they shared. "I do not know what is worse: starving in a cell, or facing his friend's family."

"Neither fate is deserved," she said bitterly.

Jack shook his head, looking out for the guards as he picked up another ear of corn. All around them, slaves talked as loudly as they dared. It felt as if they could detect the closeness of the guards. When the guards were farther away, they relaxed. When the guards got close, they hushed.

When her shift neared its end, Kirby dusted the remnants of the husks on her pants, blinked away the sweat of another long afternoon's work, and pushed away her empty wagon. Risking a glance behind her, she found Drew on the other side of the Shucking Room. She caught his eyes. Their meeting was the only thing driving her through the day.

Hopefully tonight, things would change.

Chapter 10: Tolstoy

Tolstoy stood by the windows in his quarters, looking out over a moonlit New City. Below him, in between the buildings and houses, lights danced and flickered as people walked down the alleys and pathways, preparing for a night's rest after carrying out his orders. Directly below, the stoked bonfires glowed brilliantly, but not enough to reach the Feeding Pen, where the guards fed The Plagued Ones every evening. On the eastern side of the city, the tall buildings sat dark, awaiting the laborers who would toil away in the morning, supplying the flow of traders.

The city was a carefully constructed machine, built on the backs of the humans, the devices carefully put together by The Gifted, and The Plagued Ones protecting it. It was as perfect as Tolstoy could make it, for a city mostly occupied by humans.

He sighed.

He knew the city had flaws.

The humans were selfish, prone to thoughts of escape. They were unable to see things larger than themselves. Too often, the guards used violence to ensure their cooperation. The slaves were animals, trained by fear, hunger, and lust, much like The Plagued Ones.

They valued their lives at more than they were worth.

At night, looking out over the moonlit city, it was easy to imagine it filled with his people, his Gifted, rather than humans who tarnished its image. One day, Tolstoy would build a grander place, with dozens of intelligent beings like he and the other Gifted. He would build a city where they could construct incredible machines and create the world they deserved, rather than the ruined world they'd inherited.

A voice reminded him that Amelia was next to him, watching.

"The city is beautiful at night, isn't it?" he asked her.

"Indeed, it is," she said.

"Sometimes, when I look out over the city at night, I am reminded of some of the cities from years ago, before the world went dark," Tolstoy admitted.

"But this city is better," Amelia said without hesitation.

"Do you think?" Tolstoy cocked his wart-covered brow, looking sideways at her.

"Our violence is less rampant," Amelia said. "We have a population we can control. The humans might not all be happy, but they are civil. They work toward a common cause. They help us develop things the world has not seen in years."

Tolstoy smiled. "I wish that everyone thought the same as you, as us."

"Perhaps in time," Amelia said, thinking on it.

"Or one day, perhaps the humans will be extinct," Tolstoy said with a shrug. "It is hard to know."

"But we will remain," Amelia said confidently.

They watched over the city next to each other for a moment, fixating on some of the lights.

"One day, more of those lights will belong to our people," Tolstoy said. "We will have a city filled with The Gifted, next to the city of humans who work for us."

"It is a hope, as much as a dream," Amelia said wistfully.

Chapter 11: Kirby

Kirby snuck next to the back of the small, dank buildings under the cover of moonlight, avoiding the doorway-shaped patterns of light spilling from the alley's opposite side. Through open doorways, she saw people finishing dinner, tidying up, or tending children.

No one saw her for longer than a moment.

She hoped.

All around, in the narrow walkways between houses, people lingered, talked, or carried torches from one place to the next. More than a few groups headed toward the bonfires in the courtyard. A few glanced at her as they passed, or parted to let her through. The slaves spoke more loudly than they would've dared during the day, under the scrutinizing glares of the Head Guards. Darkness inspired confidence, but it wouldn't ward off death.

Kirby knew that as well as her name.

She kept her head down, avoiding an interaction some-one might remember.

Reaching the end of a narrow alley, she veered south, her heart beating a frantic rhythm. She was farther than she'd ever been into the city. She hoped she was going the right way. The small houses went as far as the eye could see, but in the distance, she saw taller buildings, silhouettes under a ghostly moon. Somewhere far in the distance, over the wall, she heard the deathly shriek of a demon.

Someone crashed into Kirby.

She bit down on a surprised cry.

An angry man backed away from her, spouting curses.

A Head Guard.

"Stupid forest-dweller!" the burly man yelled, brushing off his shoulder as if she possessed some ugly disease. He spat on the ground. "Watch where you're going!"

"I'm sorry," Kirby mumbled, in the submissive tone she had perfected, since Cullen died.

She put her head down, awaiting the cost of her mistake.

"I ought to lay a beating on you," the guard grumbled, glaring at her in the darkness. The stink of alcohol filled the space between them.

Kirby's heart thundered. She kept her face in the shadows, lest he see something on her face he didn't like. Or something he did. After a few more demeaning curses, the Head Guard sauntered off, muttering. She looked over her shoulder, watching him turn out of sight down an alley.

In the distance, she heard him scolding a few more slaves. It sounded as if he had forgotten the incident.

She hoped.

She took a few more alleys, moving in a diagonal, southwestern path, until the chatter of slaves faded, the cloying odor of mold and feces wafted across her nostrils, and the lights transitioned to black. She was in an abandoned part of the city in which she'd never been. She saw no guards or people. But that didn't mean she was safe. An echoing yowl from over the wall reminded her that even with no guards around, there was no escape. Ahead of her, she saw the cluster of tall buildings she'd seen from a distance, but she saw no sign of anyone — or any*thing* — else.

Maybe she had misheard Drew's hastily whispered directions.

Maybe she should turn back.

Kirby swallowed as she passed between the last of a few small houses and approached a row of five, tall structures.

A new smell hit her — the smell of something charred, something burned. That odor reminded her of the ship on the shore of New Hope, where she'd hunkered and waited for companions who were never coming back. The smell lingered in the air as she kept walking.

Hands grabbed her.

Kirby stifled a cry and raised her fists, ready to fend off an attacker.

"Kirby, it's me."

Drew.

"Come this way, the others are already here."

She followed Drew around the base of the tall building, almost losing him before finding him again in the moonlight, near the back wall of the building.

Three other shadows waited. Had Kirby not been meeting someone, she might've thought they were statues. None moved as Drew introduced her.

"This is Kirby."

The others nodded.

"If guards come, we need to run in different directions," Drew warned.

One of the other shadows shifted. A woman's voice spoke. "Is your friend coming?"

"He should be," Kirby said. "I told him what you said."

She listened for another set of approaching footsteps. Bray knew better than to light a torch. He was savvy. But what if someone had seen her giving him a whispered message, in the alley after dinner? Cullen's terrified cries came back to her as she anticipated a similar fate for Bray — for all of them.

Her heart seized as a shadow skulked around the back of the building. The people near Kirby tensed.

"Kirby, are you there?" a familiar voice hissed.

"I'm here," she announced to Bray. "I'm safe."

Bray crept into the circle of shadows, limping from the

severe beating he'd received all those weeks ago, when Cullen had become a mangled corpse.

"Did any guards follow you?" Drew asked.

"No," Bray assured him.

"Good," Drew said. "Let's get started."

Chapter 12: Kirby

"What are your names?" Kirby asked the three shadows huddled behind the building next to Drew.

"Names are dangerous," the woman said.

"I agree," Bray said next to Kirby. "But you know ours."

The shadows shifted. No one spoke right away. Finally, Drew told them, "I trust Kirby with my life, as I've told you. And she has guaranteed her trust of Bray."

"Too many have died from similar guarantees," the woman said with caution.

"Like I said, you can trust them," Drew said. "They would give their lives to escape, as we would."

The woman remained silent for a moment, contemplating. "I am Clara, and this is Giovanni and James. We are the representatives of our group."

"What group?" Kirby asked.

The man next to her, Giovanni, said, "We prefer to avoid names. But if you need to call us anything, call us The Shadow People."

Kirby nodded as she took in the information. Gesturing at the buildings around them, she asked, "What is this place?"

"This part of the city is nicknamed Ashville. It is not a clever name. Many years ago, before most of us were born, these buildings were burned," Drew said, waving a shadowy hand in the dark.

"No one goes here," Clara said. "It is a place of bad luck. Even the guards tend to stay away." She fell quiet for a moment, adding, "Though they would retrieve us, if they knew we were here."

"It is a place where they conducted experiments," Drew explained.

"Experiments?" A shiver ran the length of Kirby's body.

Clara said, "In the years when our grandparents were young, The Gifted performed procedures on the slaves. Some say they tried infecting them with the spore. One day, one of the slaves broke free and released the others. Together, they set the place on fire. Unfortunately, guards found them, and they were forced to hide in one of the buildings. They perished in the flames, rather than coming out and doing what The Gifted wanted."

A quiet hung over the air as Kirby and Bray processed a new horror.

"Thankfully, that project ended a long time ago, and The Gifted are focused on other inventions and pursuits," Clara said. "For now."

"But that doesn't mean it won't happen again," James said disgustedly. "We are expendable. We are the scum on the bottom of their shoes, worth less than the dung in the Feeding Pen they collect and burn."

Kirby nodded. She'd heard enough of Rudyard's remarks to know that was true. And she'd certainly seen enough.

"Drew said you are working on a plan of escape."

"Not an escape," Clara clarified. "A revolt." She looked back and forth between Bray and Kirby. "The people in this city have been beaten down enough. They are ready to fight back."

"How many people are in your group?" Kirby asked, feeling a surge of hope as she heard those words.

Clara hesitated. "About two hundred. We have people throughout New City, in the shops, in the fields, and among those who tend animals. We have more than you see here, obviously."

Drew said, "The group has been meeting for a while, trying to determine the best plan. I joined a few months after I was captured."

Kirby asked Drew, "Do you have weapons?"

Drew nodded in the dark, anticipating her question. "We have a stash here in Ashville. Most are crude shanks, made from pieces of metal stolen from the machine shops, or tools stolen without the guards' knowledge."

"Most were gained at more risk than they are worth," Giovanni added. "We have enough to arm about half of our people, but we still need more."

Kirby had hoped for guns. But it was a start, and much more than she had when she was rotting in a cell, ready to die.

"Maybe we can get more weapons in the building," Bray said. "The Gifted must have some. They certainly have ours."

"We have thought about that, of course. Too many locked doors stand between us and those weapons," Clara said. "Getting to them would mean getting over the wall and passing The Plagued Ones. Even if we got into the building, we have to contend with the guards on the first floor, and who knows what else. It is rumored there is a weapons stash on the first floor, but it is secured by a strong door, as well as the entrance to the building. We would be better off running into the forest and escaping. Even if we needed a last resort, we do not have an escape route."

"That is another problem," James said.

"Most of us were born here, or taken long ago," Clara said. "Some of us know the area, but it seems as if things are always changing. Did you see anything outside the city that might help us?"

"We came from the north. We found nothing but demon dung," Bray said, disgustedly.

"That is our problem. No direction is safe from The Plagued Ones," Clara said. "The closest people are more than a day's walk, and none would harbor or help us. They profit from their relationship with The Gifted."

Changing from a subject with no good answers, Giovanni directed a comment at Kirby. "Drew told us the guards in your homeland helped you escape."

"It is true," Kirby said. "The guards allowed us access to the ships. Some were sympathetic, while others demanded favors. Perhaps some guards are sympathetic here."

"Unfortunately, that won't work, either," Clara said. "Most of the Head Guards were born here. They get the power of a made-up title. They get amenities. They learn to look down on the others, the way The Gifted look down on all of us. They are untrustworthy, because they gain from our subordination. And they have knives, to ensure we cooperate."

"The Gifted are only concerned with making their goods to trade, so they can keep the city functioning," Drew said, disdain bleeding through his words. "Keeping the guards happy furthers their aims."

"How many Head Guards are in New City?" Kirby asked, though she had a vague idea.

"About a hundred," Clara answered. "Our small group outnumbers them, but it doesn't matter. If something happens to the guards, Rudyard will send The Plagued Ones through the gate, or The Gifted will use the weapons they surely have in the tower to kill us. And we are not certain what the other slaves would do."

"Too many in New City are complacent," Drew explained. "They would rather live in the city than fight for it. They believe the guards' lies that the forest is full of greater dangers. Our city is fragmented."

Kirby nodded as she recalled the words Esmeralda had told her. "Has anyone ever escaped this place, or tried to revolt?"

The people in the shadows remained quiet for a long moment. Finally, Clara spoke.

"About five years ago, some other people organized an escape attempt, unbeknownst to us. They met in secret, as we are doing now. They determined the amount of time they needed to get far enough into the forests to get away. Or, so they thought."

"What happened?" Kirby asked.

Clara continued, "As you know, The Plagued Ones eat their dinner in the evening, and hunt animals at night in the forests around the perimeter. Even still, a lot of them linger nearby. These people secretly broke a hole in the wall, wide enough to climb through. They planned on leaving early in the morning, hoping The Plagued Ones had filled their stomachs. The slaves hoped to have half a morning before the Head Guards did their count, so they could run far enough into the woods to be forgotten. They hoped for a miracle. It was a foolish plan. They had no weapons."

"Did the mutants eat them?" Kirby guessed.

"The Head Guards found out about their plan the night before it happened. They waited by the hole. And they caught all of them." Clara swallowed. "They brought them to the courtyard and fed them to The Plagued Ones, while the rest of the city watched."

The air became impossibly quieter. Kirby stared cautiously around at the shadows near the building, as if one might move.

"How did the guards find out about their plan?" Bray asked.

"Most of the people in New City can't be trusted," Drew said. "Too many open their mouths, repeating what they hear. They hope to curry favor. The Head Guards, Rudyard, and The Gifted prey on peoples' hopes. They breed a culture of informants where every word is watched."

Turning to the topic of the meeting, Clara faced Kirby and said, "Drew thought you might have some insight of which we haven't thought."

Kirby fell silent for a moment, reflecting on the things they'd told her. She wanted the revolt to be a puzzle she could solve, even though it was quickly becoming clear there were no easy answers. "Bray and I have contemplated many things, of course. But we haven't settled on anything. And of course, we didn't know about the possibility of a revolt."

"We have contemplated many options, too," Clara said. "Even if we can overpower the guards, The Plagued Ones and The Gifted worry us. We do not have any clear solutions. We are torn between plans."

"We will only get one chance," Giovanni added.

"Keep an eye on what is going on here. Perhaps you will discover some new idea, in the things we have told you," Drew suggested.

"We will try," said Kirby.

Chapter 13: Kirby

Moonlight spilled over the broken, crumbling buildings, creating deep shadows between every rock and large piece of stone as Kirby and Bray made their way back. The other Shadow People had disappeared, separating down other alleys filled with the same smell of smoke and ash as the place where they met.

For too long, Kirby's meetings with Bray had consisted of brief, whispered conversations in alleyways, where they met and parted, or cautious looks in the fields. Walking next to him reminded her of riding or hiking through the forest with William, sharing their days and their nights together. Reaching over, she pulled him into an embrace.

"We will find a way out of this life," Bray promised.

"I hope so," she whispered, holding him.

"At least we are no longer alone," Bray said. "With the help of a group, we are in a better position."

Blotting her eyes before they could release tears, Kirby said, "But that does not mean it will be easy."

"Do you trust them?" Bray asked.

"I trust Drew with my life. And he trusts the others," Kirby answered, letting go and looking around. "That is enough, for now."

Bray nodded.

"A revolt will need much planning," Kirby said. "We are up against a problem with many layers. Kill the Head Guards, and The Gifted send the mutants in to devour us.

Kill the mutants, and we still have to contend with The Gifted. The Gifted surely have more guns in the tower. If they discover us, shivs and hand tools will not go far against them. And who knows what they might do to William?"

Bray sighed at a detail he had temporarily forgotten.

"I knew the city was fragmented," Bray said, "even before they said the words. I saw it in the eyes of the slaves that chanted this morning with the guards. It is clear that some of the slaves go along with their fate, because they are told lies. Or because they don't know better. Who knows what they might do, when a revolt happens?"

"Too many people get used to their mistreatment," Kirby lamented. "They think it is the only way."

"I have seen people indentured to others in Brighton," Bray said. "They put up with beatings and vile words that would provoke a fight in others. Some they think they deserve it. Others start to believe that way, after too much time in another's service."

"Enslavement has many evils," Kirby agreed.

"It is too bad your plan with the guards will not work here," Bray said.

Kirby recalled her last moments in her homeland. When she closed her eyes, she could see the sweating bodies of four hundred of her people, as they ran to the docks. She saw the expression of joy on their faces as they sailed from the harbor of her homeland for the last time, the wind kissing their skin. But those moments hadn't come without their scars. Some of her people had traded possessions, favors, and even their bodies. Her people had paid a price for their freedom to the guards, some of who had taken their toll in blood and tears. Those scars haunted Kirby, as it had haunted the others for as long as they were alive.

"What worked for us there, will not work here," Kirby reiterated. "Clara was right. The guards here would rather kill us than allow us a breath beyond New City — especially

Ollie and Avery, and some of the guards who beat us. They will not help us."

"I'd like to pay them back for what they did to Cullen, and to the slave yesterday," Bray muttered.

"Maybe one day, we can," Kirby said. "But we will need to be careful in how we execute it."

Bray went quiet a moment, thinking. "It seemed as if they had a few gaps in their plans. They said they were short on weapons. And they mentioned their lack of recent knowledge of what's beyond the walls. Perhaps those are things we can help with."

Kirby nodded. "Maybe we can work on those problems, while we think of some other ideas. In any case, I do not think we will find any immediate answers in the shadows. If we don't get back, someone will miss us."

They fell into a silence as they walked a wide alley between rows of tall buildings with less rubble, and plenty of shadow. When they had gone far enough that they could see the first rows of lights, they paused. Bray glanced up at the tall, glass-covered building in the distance, which was mostly dark, except for a few ominous flickers in the windows. Kirby didn't need him to voice his thoughts to know them.

"We will get out of this life of enslavement," Bray said. "And we will find William."

With a final embrace, they parted.

Chapter 14: William

William looked out the windows of the fifteenth floor, sickness in his heart. The information he'd received this afternoon was as cold and suffocating as the robe he wore. He couldn't get his mind off the strange things The Gifted had done to humans.

He didn't even know what to call The Gifted anymore. They weren't men, and they certainly weren't demons. Any hope he had at playing along with them felt as if it had been thrust away.

He couldn't live a life like this much longer.

He might pretend he could, when he lay awake at night, imagining that Bray and Kirby were safe, even though he knew they weren't. Cullen's death was proof of that.

Sooner or later, he would be complicit in some atrocity he couldn't fathom. He needed to escape.

William felt useless. All this time in the building, and all he'd managed to gain was a flimsy, twisted hairpin. His achievement felt inadequate. He could get himself out of a room—nothing more.

Looking out the window, William envisioned Bray down there in one of the buildings, perhaps preparing to meet some end worse than Cullen's. Bray had made a promise of safety to William, and that promise had carried them through the forests, The Ancient City, and The Arches. That promise had led them into the arms of The Gifted, into a life of enslavement he didn't deserve.

I will find a way to get out of this place and help my friends, even if it means my end, William resolved.

Chapter 15: Kirby

When Kirby returned home, most of the slaves had finished dinner. Only a handful lingered in the alleys, chatting quietly, while others settled down for the night, cleaning their dishes, or doing laundry. A few slaves returned from the bonfires, smelling of courtyard smoke. Moonlight spilled through the open doorway of her squalid house, splashing light over the meager possessions, and Esmeralda, who sat on her bedroll, playing with Fiona. Relief washed over Kirby as she crossed the threshold and found no guards.

It seemed as if Fiona had gotten over whatever mood had ailed her in the afternoon.

"How were the bonfires?" Esmeralda asked, rocking her daughter.

"Fine," Kirby said without elaborating. "Much of the usual talk about the heat of the fields."

"It seems as if it never ends," Esmeralda said. "I do not envy your job with the harvest."

"You have a challenging job, as well, taking care of a child." Kirby smiled as Esmeralda bounced Fiona on her lap.

Esmeralda didn't answer. She looked past Kirby and out the doorway. It looked as if she had something more to say.

"What is it?" Kirby asked.

With a slight shake of her head, Esmeralda beckoned her closer. Kirby got near her bedroll.

"Ollie was here looking for you," Esmeralda whispered, around Fiona's coos.

Kirby's heart pounded. "Ollie? What did he want?"

"I do not know. He said he would find you in the morning."

Kirby looked to the doorway, as if she'd find a lumbering figure standing there.

Of course, the doorway was empty.

"I would not go looking for him," Esmeralda warned. "Hopefully in the morning, when he is sober, he will forget about you."

Chapter 16: Kirby

Kirby walked the paths with a new trepidation under a morning sky pillowed with clouds. All around her, workers rubbed the sleep from their eyes, or said goodbye to their families and children, before striding hurriedly down the paths toward the courtyard. Ollie's visit was a looming weight, sitting in her stomach. She wanted nothing more than to blend in with the other workers, like she did most days, but somehow, she had gotten his attention and held it.

She braced for a final struggle. For all she knew, guards hid in one of the alleys, or doorways, ready to do Ollie's bidding. Or maybe Ollie would pull her off alone.

Soon she reached the edges of the courtyard, where handfuls of Field Hands already waited in line. A few glanced at her. Was it normal attention, or did they know something? The smell of people's sweat mingled with the odor of cooked meat, roasted vegetables, and cornmeal. The morning was already hot, and would be punishingly so, by mid-day.

Maybe she wouldn't live that long.

She slipped near the back of the line. At the front, far from her, she saw Bray, waiting between a few workers. He gave her a nod and looked away. Of course she couldn't speak with him.

A guard belched as he came down an alleyway between some houses. She turned slowly and risked a glance, watching him mingle with a few other guards. His eyes were red and glazed. Perhaps yesterday's fight had turned into an excuse to get drunk, not that he needed a reason.

Kirby looked for evidence of yesterday's fight. Most of the dirt had been scuffed over, or walked on, but she saw a few dark stains of blood in the soil. She shuddered.

The courtyard filled with more and more Field Hands, until the line was filled with people and quiet chatter.

A loud bang pulled her attention across the courtyard. She turned to find Ollie sauntering from one of the guards' private chamber pot buildings, the door slamming behind him. He joined a cluster of guards about twenty feet from the line. No one looked at her. She waited for the moment when Ollie remembered her. Maybe he meant to surprise her with an attack. The guards laughed, but she couldn't hear what they were saying.

Perhaps they discussed *her*.

A few Field Hands wheeled some creaky wagons to the head of the line, putting them in place and scuttling off.

Kirby looked at a few of the dirty, scrawny workers. They held the same fearful expressions they always did, while waiting for the count. But she could just as easily see those expressions becoming vicious cries for blood, once the guards dragged her out of the line. The guards walked from the middle of the courtyard toward the gate. A few stationed themselves by it, prepared to usher the slaves to the fields, once Ollie and a few other guards finished the count.

"Quiet!" Ollie shouted, silencing the few remaining conversations as he veered to the back of the line.

He and a few other guards moved in her direction. Kirby stiffened, following the posture of a few other slaves, who lowered their heads, or looked away. Ollie's voice boomed louder as his boots beat the earth, getting closer. She watched him in her peripheral vision as he got within a few rows of her. When he reached her aisle, Kirby stared straight ahead, keeping her fists clenched, and prepared for what might be the last moments of her life. She felt his eyes boring into the side of her head as he walked close enough that she could smell the cooked meat on his breath.

He kept walking.

Kirby exhaled. Reaching the head of the line a few moments later, Ollie stopped and faced the waiting slaves.

"Time to move," he said.

The guards opened the front gate.

Without another order, the workers shuffled ahead, grabbing their wagons. Kirby couldn't believe her luck. She moved with the line, anticipating a duty she never thought she'd appreciate. The gate swung open, and some of the first slaves disappeared into the cornfields. She kept walking, passing a few other guards. Ollie stood near the front gate, watching the slaves with a bored expression, picking at some gristle between his teeth.

She was starting to think Esmeralda had made a mistake when Ollie furrowed his brow, turned, and fixed his gaze on her. Raising a fat finger, he jabbed it at her.

"Not you. You're coming with me."

Chapter 17: Bray

Hot sun bore down through a break in the scattered clouds, as Bray pulled his wagon through the gate and into the fields.

The Shadow People were alive in his thoughts.

He felt their presence, deep inside the walls of New City, in the torturous grunts of the workers as they pulled their wagons, or in the half-empty stomachs of the people all around him. They wanted escape as badly as he and Kirby did. They were bearings in a machine, waiting for a flaw. He could hear it in their wavering, angry voices as they described The Gifted's gruesome experiments, or the atrocities they had suffered. They were as beaten and abused as anyone. They had every reason to fight.

But they had every reason to fear, too.

He thought of the words The Shadow People had told him, about those who had tried escaping.

That tale was a gruesome example of failure.

Listening to the people grunting in line around him as they started passing the gates, he wondered which ones might be Shadow People. Did the people toiling next to him in the fields, or sleeping in the houses next door, harbor the same secrets? People all around him might be preparing to fight with shanks and tools for their freedom.

Two hundred people were much more than he'd hoped.

Still, he had concerns.

He couldn't conceive of a situation where they fought the guards, the demons, and The Gifted, and won, or convinced hundreds of frightened slaves to join them. Neither could he envision freeing William.

Their predicament seemed unsolvable.

Frustrations.

Bray considered the things they'd discussed the night before. One of the problems The Shadow People raised was lack of fresh information about the surrounding area. There had to be demons in other places they couldn't see — perhaps hordes that did not belong to The Gifted.

Bray wished he had more recent information about what lay in the other directions. He knew how important that knowledge could be.

He thought about his previous battles. More times than he wanted to remember, demons had cornered him in some unforgiving terrain in the wild, and he'd been forced to abandon a battle.

But he never bedded down without knowing his surroundings. Every time he could, he thought ahead. Bray knew how quickly a plan could become a frantic melee.

An alternate route to freedom had kept him alive many times.

He needed to find out what was beyond the city walls.

Staring at the gate as he passed it, Bray left the courtyard.

Knowledge...

Maybe that was a first step.

He glanced over his shoulder as he kept going, attempting to find Kirby, as he did too often in this vile place. And paused. All he saw were skinny workers and chatting guards. She wasn't in the same place in line. Far in the distance, past the gate and into the courtyard, two figures walked away.

Ollie and Kirby.

The line kept moving, pushing Bray along, even though Kirby wasn't in it. Bray panicked, ready to run through the gate to get her, but guards were already closing it.

Dammit!

Chapter 18: Kirby

Kirby's fear heightened as Ollie led her farther up one of the pathways. A few guards, late to the morning line, wiped the remnants of sleep from their eyes as they walked in the opposite direction toward the courtyard, and the fields.

"I'll be back in a while," Ollie told them.

The guards traded a look. One of them smirked.

Ollie looked over at Kirby, ensuring that she stayed close. They passed a few doorways where mothers tended babies, or old people tended to their hearths. Ollie swore as he sidestepped a pile of retch.

"Filthy heathens," he cursed, moving to the side of the path to avoid it.

The smell of a full chamber pot filled the air as they walked by a few more dirty houses, whose inhabitants — like all the slaves — didn't have private outhouses. A baby screamed from inside a doorway. Seeing Ollie, a mother quickly averted her eyes. No one would help Kirby, even if they wanted to.

Cutting down an eastern path, Ollie headed to a house with a closed door, digging in his pocket for a key. A foreboding she knew too well swept over her.

She knew what this was.

Kirby frantically looked around, finding several paths down which she could run. Should she fight for her last few moments of life, or would that make her fate worse? The creak of a door drew her attention back to Ollie, who motioned for her to step inside.

"Don't worry, we're only talking," he said, with a lascivious grin she didn't believe.

Kirby looked from his sweaty face to the inside of the room. Once she stepped inside, she might never come out.

Seeing the look on her face, Ollie pulled his knife from his belt and stuck it near her stomach.

"Get inside."

Kirby's heart hammered as he forced her inside the small house, which contained two beds — one large and one small. His family's house.

But his family wasn't here, now.

Several piles of folded clothes sat on a few shelves. The smell of meat hung in the air — probably whatever stank on Ollie's breath. Looking over to the small hearth, she saw a picked-over meal of animal bones and skin. On the other side of the room were a small desk, and a chair. The room was much nicer than any of the hovels she'd seen.

Leading her further, Ollie closed the door.

Kirby braced herself for a final battle.

To her surprise, Ollie left her side, crossed the room, and took the chair behind the small desk. He slid the knife back into his belt. Settling back with a sickening grin, Ollie laced his fingers behind his head, watching her uncomfortable pose by the door.

"I've seen you in the fields," Ollie said, a salacious smile crossing his face.

Kirby bristled. Of course he had.

"You aren't as stupid as some of the forest-dwellers we get in here. Or at least, Rudyard tells me you aren't." Ollie picked his teeth again.

Kirby didn't nod or make any response. She wasn't sure what the right answer was.

"Did you see the fight yesterday?"

Kirby nodded. Everyone had.

"The slave who died was one of our metal workers,"

Ollie said, watching her. "He was here for ten years, longer than most of the others." She recalled the slave named Jonah lying in the dirt in the courtyard, his face smashed in and blood running from his head. "Of course, that didn't spare him a punishment."

Kirby's face betrayed no emotion.

"He stole from a guard," Ollie reinforced. "He deserved what he got."

Breaking the silence that she'd kept since entering the room, Kirby said, "It is a shame."

Ollie watched her a moment, judging her sincerity. Or perhaps he was looking for an excuse to say—or do—whatever he planned. Sliding back his chair, Ollie stood. His breathing grew heavier as he took a step toward her.

Kirby tensed.

He had promised only to talk, but of course she knew promises from cruel, ignorant men meant nothing.

"Most of our slaves would love a chance to get out of the fields," Ollie said, hiding none of his lustful thoughts as he got close enough that she could see the glint in his eye. "But that slave threw it away. He could have had a good life here. Maybe another ten years."

Kirby felt anger as she processed the rationale behind his conversation. It was the same, sick rationale she had heard too many times in her homeland. Out of the corner of her eye, Kirby saw the closed door, wondered how fast she could make it there. Would she reach the handle before his greasy paws were on her?

"You're more resilient than some of the others." Ollie eyed her. "A few of the guards thought you'd be back in the cell by now." He laughed, but she saw a hint of reservation behind it. He probably thought about the fight she'd put up outside the long building, and the bruises she'd given him.

Kirby said nothing. A single word might speed up what he had planned.

She clenched her fists.

"I told them you knew better than to fight with me again." Ollie smiled, cocking his thick, ugly skull sideways. "You know better, don't you?"

His words felt like slick, sweaty caresses. He leaned close enough that she could smell his dirty skin, and see a few red sores around his mouth.

"Those who make my time pleasant, live pleasant lives," he said, through dry, cracked lips.

Kirby would bite those lips off before they touched her.

She tried backing up a step, hoping to get enough leverage that she could throw a punch, or a knee, but she was up against the wall. With nowhere else to go, she stared at him.

Ollie's hands were at his side, clenching and unclenching, prepared to grab.

The doorknob made a noise and turned.

The door?

Kirby and Ollie's heads jerked.

A young, mop-haired boy peered into the room.

"Daddy?" he asked, stopping when she saw Ollie leaning against Kirby. "What's going on?"

"None of your business," Ollie snapped. "Get out of here."

A frizzy-haired woman stepped in behind the child, grabbing his shoulders. "I told you to stay out, Junior," she whispered. "When the door is closed, we can't come in. You know that."

"But I wanted to show Daddy the water we got," the child protested.

"I'm sorry," the woman told Ollie. "I told him we were going to Annie's."

Some of the lust fled Ollie's eyes as he appraised the two newcomers, and Kirby's eyes traced a path over their shoulders to escape.

"We're all set for our laundry, Daddy," the mop-haired kid said, holding a bucket in front of him. "We're going to do it while you're at work."

Ollie's face was torn as he looked from the frizzy-haired woman to the kid. "Give me a moment. I'm almost done." He cranked a thumb toward the door. "Shut the door behind you."

The frizzy-haired woman watched Ollie for a moment, before putting her arms around the child and ushering him out of the house. She gave Kirby a hard stare before she left. Ollie returned his attention to Kirby. Frustration crossed his face as he tried to recapture his lustful thoughts, but failed.

Angered, he took a step back.

"What do you know about metal work?"

Kirby was surprised. "Metal work?"

Ollie seemed annoyed to repeat himself. "Do you know it or not?"

Kirby nodded. "I have worked with metal where I used to live." The words weren't entirely true, but she sensed an opportunity.

"Rudyard wanted me to fill the position we lost," Ollie said. "Keep me happy, and you'll keep your job. Fuck up, and you're back in the fields." His eyes roamed from Kirby's face to her shirt. "Or maybe I'll find another use for you. I'm not through with you."

Chapter 19: William

Mid-day sunlight broke through the clouds, beaming through the glass windows of The Library Room, reflecting off the strange metal devices situated around the room, and illuminating the bookshelves by the walls.

William sat at the large, opulent table, filled with appetizing lunch dishes that Tolstoy had ordered. All around, The Gifted sat, murmuring their pleasantries and smiling through their warts. They passed dishes of sliced peaches, meat, strawberries, and apples. A few smiled as their eyes passed over William, sitting in his usual spot in his new attire.

"The robe fits you well," Herman said, with a shake of his head.

William looked down at the robe, which still felt as if it belonged to one of the snobbish scholars in Brighton, rather than draped over a captive boy's arms. He forced a smile.

"You look esteemed," Tolstoy agreed, with a sage nod.

William returned his eyes to his plate, wishing he could melt into his food.

"A man who dresses well succeeds," Barron said with a laugh. "An old adage you might not have heard."

William politely nodded.

Directing his attention to the others, Tolstoy said, "I met with Rudyard earlier this morning. He says we had a problem with the slaves yesterday."

"A problem?" Amelia asked, frowning as she chewed.

William looked toward the empty seat at the end of the table. Of course, Rudyard wasn't there. He was normally too busy taking care of whatever he did in the city.

"The guards solved the issue, whatever it was," Tolstoy said.

"What happened to the offenders?"

"One was killed, one was beaten," Tolstoy said, as if he discussed a bothersome pest. "The guards acted in our interests. The city is running smoothly again."

"Good," Herman said. "We need to keep production up."

"Rudyard says we have lost a few to sickness," Tolstoy said. "With the change of the season, I expect we will lose a few more. Rudyard will have the Semposi bring in more workers."

You mean slaves, William thought angrily.

William's stomach twisted in knots as he recalled the encounter with the savage, uncaring men in the forests. Thinking of them led him to thoughts of Cullen's twisted, mangled body, and the story of how Cullen's brothers had died.

The Gifted weren't just the cause of the pain in New City.

They caused pain in the forest, too.

They might not drag people from the woods, or beat them, but they were the people that gave the orders to rip them from their homes. They were the demons that sat on well-constructed chairs, ensuring everyone outside the tower lived lives of pain, suffering, and misery.

A knock at the door interrupted his angry thoughts.

"Ah, that must be dessert," Tolstoy said, turning to face the door. "Come in."

The door opened, revealing two muscled guards carrying trays of colorful bread, filled with fruit. William recognized two of the men that usually kept watch on the bottom floor, as he had learned. Bringing the desserts to the table, they set them down at various points in front of The Gifted.

"Are we too early?" one of the guards asked.

"No, the timing is perfect," Tolstoy responded.

"Do you need anything else?"

"That will be all," Tolstoy said with a dismissive wave. The men left.

Tolstoy ignored their departure as he reached for a dessert and passed a dish along to Herman.

After chewing a mouthful of bread, Tolstoy said, "Rudyard mentioned we need to keep an eye on our rations, as the seasons change."

Barron tapped his fork on the table, reemphasizing the point. "The slave's stomachs should be full enough that they can do their work. Not an ounce more. Gluttony leads to laziness. And laziness slows progress."

"It is unfortunate that we need to worry about such things," Tolstoy said. "Perhaps one day, the slaves will understand the importance of our work."

William pictured the scrawny, dirt-covered slaves he'd seen picking corn on that first day. Not one had contained an ounce of fat on their sinewy bones. His anger grew as he looked around at the bulbous-headed men and woman, whose full plates and full stomachs gave them the energy to push words past their arrogant lips.

He wanted to take back his Tech Magic guns, pull the metal buttons, and send them all to whatever came after. The Gifted weren't human, but they weren't immortal — not really. They could die. They knew their faults, just like the humans who lived in the woods. They knew better than to wander into danger. That was why they stayed in this opulent tower, giving pompous orders and reading their books.

They were above danger, because they lived a protected life.

Or were they?

William looked down at his ugly robe.

Maybe through all their intellect, they'd already made a mistake. William pondered that thought.

Not one of the slaves in those squalid buildings had a chance at reclaiming their freedom. They were trapped in a system that wouldn't release them. But he wasn't. The Gifted had let William inside their twisted den—a simple infected boy.

What if he could find a way to rid New City of their leaders? What if he could erase the power that kept the slaves contained?

The idea felt far-reaching and impossible. But it was an idea, and the longer he thought about it, the more he realized that an idea born of anger might be a clear-headed solution.

Maybe there was another way to help his friends.

Sitting at the table, staring at all the smug, arrogant faces, William couldn't dismiss a nagging thought.

The Gifted had to die.

He had to kill them all.

Chapter 20: Kirby

Whirs and clanks filled the air. Smoke from the city's shops permeated the loud, sweltering room and lingered in Kirby's nose.

All around her, slaves toiled, dripping sweat. Some wore thick gloves, or aprons over their usual clothes, while a few wore crude masks. Some workers manipulated long sheets of metal in larger machines, curving or cutting, while others fashioned smaller bits. About half the workers were women. A few people peered at Kirby between their duties, even though she had already been in the building for a little while.

Near the back of the room, several long workbenches sat at a small distance from the wall, with bins for scraps and piles of metal placed between them. Some of the benches contained smaller metal machines, with sweaty people using them, or using hand tools. Racks hung in orderly rows on either side of the room, containing the tools not in use.

The woman named Rosita, with whom she'd been paired, led her to the back. Rosita's face was ruddy, flecked with sweat. "We work mostly with sheet metal in here. I've heard you have some experience."

"Yes, I have experience, but it has been a while," Kirby said.

She hoped the lie wouldn't bury her.

"We wondered if someone would fill Jonah's spot," Rosita mused, loudly enough to be heard over the whir of the machines. "We thought they would increase our workload."

Kirby nodded. She knew the loss of a worker could affect the others. "I was in the fields."

Rosita nodded. "I remember you. You arrived a few weeks ago." Handing Kirby a leather apron and gloves, she said, "You'll want to wear these."

Kirby donned the clothes. As she put them on, she glanced sideways at a few guards who chatted outside the doorway, past the bevy of machines. They seemed glad to be away from the sweaty slaves.

Pointing around the room, Rosita explained, "We have blacksmiths in other buildings that forge tools, or make molds, but most in this building work on lathes or English wheels. The people on the benches, like us, mostly use hand tools: shears, metal brakes, and a few other implements."

Kirby nodded. She'd been around some of the machines before, though she'd never used them.

Rosita explained, "Right now I am working on a project for The Learning Building. We're fashioning some sheets of metal to reinforce the windows on the lower floors. You can help." Pointing to a stack of metal on the floor, between the workbench and the bin next to it, she said, "This is the material we'll use."

Kirby examined the pile of metal. Most was in square or rectangular shapes, looking as if it had been pulled from the rubble in ruined cities.

Answering Kirby's unspoken question, Rosita said, "The metal was traded from people in the forests. The guards bring in new batches to ensure that we don't run out." Pointing at a piece of sheet metal leaning against the wall, she said, "That is the piece we are matching to make the barricades for the windows. It is our template. We don't have to be exact, but the guards — and Rudyard — want it close."

"I understand," Kirby said.

Gesturing at a long rectangular tool affixed to the

workbench, Rosita explained, "That's our metal brake, which helps us keep straight lines. For this project, I have had luck with metal shears. We only need to make sure the metal is large enough to cover the window frames. The guards aren't concerned with the edges." Rosita nodded to a pair of thick metal clippers on the nearby bench. "Can you help me with a sheet?"

Rosita directed Kirby toward the next sheet in the pile, which she helped pick up. With Kirby's help, Rosita propped up the metal, making a straight line down the side with her shears, matching the template piece. When she was finished, she said, "We put the scraps in a bin over here, to be used by some other metal shops. Other workers take the bins away during our shift, as they get full."

Rosita tossed the long, skinny pieces of scrap in the bin nearby. Peeking over into the bin, Kirby saw a few other scraps at the bottom, in various shapes and sizes. Most were thin and small enough to give her ideas. She glanced outside the building. Past the slew of workers and machines, the guards chatted, looking in the room only occasionally.

Ensuring that no one saw her gazing too long, she looked back at Rosita, helping with another cut.

"Can I work on the next piece?" Kirby asked Rosita.

"Sure," Rosita answered. "Give it a try. When you are good enough, you can work by yourself."

Chapter 21: William

"Where are you going, William?" Amelia called over.

"I'm just taking a break," he said, straightening his shoulders, as if he were proud of his robe. He gave her a friendly wave as he walked into the room with the glass cases. After he left, Amelia ambled over to chat with Barron. A few other Gifted grumbled, or held quiet conversation.

Using his moments alone, William walked to the glass cases.

Peering through the first, he studied a circular, glass bauble. The weapons and trinkets in the glass cases were more familiar than they were a few weeks ago, but instead of filling him with wonder, they filled him with sadness. Rather than picture the mysterious tribes who made them, he couldn't help thinking of how they were dead. Who knew what ends they had met?

Perhaps some died at the hands of The Gifted.

Knowing what he knew now, William wouldn't be surprised.

Moving along, he studied one of the long knives with cryptic carvings on its handle, gleaming underneath the case. Next to it was a sideways bow with a long, wooden handle. He'd only seen one thing as strange in his travels, but not in a while. Beside them, he saw more knives and swords. Some had obvious uses. And it wouldn't take much practice to learn the ones that were new to him.

But how would he get to them?

He peeked over toward the doorway, ensuring that no one was in view before tapping softly on one of the cases. The glass was thicker than most similar barriers he'd seen. He didn't see a lock, or a place where he could pry the cases open. He recalled one of the buildings he'd been in long ago, filled with broken pieces of stone that came up from the floor, surrounded by glass. He'd been told that place was an Ancient museum. Such places were used to preserve artifacts, instead of using them. The concept was strange to William, but it matched what The Gifted had done here.

The weapons were protected in a way that was difficult—nearly impossible—to get through without sheer force.

And breaking the glass was a surefire way to get noticed, or killed.

He'd be overwhelmed before he could take down more than one or two of his enemies. He needed to kill all of The Gifted—not just a few.

Through the doorway, he caught a glimpse of Barron speaking with Amelia. More Gifted sat in their chairs around them. Looking at their large, imposing figures, William knew he couldn't single-handedly kill all of them with primitive weapons. He might kill one or two before the others reacted, but they would overwhelm him. They might have weapons he couldn't see, and they certainly had guards.

He wanted the weapons in the room to be the answer, but he didn't see how.

A foolish fantasy played in his head. Maybe he could sneak up at night, barricade himself in the room, and break the glass cases. He could create a stronghold with his weapons and battle off anyone who came to harm him. He would be king of the shimmering tower, if only for a while.

But that was a way to death, even if death didn't come quickly. He would starve, or The Gifted would send more guards or demons than he could handle. They would beat down the door and overwhelm him.

They would kill him before he raised a rusted knife.

Or maybe they'd keep him alive, so he could watch his other friends killed.

The glass cases weren't the answer.

He needed a better way to ensure that he wiped The Gifted from the earth. He needed a way that might lead to his friends' freedom, as impossible as that sounded.

He needed Tech Magic.

Chapter 22: Bray

Bray hurried down the alley. Around him, slaves carried buckets of water to or from their houses, or cleaned up from lunch. A few children played games with stones in the alley, stacking them and knocking them over. Relief crossed his face as he found Kirby.

"I saw you pulled from the line," Bray said. "What happened?"

He looked her up and down, thinking she might have an injury he couldn't see.

"Ollie took me from harvest duty," Kirby explained. "He took me to his house." Seeing the worried look on Bray's face, she added, "He did not touch me, though that was his intent."

Kirby told him about being brought to Ollie's quarters, as well as the task she was assigned. She also relayed Esmeralda's story about a vicious attack she had suffered. Bray's anger roiled as he heard about Ollie's demeaning words and his searching hands.

"If his family wasn't there, things might have gone differently," Kirby said.

"I will slit his throat before he touches you again," Bray promised.

"You will not have to," Kirby said. "I will kill him myself."

Bray cooled his anger. Kirby had never needed his protection, as much as he wanted to give it.

"I know men like him," Bray said. "He will keep trying, until he succeeds."

"You think I do not know that?" Kirby's eyes filled with the same rage he had seen that first day in the courtyard, when a guess had become a stinging reality and they were enslaved. "I will deflect him as long as I am able. I have dealt with many men like him. When the day comes that he touches me, I will kill him."

"You will die if you fight back," Bray protested.

"Would you have me submit?" Kirby's eyes moistened with an anger that could quickly turn on Bray, if he pushed.

"I'm not asking you to let that happen," Bray clarified.

"If I let him do what he wants, I have already lost," Kirby said, her voice wavering. "I will not let it happen. A beating, maybe, but not this."

"I understand," Bray said, and he did. "I will find a way to work nearby. Perhaps The Shadow People can get me into the metal shops."

"If The Shadow People had that power, don't you think they would have offered?" Kirby asked, shaking her head. "Obviously, the guards will not help us. Such favors are beyond our reach."

"Maybe I can—" Bray opened and closed his mouth as no good answers came.

"We have no control over where we are. We both know that." Kirby's eyes showed her internal struggle. "I will handle myself for now. In the meantime, we will keep working on the topics we spoke about last night. It is the only way." Shifting the conversation to a potential plan, she said, "I am already getting ideas from my day in the machine shop. If I can figure out a way to ferret some scraps from the shop, we might have a solution to our weapon problem. Or at least something that will help."

"Shanks, to fill in our weaponry," Bray caught on.

"It is not a solution, but a start. Taken over time, some

pieces of metal might add up. Perhaps we might even have enough so each person's hands are filled, when the time comes."

"I have some ideas, too." Bray briefed her on some of his thoughts from the fields.

"You are thinking of an escape route, if the worst happens," Kirby summarized.

"I remembered what James said," Bray commented. "If we have a better idea of the terrain, it can only help."

Kirby nodded. "Certainly."

"These slaves are not fighters, like us," Bray continued. "Or at least not all of them. If we start a revolt, we might succeed for a while, but at some point, we might have to flee. A few moments' lead can mean the difference between living and dying. We both know that. We need an alternate route to freedom."

"What does that mean for William?" Kirby asked, raising a topic that had plagued Bray.

"Unfortunately, it sounds as if we will have to help ourselves before we help him," Bray said.

Looking up at the shimmering tower, Kirby said, "We will do what it takes."

Silence came over the conversation. Something else was on Kirby's mind.

"What are you thinking?" he asked.

"I am thinking of the others in New City, like Esmeralda," Kirby admitted. "For every one of the two hundred Shadow People, there are many more that remain silent, scared to leave, or trapped in a position where they cannot run. Hopefully, we can help them, too."

"You think they all deserve a golden palace in the clouds," Bray inferred.

"Everyone does," Kirby said.

Bray fell silent a moment. "We should get back to lunch and to our afternoon duties."

Kirby nodded as she looked around.

"Be careful, Kirby," Bray said, touching her arm.

Kirby watched him for a moment, anger and sadness in her eyes. He squeezed her arm.

And then she broke away, walking off down the alley.

Bray lingered until she was out of sight, fearing it might be the last time he saw her.

Chapter 23: William

William sat on one of the long, soft beds in his room. Amelia had suggested he read through a pile of books she had given him, but he was disobeying. It was a small act of defiance that probably didn't help him, but it felt good. Looking out the windows at the bright sunlight, he allowed himself to remember what it was like hiking through the forest, Bray and Kirby at his side. They had so many memories that too many blended together.

But one particular memory came back to him.

He recalled a bright, spring day when the leaves were budding on the trees and the sting of winter had gone. The weather had been perfect.

William had sat next to Bray and Kirby on a mountaintop, surveying the crumbled spires of a distant city they had yet to explore. With the sun hot on his face, a warm belly full of rabbit, and a flask full of water, William thought that city could contain anything. William had listened as Bray told exaggerated tales of the wild. He and Kirby had laughed, poking holes in Bray's stories, making lighthearted fun. William remembered never wanting that moment to end. It was a simple moment, memorable in its happiness.

It was so easy to take those days for granted when you didn't know they were ending.

But now he had hope.

He had a plan, even if he didn't know any details.

A knock at his door reminded him that Amelia was

coming for him. She had told him they would continue practicing letters.

"Come in," William called, broken from his reverie.

Surprise hit him when he saw Barron standing there, his bulbous head tipped to the side. He trudged in, his robe swaying around him. "It's been a while since I've been on this floor," he said, nostalgically, looking around.

Fear lodged in William's throat as he recalled the hairpin underneath the dresser. Not wanting to prolong a visit, he crossed the room. "Where's Amelia?" he asked, in an innocent tone.

"She is upstairs. I offered to take you to the drafting room. She thought you might benefit from my explanation of what I am working on. Later, she will work on your letters, as she promised."

William nodded through the lump in his throat. "Okay." He took a step toward the door, hoping Barron would follow.

"You seem intrigued," Barron said.

"I am just excited to hear your explanations," William said, keeping his expression innocuous.

"Of course. Come with me." Barron waved a hand. "Perhaps you will get bitten by the same bug of knowledge as I have been."

**

William stared out the third-floor windows, overlooking the balcony and the crop fields beyond, Barron at his side.

It seemed as if Barron could speak about the plans forever, audience or not. His eyes sparkled with an energy that William had only seen a few times—while they ate dinner, discussing their books.

Or when he watched Cullen die.

William wished he could disappear into his head, like

he did when he read upstairs. Instead, he gazed out the window, past the balcony and out into the crops.

"What do you think of my revised plans?" Barron asked, snapping William to attention.

"I like the pontoons," William said, repeating the funny word that Amelia had told him.

"They will help us set the plane on water, when no other option is available," Barron repeated.

"I understand," William said.

His attention drifted outside, where a string of strangely-clad men emerged from the distant woods, pulling a caravan of covered wagons. He watched as they toted their goods through the grass field at the forest's edge, heading toward the dirt path between the crops. A few demons clustered by the edges of the path, watching the approaching newcomers. If only he had a way to harness the twisted men's power.

Of course he couldn't, while trapped in a building.

Mistaking William's silence for reflectiveness, Barron said, "It is an adjustment, living with our intellect." Smiling at William, he asked, "Have you found it so? You are learning things at a rapid rate."

Considering his answer, William said, "Yes."

"Too many thoughts enter our heads at once. Sometimes, we have to choose which ones to follow. But we pick things up much faster than any human. We have intelligence of which they can only dream. Much more than The Plagued Ones outside."

William made a show of his smile.

"I get ideas at the strangest times," Barron said, evidently enjoying hearing his own voice. "Sometimes I read something in The Library Room, and it will hit me days later. Other times, I will get an idea in the middle of the night, while I sleep. I've worked some long hours on my projects." Barron's tone was reflective. "In any case, the bug for knowledge is a strange thing. Perhaps you should pick up some books on aviation and see if you have a passion for it. You will not understand all the words just yet, but in time, you will."

"I will try them," William said. Looking over at Barron's smiling, repulsive face, he said, "Perhaps I will even check some out this afternoon in The Library Room."

But William already had a passion, and a goal.

He would check out those books. But the only thing he would think about while he stared at them was how he'd destroy The Gifted.

Chapter 24: William

William sat at one of the smaller desks by the window, staring at a page he wasn't reading. Bright sunlight splashed across the page, illuminating some of the simpler sentences that he was starting to grasp. Across the room, Amelia perused the bookshelves, taking out a few worn tomes, compiling a new stack for him to study, based on Barron's recommendations.

If he weren't so afraid of her, he might have thrown her books in her face.

Instead, he steeped himself in thought.

Tech Magic. That had to be his answer. But where could he get it? It was possible The Gifted had weapons in their rooms, but it wasn't a certainty. Guards were stationed at the building's entrance, and on the seventeenth floor, beneath The Library Room. All of the other floors were inaccessible without an enormous risk. The only time he might sneak into a room unsupervised was at night, when The Gifted were in their quarters, or in the afternoon. But opening the wrong door might lead him into a vicious encounter. He'd learned where a few of The Gifted's rooms were, like Tolstoy's and Amelia's, but not all of them. And neither of those floors promised weapons. He certainly hadn't seen any weapons in Tolstoy's room.

Frustrating thoughts.

He considered what he knew. The square, secure box on the ground floor had once contained their confiscated swords and Tech Magic guns. But who knew to where those weapons had been relocated? The box had been empty when they'd arrived; certainly The Gifted had moved them. If there were a storehouse past the guards, he'd never make it without a weapon to get him there.

One weapon, to have a chance at getting more.

William's circular thoughts led him nowhere.

The only weapons of which he was certain were those in the glass cases.

William shook his head as his gaze drifted over the desks and out the windows. His eyes roamed back to Amelia's desk.

A thought struck him.

Amelia's gun.

He'd forgotten about the old, sentimental relic.

Even if that gun was still there, it was empty. Amelia knew better than to keep ammunition with it. It wasn't loaded before, and she certainly wouldn't have armed it so that a desperate, captured boy could get a hold of it. It would be foolish to risk his safety for an empty gun, which would be just as effective as the microscope, or any other weapon only good for hitting someone.

But some hope returned as he considered something Amelia had said: *"It should work. I keep it clean, even though I no longer have the need to use it."*

If it worked, she must have ammunition.

And where might she keep the ammunition for a sentimental gun?

In her room.

William's heart pounded as an idea solidified. Perhaps William had found the first secret to his escape. Rummaging through one room was much less risky than fruitlessly searching through several. If he could find ammunition, it would be worth the risk to go to her floor.

William had hope, now that he had a destination.

He just needed to figure out how to get there.

Chapter 25: Bray

All around Bray, workers dispersed, splitting off to their homes, grateful for the only reprieve they got in this hellish place: dinner and a few hours with their families. Those brave enough to leave their homes after supper spent their time by the bonfires, after the demons had fed.

He looked down at his dirt-caked fingernails. He needed a wash. Returning to his house, he found Teddy using a bucket in the corner.

"I got our water," Teddy said, cleaning himself with a rag.

"Thanks," Bray said, shucking off his sweaty shirt. "It seems as if the dirt always finds a way to our skin, regardless of what we wear."

"Isn't that the truth?" Teddy asked. Finished cleaning up, he passed the bucket to Bray. "I saw Kirby in the metal shops today."

Bray nodded. "They pulled her from the fields this morning and gave her a new role." He kept his answer brief.

Teddy said, "It is hard work, as all the jobs are. Her hands will get used to a new ache."

"How were the sewing rooms?"

"The same as always: too much clothing to finish, but never enough time to do it. The guards treat each day more urgently than the last."

"They're pushing us harder with the crops, as well," Bray muttered.

"It will get worse, as the season ends," Teddy said empathetically.

Bray cleaned in silence for a few moments as workers outside hurried to their homes. With a few moments before the demon bells started ringing, Teddy sat back on his bedroll.

With a sigh, he said, "Back in the earliest days, there were far fewer jobs in New City." Teddy wiped some water from his face. "Most of the earliest people spent their days clearing the rubble from the crop fields, or planting seeds that didn't always take. Some spent time building the wall, or constructing the houses where we now live. Others lived in The Learning Building, serving The Gifted."

Bray nodded. He looked out the door and up to the tall building, as if he might see past the glistening windows and find William.

"Back then, The Gifted kept swarms of The Plagued Ones nearby for protection, while they let out the rest to hunt in the forests," Teddy said, looking out at the guards carrying bells toward the gate. "They didn't hand feed them the way they do now."

"That life seems more suited for an animal like a pig or a cow," Bray grumbled.

"It is an unnatural life," Teddy agreed. "The Plagued Ones might listen, but they are always on the edge of hunger. They fight their instincts by living this way."

They watched a few more guards pass by.

Shifting on his bedroll, Teddy said, "Life was simpler back then. Not as many machines to keep up, or guards to make our tasks harder."

Bray asked, "How do you know so much about those first days?"

"When I used to go out to the bonfires, I'd hear stories passed down from the workers' families." Teddy averted his eyes. "The Gifted also used to tell tales when they came down here years ago. Now they stay up in the tower. They're more secure in the life they've built. Or maybe they value their safety too much."

Bray nodded. He knew the safeguards all too well.

Looking at Teddy, Bray said, "You know a lot, for someone who mostly keeps to himself."

"I might be quiet, but I pay attention," Teddy said. "I hear many things."

"In the shops, I imagine," Bray said.

Teddy nodded.

The bells started ringing. With too much commotion to talk, they turned their attention out the doorway.

Chapter 26: William

"I can't believe how much better you've gotten at writing, in only a few weeks," Amelia marveled at William, as the daylight waned through the windows. "Your letters are more legible than some of The Gifteds'."

"My name looks different than I ever would've expected," William said. Not for the first time, he marveled at the strange symbols for the word he'd been saying all his life.

Amelia pointed to the word she'd written underneath his, which started with the symbol 'A'. He compared both names.

"My name is a little longer than yours," William said.

"Only by a letter," Amelia clarified.

"I still don't understand why some of these letters appear twice," he said, frowning as he looked at the middle of his name.

"The language can be complicated in its rules," Amelia said. "In fact, our language is one of the most difficult to learn. But you have done it correctly."

William stared at the strange symbols, wondering who had decided those rules, and why everyone else had agreed.

"Are you ready to go downstairs for sleep?" Amelia asked.

William looked around. In the time they'd been writing, most of the other Gifted had left for their quarters. Thinking back, William recalled a few goodnights he hadn't acknowledged.

"I'm ready," he said.

Finished with the lesson, they put away their materials.

"You are fortunate to have such a library," Amelia said, gesturing at the bookshelves, as they put some books away. "The price of some of those books was steeper than you might imagine."

"It is hard to think about how many different places you must have foraged to get them."

"In some of the earlier days, we took large risks. Sometimes, we went into buildings that were mostly collapsed, sifting through the rubble. The price of knowledge is never cheap. But knowledge leads to greater things, as you know."

William nodded.

"Let's get going," Amelia said.

William followed her out of The Library Room and down the stairs. He looked out the windows into the cornfields, watching the windmills churn through an evening breeze that he missed as dearly as his friends.

Passing one of the landings, he glanced over at Amelia's doorway. He looked away before he caught her attention. As they took another flight of stairs, William put a hand to his stomach, stifling a cough.

"Are you okay, William?" Amelia asked, pausing with concern.

"I'm fine," William said, continuing.

"It sounds as if you are getting sick."

"I'm okay," William said, putting on the happy smile that he'd practiced for weeks.

"Some of us get illnesses as the summer season ends. Perhaps you should sleep a little later tomorrow," Amelia suggested. Reaching the landing to his floor, she opened the door to his quarters.

"I'm sure I'll be fine," William said. "I don't want to miss a lesson."

Chapter 27: Bray

Bray cracked his neck under the morning sun, tossing a piece of corn into his wagon.

Loud chatter drew his attention to the end of the row, where two guards moved faster than usual, striding in the direction of the forest. A moment later, a few more passed, accompanied by Rudyard. Grabbing his wagon, Bray wheeled it down the row and stopped at the edge of the dirt path, where he could get a clearer view.

Deep in other rows, slaves pulled fresh ears from tall stalks. A few looked over as they saw something more interesting than a wagon full of crops. Bray waited until they looked away before he peered after the guards and Rudyard, toward the forest.

A few of the men called the Yatari engaged in conversation with Rudyard and his guards at the head of the path. They held large bags in their hands. The Yatari spoke with animated expressions, raising their shoulders and arching their backs. Rudyard said something. A moment later, a Yatari that might've been a leader let one hand off of his bag to motion over the wall at New City, waving his hands angrily.

A few interested demons crept to the edges of the path.

Rudyard pointed at them, making a show of power.

The Yatari handed the bags to Rudyard and the Head Guards, who started back down the path, toward the gate. Bray ducked back into the row, waiting for Rudyard and his guards to pass. When they were gone, he saw the Yatari standing, waiting.

Maybe their discontent was something he could use.

Bray crept through the dirt rows of corn, cutting between the stalks, avoiding the eyes of slaves and demons as he worked his way toward where they stood. Many of the other slaves had wandered away, probably afraid to get too close to a cluster of guards, and Rudyard.

Or they were afraid of the demons, who kept everyone in check.

Soon he was near the end of an aisle beside the Yatari. All wore loose, white garments, with boots that seemed slightly shorter than what he normally saw in the woods. Necklaces made of strange, multi-colored rocks and shells hugged their necks. One man wore a hat made of a thin fabric, cocked to the side, covering a shock of thick hair. They spoke in strange accents, muttering, or perhaps arguing. Bray couldn't hear much, but every now and then, he picked up a familiar word.

They stood in a tight group, shaking their heads in disgust.

They were clearly upset.

Bray set down his wagon, feigning work as he watched them. A few turned their heads as they eyed the demons skulking through the crops, clearly uneasy. One drew a flask from his side, sipping nervously. Bray looked down the front of the path, near the gate. A few guards ambled about, yelling at slaves, but Rudyard and his posse had disappeared. It seemed as if they were behind the gate, getting whatever goods they meant to trade.

None returned.

Yet.

Catching the eye of one of the Yatari, who stood at the rear of the group, Bray made a show of glancing up at the sun, wiping the sweat from his brow.

"Another hot day," Bray said, only loudly enough that the man could hear.

The man shifted uncomfortably, but he didn't respond. The other Yatari kept their focus in the direction of New City. Bray's eyes roved over the man's necklace. What he'd thought were rocks or shells were actually bones, or teeth. Seeing them, he recalled the Semposi, pulling settlers from the forest and using them for trades, or other purposes the gods only knew. But these teeth were too battered, too yellowed, even for settlers or barbarians. Most were chipped.

Taking a guess, Bray asked, "Are those Plagued Ones' teeth?"

The Yatari man shifted uncomfortably, adjusting his pack. Feeling the weight of Bray's unanswered question, he nodded.

"I used to slay them," Bray said, spitting on the ground.

The Yatari man's friends gave him warning stares as the Yatari man nodded again.

Bray smiled. "They are vile creatures. I might be forced to live among them, but I'd rather they were at the end of my sword. At least you have found some use for them."

The man refocused on the path in front of him. Bray was the property of another, bound by death and punishment. Of course, they wouldn't speak to him.

"I've killed over a thousand of them in my lifetime," Bray said, trying to hide some of the frustration in his voice. "Though that doesn't help me much here."

He was surprised when the man answered in the same strange accent Bray had overheard. "The necklaces scare away the barbarian tribes. They help us avoid danger."

Bray nodded. With a knowing smile, he said, "A good idea. I wish I had thought of that myself."

The Yatari man seemed pleased at the compliment as he scratched his tan face.

Making a show of wiping away his sweat, Bray said, "It

seems you are a bit more used to the temperatures than I am. I'm from up north. It was much nicer when I had more trees to hide behind. And a sword to slay the nagging beasts." He looked sideways, where a demon lurked between some stalks, watching them.

"I don't envy your work," the Yatari man said sympathetically, before looking away once again.

Bray leaned around the last corn stalk, checking for Rudyard and the guards. Deep in the distance, some guards chastised one of the slower slaves pulling a wagon toward the path, but no one else approached.

The Yatari man lifted his flask to his mouth again, taking another sip.

"That wouldn't happen to be snowberry, would it?" Bray grinned, recapturing the man's attention.

"Snowberry?" the man asked. "I'm not sure what that is."

"That's what we drank in the taverns where I'm from." Bray shook his head. "I couldn't tell you the last time I had it."

The Yatari examined his flask, as if he wasn't used to getting a question about it. "It's Gutrot," he said finally.

"I'd kill for something other than lukewarm piss-water," Bray lamented.

Pity crossed the Yatari man's face as he looked at his flask.

"Not a good idea," one of his friends grumbled. "They don't want us talking with them."

Those words seemed to stir something in the Yatari man, whose eyes flashed a moment of anger. Putting his anger into a step, the man strode into the corn to talk with Bray. "Fuck them."

He handed Bray his flask.

The other Yatari shook their heads, clearly nervous. They kept their eyes focused on the path, making it clear they didn't agree with the first man's actions. Bray tilted back the flask, swallowing a sip of the beverage. It was bitter and had a strange aftertaste, but it warmed his stomach.

"Thanks," Bray said gratefully, handing back the flask. "What's your name?"

"Xavier," the man said, with a quick nod.

"You live by the ocean?" Bray said, remembering some information he'd heard.

Xavier studied him, surprised. "You know of us?"

"Only what I've heard from here," Bray said. "As I said, my people came from up north."

"What is the name of your people?"

"We don't have a name," Bray said, thinking about it. "But we're from a town called Brighton."

"Brighton?" Xavier asked, clearly intrigued.

"It is a township many days walk from here. We were a ways from home, traveling, when the Semposi chased us," Bray said. "The Gifted captured us not long after. Now we are slaves."

Xavier shook his head, as more pity crossed his eyes.

"I heard your people have boats," Bray said. "One of my friends used to sail the ocean."

Xavier looked over at his friends, a few of whom had been casually listening, and were now eavesdropping closer. "What types of boat did your friend have?"

"She had several. I don't know the names, but they were large," Bray said, making a grand show with his hands. "A storm ravaged them. Most have turned to wreckage." He frowned as he thought on it. "Although, a few parts could probably be salvaged, if someone had the right knowledge."

Looking back at his friends, Xavier asked, "Do you know where these wreckages are?"

Noting the curiosity on Xavier's face, Bray said, "I suppose I could remember. They landed where my friend traveled, a long way from here. I will warn you, it is not a short trip."

Xavier traded another look with his friends. "Still, that information would be worth something to us."

"I would accept a gift, if I was allowed," Bray said with a grunt, looking down at his wagon. "But the guards would beat me if they found something I wasn't supposed to have."

Another flash of anger sparked in Xavier's eyes. "Perhaps another drink, then."

"Thank you, friend," Bray said, as he accepted the flask and took another long swig. Making a show of pondering something, he said, "Perhaps there is something you can help me with."

Xavier's reluctance returned.

"I traveled with a few other friends, before I came here," Bray lied, shaking his head. "They went in another direction. I was hoping for some assurance that they were alive."

Xavier looked carefully around. "There are many people in the forest," he said evasively.

"Of course. I was hoping if I described them, you might have some information."

"What do they look like?"

"One was portly, with a large mustache. The other had a beard that came to his waist," Bray lied. "My hope was that they ended up in a place better than this."

"I have not seen them," Xavier said. "Which direction did they head, and when did you last see them?"

"They headed east, a few weeks ago," Bray said. "We were split up."

Xavier chewed his lip. He seemed as if he was torn between answers. Or perhaps he had figured out Bray's motive. Choosing his words carefully, he said, "If your friends went west or south, they might have become a meal. But if they headed east, between the mountains, they would have found a path free from The Plagued Ones. There is less game for them to hunt."

"Over there?" Bray asked, nodding discreetly over the

field of corn and in the direction of two distant bumps on the horizon.

Xavier nodded. "Not as many animals lurk there. The Plagued Ones in this city like to hunt in the north, or to the west."

"How far is the pass?"

"Less than half a morning's walk." Xavier flashed a cautious glance. "It is the path we take when we come to trade. It is safe from The Plagued Ones." Carefully, he added, "If your friends made it that far, they might be safe."

The Yatari nodded, watching Bray expectantly.

"Thank you for the reassurance," Bray said to them. "Now, I owe you some directions."

Chapter 28: William

Pillowy, circling clouds covered some of the morning sunshine as it filtered into William's room, casting stripes of light over the floor.

William sat at the edge of his bed, listening to Amelia's footsteps getting closer. He started in on the hacking cough he'd practiced several times since she'd left the night before. The noise echoed across the room, bounced off the walls, and hopefully made its way out in the hallway. He heard Amelia pause before she knocked.

"William? Are you all right?"

He waited a moment before responding, "Yes. Come in."

Amelia peeked in on him with concern. William kept to the edge of the bed, holding his raw, red throat, irritated from his forced coughs.

"You don't sound any better than last night," she observed.

"I don't feel too bad," he said, making a face that showed otherwise. "I am ready to head upstairs."

Amelia didn't seem certain, but she didn't say anything as William slowly got off the bed, accompanying her to the doorway. Pulling in a heavy breath, he let out another brutal hack. This time Amelia stopped, shielding her face.

More worry overtook her expression. "It sounds as if you might be getting a sickness. Those types of illnesses are easily spread to the rest of us."

"Spread?" William asked. "Sicknesses are a will of the gods, aren't they?"

"The gods." Amelia laughed. "That is not the way sicknesses work. Humans get them first, and spread their illnesses to us. If we are together in the same room, more of us are apt to get sick. It might be a little easier for you to recover, because you are younger, but severe illnesses are a worry for us older Gifted. Our brains might be intelligent, but our bodies are still susceptible." Taking a step away from him, she said, "It is probably better if you rest a little while today, away from the others."

William made a show of his disappointment. "I was looking forward to writing more letters today."

"There will be plenty of time for that later," Amelia said, putting a hand over her mouth. "I will have breakfast sent to you here by the guards."

William held his stomach.

"Are you feeling sick to your stomach, as well?"

He nodded.

"Probably an effect of your illness. Maybe you should skip breakfast. I will have the guards bring up lunch, when they come back with our second trip for dessert."

William put on a disappointed face.

"You need your rest, to recover," Amelia said. "You should try to sleep."

William nodded, maintaining his dejected expression as she opened the door and walked out. Before she left, he forced his way through one more loud, sidesplitting cough. He saw her wincing as she shut the door.

And then William was alone.

William listened to Amelia's footsteps as she treaded up the same stairs, presumably going to The Library Room. For a while, doors opened in the floors above and below, as more of The Gifted headed to the eighteenth floor. A few conversed quietly. And then the building fell preternaturally quiet.

William waited a long while, until after he heard the guards bringing breakfast to The Gifted.

Only when they returned to the ground floor did he get off the bed.

William tiptoed to the doorway, listening, before retrieving the hairpin from beneath his bureau. Turning it in his hand, he swallowed. It had been weeks since he'd held it, and just as long since he'd considered using it.

He was deathly afraid he might kill his friends with a mistake.

But they might die, regardless. And if they did, he would never forgive himself for his inaction.

Swallowing a nervousness that he feared would accompany him forever, William crept to the door and unlocked it.

Chapter 29: Kirby

Kirby balanced a piece of sheet metal on the workbench, picking up her shears. Nearby, Rosita completed a cut, tossing her finished piece into a stack. The pile of finished sheets they'd started this morning had grown to almost twice its size. A few times, other slaves entered the shops under the guards' direction, taking away the completed piles. But there was plenty of time in between.

That was the time in which Kirby was interested.

Cutting the sheet in front of her, Kirby forced her way through a stubborn piece. Each sheet seemed to vary in condition. Every so often, she saw a sheet that contained some stain or smell she couldn't identify. Most smelled of the decrepit buildings of which they'd once been a part, while others contained a hint of animal dung. One or two contained the crusted, dried skin of a carcass.

"The traders don't always clean the metal, before we get it," Rosita explained, nodding as she saw Kirby picking at a stubborn brown spot with her gloves. "We've seen all types of things on them."

"I believe it," Kirby muttered.

"One time, we found one with what must've been a skull's worth of blood, stained on the side," Rosita said. "Another time we got a batch that smelled like The Plagued Ones. I think the whole shop smelled that day." A thin smile crossed her face.

A loud, rhythmic clanging echoed across the room,

interrupting Rosita's conversation. Kirby looked over to find a dirty slave working a small piece of metal through a machine. Rosita returned to her work. The workers in the machine shops talked less, unable to compete with the constant sounds of the workers around them. Occasionally, a guard poked his head in, asking a question or making a demand, but otherwise the din was constant.

Kirby noticed the guards mostly stayed out of the building, so they could talk and share jokes away from the noise of the shop.

Finished with a long cut, she pulled a finger-width scrap from the end of the sheet and carried it over to the scrap bin. Peering in, she saw a growing pile that the slaves hadn't carted away. She looked over her shoulder, watching the guards chat away.

Kirby set the metal in with the others.

She overruled a dangerous impulse.

It was too soon.

A loud laugh drew her attention to the doorway.

A lumbering form stood among the other guards. A bitter taste filled Kirby's mouth as she saw Ollie, holding up his hands in some lewd gesture. He glanced over, meeting her eyes. She quickly averted them. The memory of his stinking, sour breath and his roaming hands came rushing back. Her pulse pounded. He might come inside when he was through talking, pulling her away from her task.

The moment she feared might be closer than she knew.

Kirby kept her head down, clenching the shears in her hand as she cut with new vigor.

She risked another glance at the doorway.

The laughing stopped.

The guards were on to some new, crude story.

Ollie was gone.

Chapter 30: William

Alone on the stairs, William paused.

Fear pierced his heart like a stake.

Traveling down the stairs in the nighttime was fear-inducing enough, but traveling in the daytime provided its own set of worries. He had no cover of shadow, no place to hide, should someone discover him. The amount of time it took to unlock a door ruled out ducking into a room. He would have to go down three flights of stairs to get to Amelia's quarters — three flights of quietly sneaking and hoping no one came out.

Something else frightened him.

Tolstoy's room was on the way.

Tolstoy was probably inside his quarters, poring over his books and his drawings, doing the gods knew what else. *Perhaps planning more of his experiments.* William's fright became a sickening fear as he looked up and down the surrounding flights of stairs. The stairwell was quiet. He heard nothing, other than the faint hum of a machine from somewhere outside.

William crept down the flights of stairs.

Next to Tolstoy's door, he listened for sounds — a footstep, a cough, or the slide of a chair's legs across the floor. He heard nothing. He pictured the large, wooden desk on the far side of the room, with Tolstoy's imposing figure occupying it. Tolstoy was so intent on his work that he was silent. Or maybe he wasn't in there at all. That gave William a frightening afterthought.

What if he encountered Tolstoy on the stairs?

He ran through a stream of excuses.

Amelia left the door open.

I was looking for breakfast.

I was coming to your room to ask you a question.

No excuse seemed legitimate enough.

He wasn't supposed to be out.

Soon he had passed the landing and was beyond the door's sight. William breathed a sigh of relief as he crept past a few more landings and reached Amelia's door. He paused, ensuring he heard no noise, and then worked on the lock.

Finished unlocking the door, William swung it open slowly.

Amelia's room was empty. Unlike Tolstoy's, which sported magnificent furniture and an impressive array of pictures and drawings, Amelia's room was simple. The sheets were turned down on her bed. Several pieces of clothing hung haphazardly on her bureau, or dangled from drawers. She wasn't as neat as he would have expected, from someone who appeared so ordered.

William didn't pause on the threshold. Sneaking inside, he closed the door. On the far side of the room, he saw a small desk that looked to be about in the same spot as Tolstoy's. It seemed as if she didn't use the desk often—only a few closed books sat on its surface. Next to the desk, however, was a square box that resembled the one downstairs.

Glancing over his shoulder, William tiptoed across the room, past the bureau and the disheveled clothes, and made his way to the box. He bent down, certain that he would encounter resistance and another lock he had to force his way into.

The box was open.

It made sense, when he thought about it.

The Gifted had nothing to fear from each other. And they had little to fear from the guards. Locking their rooms was probably a precaution. High walls, a demon army, and vicious guards repelled their prospective enemies. The slaves were far enough away that they were considered no danger. No one could get to them.

Until now.

William opened the box, wincing at the small noise, and peered inside, finding a few small shelves. William frowned as he found an array of objects, no two the same. Taking great care to memorize the location of the objects, he pulled out a few and inspected them. William turned an aged, brown flask in his hand that looked like it hadn't been used in many years. Next to it was a tiny bag in which someone might've collected coins, now empty. William paused as he recognized three letters on each item, all of which were different. He frowned as he noticed the symbols didn't appear in Amelia's name, or even his. Nearby were several strings of jewelry — metals that were in various shapes and conditions.

William kept digging, sorting through things that looked as if they were keepsakes. He felt a pit in his stomach as he recalled the gun upstairs, and Amelia's explanation of where she'd gotten it.

Dead people's possessions.

William's fear almost made him leave, until he spotted a small, metal tin sitting underneath a strange looking flask.

He reached for the items, taking care not to knock anything over as he did.

He looked at the flask. Shaking it gently, he realized it was filled with some sort of powder. A long tube sprouted from the top, containing some residue that looked like some of the black, ashen material he'd seen in the shells of the gun casings he'd used with Kirby.

Setting aside the flask, he opened the tin.

Inside were a handful of balls and some caps. He'd never seen the caps before, and the balls looked different than anything he'd encountered, but they might fit the gun he'd seen upstairs.

It looked as if the objects went together.

This must be what he needed.

He had no idea how to use them, but he'd figure that out later. With a quick glance behind him, he emptied the balls and the caps into his pocket, replaced the metal box with the other keepsakes, and pocketed the flask.

With everything else back in place, he snuck out the door.

Chapter 31: William

Back in his room, William caught his breath. His heart pounded so heavily he thought it might burst through his chest. But he'd done it. He'd found what he was looking for. He felt a burst of elation as he reveled in his accomplishment. But his success wouldn't last long, if he were caught.

William cocked his head, listening for the sound of fast footsteps. The Gifted might not have been in the hallway, but their presence was everywhere—in the smell of the wooden furniture in his room, in the walls, and in those ominous windows that contained the ashes of the slaves. Looking through the glass, he shuddered as he pictured those dead people forever trapped in the building, doomed to overlook the place in which they'd spent a life of enslavement. He wouldn't be the same as them.

And neither would his friends.

With his breathing calmed, William fished the hairpin from his pocket and quickly returned it to its place underneath his bureau. Returning to his bed, he pulled out the small, round pieces of metal and the caps from his robe pocket, as well as the flask. He set out the balls and caps. Each ball had a corresponding cap.

They must be rounds.

The rounds were just as magical now as they had been when Kirby had first given him a gun, all those months ago. Looking at them closer, his brow furrowed. The rounds didn't seem as old as the gun. In fact, they seemed as if they had been preserved, or perhaps found later. But that made sense. He considered what Amelia had told him. The gun was several centuries old. Other rounds would've been expended over the years.

Maybe she had stolen these rounds from somewhere — or some*one*.

His eyes roamed over the balls with wonder.

His face fell.

William counted seven rounds and caps.

Seven.

That wasn't nearly enough to kill ten Gifted. William's heart beat in his throat, as he questioned his success. William had fired guns enough times to know that not every round hit a target. And sometimes, a shot wasn't fatal. He might wound someone, without killing the person. The Gifted might have their wart-covered hands wrapped around his throat before he got a chance to finish what he started. Or they might kill him in some other, horrible way.

Foiled plans.

Staring at the small, metal balls, his heart sank. He had taken a risk with no guarantee of success. He recalled the condition of the keepsakes in Amelia's quarters. He had been careful to replace them the right way. Still, even if she didn't look at them regularly, sooner or later, she'd discover the items from the tin, and the flask, missing. And when she did, William's would be the first name that came to mind.

Who else would steal them?

Amelia might not know the specifics of how he managed to get that ammunition, but suspicion would lead to discovery. And then William would die.

William had the panicked thought that he should slip back out and replace them. But that came with an equal risk of getting caught. William swallowed, picked up one of the rounds, and turned it over between two fingers.

He couldn't get his mind off the antique, metal gun.

He wanted it in his hands.

He had gone too far in his plan to turn back now.

He would wait a day or so, to ensure The Gifted hadn't detected anything, and then he'd get it.

Chapter 32: Kirby

"We are almost done for the day," Rosita said, wiping some sweat from her forehead as she tossed another sheet of finished metal on the pile.

Kirby nodded as she looked at the doorway.

The guards were there, supervising, but none of them looked over.

Ollie was gone.

Still, she couldn't forget his eyes on her earlier.

Ollie's looming threat lingered, long after he was gone. At any moment, he might come back and pull her away, to the smirks of the guards and the fearful stares of the other slaves. No one would help her, when he pulled her off to do whatever his greasy hands desired. She couldn't get her mind off the ominous words he had spoken, when she had been in his house.

I'm not through with you.

In here, she might have a chance at defending herself, but outside, in an alley or in her home, she was defenseless.

She thought about what Bray had said about finding an escape plan. A revolt was the ultimate goal. But what if Ollie attacked her beforehand?

Kirby wouldn't die without a final fight.

She looked around. Most of the workers finished up their last, hard duties for the day. Soon, they would wind down, take off their work garments, and prepare for an evening of relative freedom. Finished with a long piece of metal, and finding no eyes on her, Kirby swallowed. She looked around.

This time Kirby didn't stop her impulse.

She used her shears to make an extra snip. A piece of metal the size and shape of a finger fell into her waiting hand.

She looked around again.

No one was watching.

Clenching a fist around the scrap, Kirby stuffed the sharp metal in her pocket.

**

The metal scrap felt like a bomb in her pocket as Kirby took the alleyways home. Every laugh made her turn; every footstep made her think someone followed. More than one pair of eyes seemed as if they fixated on her, even though she doubted that was true. She kept a wide berth as she turned every corner, afraid that hands would grab her and frisk her.

She might be paranoid, but she had something to hide.

Protection.

That's what the metal was supposed to be, once she shaped and sharpened it.

But right now, it felt like a burden, an easy way to death, if she weren't careful.

When Kirby returned home from the machine shop, Esmeralda stood outside, hanging laundry. Four other women stood nearby, chatting quietly. Two held babies in their arms, while another held the skinny arm of a toddler. The fourth held Fiona.

Hiding her nerves, the piece of metal still in her pocket, Kirby said, "Hello."

The women nodded. One of the women shifted the baby on her hips.

Noticing Kirby, Esmeralda turned from her laundry and said, "Kirby, these are my friends Marla, Cindy, Louise, and Gayle."

The women politely smiled.

"They stopped by for a visit," Esmeralda said. Turning her attention to her friends, she said, "Kirby works in the machine shops. She was transferred from the fields."

"My husband works as a blacksmith," Marla said, with a knowing nod. "He probably works near you."

"I was just assigned," Kirby said evasively. "I don't know many people yet."

The woman with the toddler, Cindy, winced. "I worked there before I had Cecilia. I can still hear some of the clangs when I lie down to sleep. The noises can be loud."

Marla said, "You'll want to plug your ears with a piece of clothing. That's what my husband does. He says it dampens the ringing he hears at night."

Kirby nodded, grateful for the tip.

"We should probably get back," said Marla. "Our husbands will return soon."

The others agreed. Gayle handed Fiona back to Esmeralda, before shuffling off, motivated by the other slaves returning to their homes. Kirby couldn't recall a time where the people in New City didn't feel the pressure of the guards' schedule.

With the women gone, Esmeralda smiled. "I washed our bedrolls," she told Kirby, gesturing toward the items hanging to dry as she hugged Fiona. "They should dry by this evening."

"Thanks," Kirby said, and she meant it. With so much time spent in the metal shop, normal tasks seemed like a tiresome burden.

Keeping her voice low as they entered the dwelling, Esmeralda said, "We were talking about some of the times we've spent with our little ones. Those moments will be over soon."

Kirby nodded. "The years go by quickly."

Esmeralda shook her head. "That is not what I mean. The guards came and talked to us this morning." Esmeralda looked as if she fought back tears. "They will transition us to work duties soon, while the caretaking women watch the kids."

"I am sorry to hear that," Kirby said sympathetically.

Esmeralda sighed. "I was hoping I might get more time."

"I am sure Fiona will adapt to the change," Kirby reassured her.

"She has no choice." Esmeralda looked at Fiona with guilt in her eyes. "And neither do I. One thing is certain: I will miss her during the day."

Kirby nodded empathetically. She didn't know what was worse — living through suffering conditions, or adapting to them. Esmeralda wiped her face as she held her child.

Hoping to distract her from a depressing mood, Kirby asked, "Do those women live close?"

"A few," Esmeralda said. "Marla and her child Jayden live two rows to the north. Cindy has the toddler named Cecilia. She lives a few rows behind us. Gayle and Louise are from farther back in the city. Last year, we had a few more infants nearby, but they moved."

"Moved?" Kirby asked. "I did not think we had any choice as to where we lived."

"We don't normally. Caitlyn and Jeremy switched to a house on the eastern part of the city, when heavy rain collapsed their roof, flooding their house and damaging the walls. The rain changed the stream near the house, so it floods every time it rains. It was an unlucky accident. The guards decided to move them rather than repair it. Their old house is the corner house at the end of our row." Esmeralda's eyes grew reflective as she pointed.

"It sounds as if you know the people here well," Kirby said.

"I have some free moments, in between caring for Fiona." She shrugged. "I notice things. Of course, I will not have that luxury much longer."

Kirby felt sympathy for Esmeralda. But an idea percolated, as she listened to Esmeralda talk. Perhaps the flooded house might be a place where she and Bray could meet.

Chapter 33: Kirby

Kirby ducked into the small, dank house under a caving roof. Piles of rubble lined the floor. What was left of the ceiling was lined with cracks, allowing moonlight to seep through the dwelling. Her feet splashed into a few long-standing puddles as she crept far enough inside to be concealed by the house's fractured walls. The place was damp, but it was safer than meeting in an alley, or in a dark corner where others might see. The shadows around it kept the lights from the other houses at bay. She saw no one near.

After a little while, a lone figure came down a perpendicular alley and ducked inside to join her.

"Bray," she whispered.

"Where did you find out about this place?"

"Esmeralda mentioned it," Kirby said. "It flooded a while ago. She doesn't know I'm here, of course."

"How was the machine shop?" he asked.

She could hear another question in his voice. He wanted to know about Ollie.

"Ollie didn't bother me," Kirby said. "I saw him once, but he left me alone."

She could feel Bray's relief bleeding across the dark space between them.

Pulling the piece of metal from her pocket, she held it in a bit of ambient light. "I was able to take this."

Bray's eyes widened as he imagined danger. "Did anyone see you?"

"If someone saw me, they would've pulled me away," she said, trying to reassure herself as well as him.

"Do you think we'll be able to get more?" Bray asked.

"I am learning how things work," Kirby said. "The guards keep an eye on us, of course, but there are opportunities. I think I can get some more pieces out and away."

Bray nodded, but she saw the concern on his face.

"This is not the first time I've done something like this," Kirby assured him.

Bray shifted in the darkness as he kept watch out the small, dank building and Kirby stuck the metal back in her pocket. Determining that no one walked nearby, he said, "I spoke with some of the Yatari today."

"The people who build boats," she remembered.

"I traded some information. I think I have that escape route I was hoping to figure out."

Kirby's spirits rose as Bray described what had transpired with the men, along with the information he had traded. For a moment, she forgot about some of the other dangers of the city, as she listened to some of his inspiring words.

"How far is this mountain pass?" she asked.

"Less than a half day's walk," Bray repeated.

"At a faster pace, it would take less time to reach it," Kirby said, excitement in her voice. After a careful thought, she added, "Though, if mutants follow us, it won't matter if the area is free of them."

"Probably true," Bray said.

Kirby fell silent a moment as she imagined two hundred slaves fleeing through the narrow pass. "I am trying to picture a worst-case scenario, in which we are forced to use this path. Having steep hills on either side might make it difficult to flee. Or to fight."

Bray explained his reasoning. "Aside from the assurances the Yatari gave me, I've fought plenty of battles in similar terrain. If we are lucky, the demons will come from one direction. Most will stick to the clear path to reach us. If we keep the demons on one side of us, the high ground on either side might help us. We can topple them, so they cannot surround us. It is not a guarantee of success, but it is better than running into the wild blindly. And it is certainly more than we had yesterday, when we knew nothing outside of the walls and the crop fields."

Kirby nodded. She knew nothing was certain, but the information was definitely useful. "Do you trust the Yatari?"

Bray nodded. "They seemed sincere. I think they feel for us. Not enough to help us, but I believe what they told me. And I told them nothing incriminating."

"It was a clever move," Kirby said. A wave of nostalgia swept over her as she thought of the boats in New Hope. As broken down and unusable as they were, she doubted she'd ever see them again. "Did you tell them the truth about the boats' location?"

"I told them the boats are far. I am uncertain whether they will go, but I did not lie," Bray said.

"Those boats will do nothing for anyone," Kirby said, falling silent for a moment as she reflected.

"Exactly what I thought," Bray said. "But it was enough to get the information I needed."

Patting the ground around her, she searched with her hands through some of the rubble. Finding a round, smooth stone the size of half her palm, she held it up to the moonlight.

"What are you doing?" Bray asked.

"Finding something to use to sharpen my piece of metal," she said. "Later — perhaps while Esmeralda sleeps — I'll fashion it into a weapon I can use."

High spirits overtook Kirby. She had survived another day, spirited away a weapon, and had plans to get more. And Bray's information brought them closer to a plan.

"Between what you've found out, and my getting some metal, our plan might be closer to fruition than we think," Kirby said optimistically.

"Perhaps we should talk with The Shadow People," Bray said.

"I will see if I can catch Drew's ear tomorrow."

Chapter 34: Bray

When Bray returned home, Teddy knelt by the fire, cleaning some of their dented pots and pans. The house was otherwise empty. As usual, no one else had wandered in to mingle, as Bray often saw at other dwellings. In Bray's time here, he had only seen the guard who brought him here and the guards who passed out rations near the door. Teddy was careful, as always.

"How was your walk?" Teddy asked.

"As pleasant as it gets, after a full day of standing," Bray said, stretching his sore back.

"Sometimes the hottest days make for pleasant nights," Teddy said, sounding as if he'd used the line before. Or maybe it was what he'd told himself, in those days before his isolation. He scraped a stubborn food stain away from a pot.

A few conversations drifted over from the courtyard, where several large groups of people hovered around the bonfires. None of the backlit faces looked in their direction.

"They are talking about our lowered rations," Teddy said, shaking his head. "The guards will be cutting down our portions in anticipation of the slow growing season."

Bray shook his head. "Dirty pig chasers. How did you hear?"

"Aside from those people? Some guards talked about it outside the sewing rooms. It happens most years, though it doesn't make it any easier," Teddy said. "Those with children have it the worst. They have to stretch their rations further. The guards compensate for the extra mouths, but never enough."

Bray nodded, looking up at the shimmering tower. Not for the first time, he wondered about William's treatment. Was he receiving plentiful meals like when they first arrived, or were his portions reduced to scraps?

Standing near the door, Bray kicked off his boots, emptied some of the day's dirt, and carried them back to his bedroll. He'd air them a while before putting them back on to sleep.

"You rarely go without them," Teddy noticed.

"Old habits from the wild," Bray said. "I'm always ready to move."

Finished with his cleaning, Teddy sat on the bedroll across from Bray, watching the clusters of people disperse from the bonfires. Quiet conversations grew louder as people finished up their talks, or said their goodbyes. Teddy looked as if he had something else to say.

Surprise hit Bray as Teddy leaned over and whispered, "I wouldn't meet in the flooded house anymore."

Bray's blood froze.

He looked outside, as if he'd stepped into some trap.

"What did you say?" Bray asked, as if he might've misheard.

Teddy kept on as if he hadn't been questioned. "Too many people have used that place in the past. It is not safe. Do not meet there again."

A few women cackled as they let out a laugh they only dared at night.

Bray watched Teddy suspiciously. Was Teddy giving another friendly warning, or did he want something?

Perhaps Teddy meant to gain the meager share of Bray's rations, his clothing, or some other benefit he couldn't see.

Bray had seen similar situations. Eventually, the secret would get out, no matter how many promises were made.

His mistake could cost his life.

Sticking with his denial, Bray said, "I don't know what you're talking about."

"I mentioned before that it was dangerous to have those you cared about in the city," Teddy said. "And I meant it. Having friends here is a burden."

Bray clenched his fists, ready to spring from his bedroll and silence Teddy, if it came to that. He was preparing an accusation when Teddy spoke again.

"I am one of The Shadow People."

Bray watched him suspiciously.

"Drew told me you are trustworthy," Teddy said, with a firm nod. "I needed to wait to be sure. I have been watching you, and reporting back to him. As you probably know, we have people everywhere."

"Who's Drew?" Bray asked, not ready to give up on the idea that he might be ambushed.

"You met him in Ashville, along with Clara, Giovanni, and James. They vouched for you. And for Kirby, too. You do not have to worry. All of this information is safe." Teddy nodded assuredly.

Some of the tension left Bray's body as they watched loud people walking past the doorway, too engaged in their conversations to hear.

"Drew came to me when you first arrived. He told me about Kirby." Teddy glanced discreetly over his shoulder. "He told me he needed to know more about you before we spoke further. Only when it was safe did he approach her and set up the meeting in Ashville. But of course, you know all that."

Bray nodded as the information lined up.

A strange feeling overtook him as he watched his roommate—his new confidant. "You want escape, too."

Teddy nodded. "No one suspects me, because I rarely leave. They think the death of my family broke me. They are right. But it will not stop me from escape, or from helping others. When the time comes, Bray, I am ready to fight alongside you."

Chapter 35: Kirby

Morning sunlight cast a bright hue over the alley outside of Kirby's house, where people emerged. Throngs of people filled the alleys as people finished their morning rituals, preparing to head to the courtyard for the count before the fields, or their duties elsewhere in the city. A few children hugged their parents, sending them off to jobs that would leave them beaten down and tired by the time they returned.

Taking a dirty bowl from Esmeralda, Kirby scrubbed away the remnants of another meager meal.

"Thank you for your help with the dishes," Esmeralda said.

"It is no problem."

Kirby's eyes burned from another night with little sleep. This time, it wasn't due to the pain of her joints, or the nightmares that always seemed to plague her, or even because of Fiona; it was because in the night's darkest hours, while Esmeralda slept, Kirby had quietly scraped away at the metal she kept hidden underneath her bedroll. Over the course of a night, she had turned a piece of metal into a weapon. She felt the sharp tip of it in her boot, pushing against her ankle, in a place where she could reach it. From now on, she wouldn't be without it.

Finished cleaning the dishes, Kirby said, "I am going to head out."

Esmeralda seemed disappointed as she played with Fiona.

"I want to make sure I'm not late to my shift," Kirby said.

"Of course," Esmeralda said, with a smile. "I will see you at lunch."

Kirby entered the mass of moving workers, all heading in different directions. She veered toward the shops, taking a diagonal path as she looked through the flurry of faces. A few guards emerged from behind their closed doors, smearing the sleep from their eyes, or popping last bites of food in their mouths. Each of those guards reminded her of Ollie, who probably kissed his wife with his foul lips as he set off for the courtyard, like his comrades. She avoided a path that might intersect with his.

Rounding a corner several alleys from the shops, she spotted a familiar, gaunt figure walking through the streets. Catching up to him, Kirby didn't look over as she initiated conversation.

"We have some information to share," she told Drew, keeping her eyes forward.

Drew nodded. "Would you like to meet tonight?"

"Yes."

With a furtive nod, Drew said, "We will see you then."

Chapter 36: Bray

Guards walked in a menacing group across the court-yard, heading for the long building.

The people lingering in the courtyard skirted out of the way.

"What's going on?" Bray asked.

"I think they are letting Gabe out," Teddy told Bray.

Bray and Teddy stood at the doorway of their house, watching the guards walk toward one of the middle rooms, fanning out around the doorway while one of them fished keys from his pocket, and the others unsheathed their knives. Unlocking the door, the guard pulled it open and stepped back.

They had only seen the slave from the fight once or twice, when guards had opened the door and thrown food in. A few times in the night, they had heard long, disconcerting cries coming from his room—sobs that sparked the curiosity and shame of all who passed by. Most had hurried past, afraid to get the attention of the guards.

But the guards hadn't paid Gabe any mind.

Now, days after his indiscretion, Gabe was still there. Or was he? It seemed as if the room were empty. Dark shadows covered most of the area they could see. Perhaps the guards would pull a starved, bloodied body from that room.

Or maybe he had escaped.

"Come out, forest-dweller," a guard yelled, clanging his blade against the inside of the door.

The noise echoed through the courtyard, prompting a few people to take up at their front-row doorways to watch.

"Come out, or I'll yank you out!" another guard threatened.

A slow groan escaped from the cell. Moments later, a few scrapes echoed from the dark room. The lingering people craned their necks, trying to see inside. The guard banged his sword again, his impatience growing.

A shaggy-haired man stepped out of the shadows, walking a few feet into the sunlight. Gabe's face was swollen and flecked with stubble. His clothes hung off him in tattered strips. If Bray hadn't seen Gabe thrown inside, he might've thought this was someone different.

Stepping out into the courtyard, Gabe squinted at a sun he hadn't seen in days.

The guards watched him for a few moments, as if he might make a vengeful lunge. But Gabe was in no such condition. His legs wobbled as he took another step. He seemed disoriented and confused. Bray knew the solitude of that dank cell, when days and nights blended together, connected only by the smell of stale piss and hours spent scratching at the door.

Gabe's treatment was undeserved.

But he was alive.

Looking around the courtyard, Bray saw wonder on more than a few faces. A few scampered back to their houses, telling others, or heading back down the streets, perhaps to tell his family.

"Some say he wouldn't walk again," Teddy said to Bray.

"He's walking now," Bray said.

Teddy blew a long breath as Gabe took another, staggering step. "It is a miracle to see him alive."

Looking at Gabe, Bray couldn't help but relive the fight. He'd never forget the chants, the guards' provocations, and the families' screams.

But something else struck him.

With the battle's end imprinted on their brains, it was easy to forget what had transpired earlier.

Gabe's friend, Jonah, had battled Roberto before he died.

Jonah's struggled had been brief and defiant, but it had inspired the crowd.

Almost everyone had rallied around their fellow slave.

Looking around at the gawking people in the courtyard, Bray recalled the anger beneath the fear. Almost everyone did their toil without complaint, but he saw rage in too many eyes, as they took their beatings. Too many sat silently through scoldings that would've prompted more than a few fights in the wild.

What if that rage could be harnessed?

Perhaps a spark was all that was needed to swing seven hundred slaves to their side to win a battle.

And two hundred Shadow People was no small number.

The Shadow People already outmanned the guards. With weapons, a battle would go quickly — especially when the attack was a surprise. Who would attack their brothers, sisters, or relatives when they started a battle with weapons against those that had enslaved them? Who would fight on the side of their oppressors, especially when a battle was going poorly? Some of the more bloodthirsty would jump into the fray without hesitation. Others would fight for their freedom, defend themselves, or perhaps get revenge. The most timid or complacent ones would swing to the side of the winner, once a revolt started. They'd want to preserve their lives.

That didn't solve the problem of The Gifted, or the demons, but it was a start.

No one would preserve a miserable system.

A few, perhaps, out of fear. But certainly not all.

Bray watched the guards flanking Gabe, escorting him across the courtyard, prodding him when he stumbled.

The sight of the beaten, bloodied man should have ripped away his dreams, but instead it gave him hope.

Maybe the revolt had a better chance than he'd originally thought.

Chapter 37: Bray

Moonlight illuminated the two figures next to Bray and Kirby as they stood behind the putrid-smelling building, waiting for the others. The tall, ashen monoliths of Ashville towered above them, reminding Bray of the danger they were in, but for the first time, he had hope they might escape this hellish place. The thoughts he'd put together in the courtyard inspired him.

The hour of revolt was a step closer.

A new set of footsteps approached, and a new face he could hardly see joined the circle. Moments later another huffing, nervous person arrived. The others shifted, making room for their comrades. Bray looked through the shadows, making enough of an identification to see it was the same group who met before.

"Kirby says you have information," Drew said to both of them, in the same, stern voice he always used.

"We have news," Kirby agreed, ready to share the things she and Bray had discussed on the way. "Possibly, some solutions."

The group fell silent as they anxiously waited.

Kirby started. "A few days ago, I was transferred to the metal shop."

"I saw you there," Drew said, with a knowing nod.

Kirby elaborated on her experience working with the sheet metal, and her access to some of the scrap bins. "I have learned enough of the routines to find some opportunities. I cannot take a lot at once, of course. But each shank will arm another person. If we are close to a solution, I am willing to take more risks."

"That would be a big help," James told her. "You are not the only one taking from the shops. We have a few others ferreting away what they can."

Kirby nodded at the information she and Bray had suspected. "Perhaps it is time to increase the amount we take."

"The guards will frisk anyone they find suspicious," Clara warned. "Be careful."

"It sounds as if you have a bigger plan than shanks," Giovanni said.

Bray took over the conversation, sharing what he had learned in the fields. "I spoke to some of the traders that do their business in front of the shimmering building."

"Which people?" Drew asked.

"The Yatari."

The others nodded. A few shifted uncomfortably.

"Not many have risked speaking with the traders," James said. "It is an easy way to death."

"I took a risk that seems like it paid off." Bray told them of the information he'd provided on the ships, and the escape route they unwittingly — or perhaps knowingly — gave up.

"You told them of New Hope," Drew said, with a similar nostalgia to Kirby's.

"I did, but what I got was more important. The mountain pass might be an alternate route to freedom. When the time is close, we can break a hole in the stone wall, as the other slaves did, all those years ago. We will have a backup plan, if the revolt goes poorly."

"I know of the pass of which you speak," Giovanni said, after a pause. "I traveled it a few times, before I was captured. I believe the Yatari tell the truth. There are fewer

Plagued Ones there, but that doesn't mean it is safe. We might bring our own death, if the wild men follow us."

"That is what Kirby mentioned," Bray said. "But it is fresh information, and more than we had before."

No one disputed it.

Taking back the conversation, Drew said, "You sound as if you have something else to say."

Bray shared what he'd observed in the bloody battle, all those days ago.

"I think we have more people on our side than we think," Bray said. "Most are too afraid to start a revolution, but they will join one, once it starts. The fight in the courtyard is proof of that. I saw the defiant looks in those eyes when Jonah attacked Roberto. I saw an obstinacy in the others that can turn into a will to fight."

Kirby chimed in. "Some of the people may flee, or be shocked when a revolt starts, but many more will fight for their lives, and their freedom. Once they see the first guards topple, their anger will erupt. A small group will become a large one. Even the most timid of them will defend themselves, if they are forced to."

"And if they don't side with us?" Clara asked, not ready to accept the proposal.

"It is a risk," Bray said. "But I think we have a good chance at succeeding. With two hundred people against the guards, we should be able to make quick work of them. That will dispose of one layer of danger."

"That is a big chance," Giovanni said, shaking his head. "A mob can turn ugly. A well-conceived plan might turn to chaos."

"Anything would be preferable to the system under which we live," Kirby muttered.

A few in the group muttered responses, but no one rebutted her argument.

"You are talking as if the guards will be standing in one

place, waiting for their deaths," Giovanni said. "That is not the case. They have long knives, and plentiful meals that give them strength. It is not as easy as you think."

"Perhaps if we ambush them in the morning," Bray said, "we can take them when they are half-awake, with full, slow stomachs. Two of us can certainly take one man. Do you know the locations of all their homes?"

"Yes," Drew said. "We have lived here long enough, and discussed that often enough, to have them memorized."

A few in the group nodded as they envisioned the scenario.

"And then what?" Giovanni asked. "Say we take down the guards. We still have The Plagued Ones with which to contend, and The Gifted, who will surely bring their guns and other weapons. They might attack us from the balcony, or even through the gate."

"By that time, we will have greater numbers," Bray said. "We will have the guards' weapons, as well as our own. We will have a mob that can take a stand in a city surrounded by walls, and filled with houses. We will have the keys to the gates, and the ability to defend ourselves, if The Gifted let the demons inside, or if they attack."

"And if things go poorly, we will have our escape route," Kirby finished.

With the proposition in the air, Bray and Kirby waited.

The group shifted.

It seemed as if no one wanted to speak first.

"It is strange talking about these things, after planning for so long," Clara admitted, breaking the silence.

"For months, we have discussed a plan, but this is the closest we have come to action," said James.

"All of us are willing to risk our lives for our freedom, but I am worried," Drew admitted. "Hundreds of Plagued Ones are no minor threat, and neither are The Gifted. The slaves in this city are workers, not fighters. Those in our revolt are better suited for battle, but many have no experience. How will they fare, if we become outnumbered?"

"I am fairly confident we can kill the guards," Clara said. "But Drew has a point about the other threats."

"Everything about this city is a risk," Kirby said. "We might die at any moment, like some of the others we've watched. We might spend so much time planning that we die before we finish."

Bray heard a frustration in her voice, born of too many nights of uncertainty, lying in a cell, or even in bed, waiting for the knife at her throat.

A few of The Shadow People shifted, uncertain, or perhaps afraid.

"I will not lie," Clara said. "The Plagued Ones still concern me. Perhaps we should give it a few days, before we commit. We can take it to some others with whom we meet."

"In any case, your plan with the weapons seems like a good idea," Giovanni said. "We can have our people step up our weapons collection. Anything you can get will help."

"We will make a decision when we meet again," Drew said.

Chapter 38: Kirby

Kirby placed the stack of metal in the pile, watching the guards at the doorway. Whirs, scrapes, and bangs echoed across the room. She adjusted the small, rolled-up pieces of fabric she'd put in her ears, which she'd made at the suggestion of Esmeralda's friends. The fabric didn't protect her from all the sounds, but it dampened them. Hopefully she wouldn't need them much longer.

Hopefully, a revolt would come soon.

Behind her, Rosita said something over the noise. Kirby turned, taking out one of the pieces from her ear to rid some of the muffle.

"We received a new batch of sheet metal," Rosita repeated, pointing at a new pile in the corner. "That will keep us busy for most of the day."

Kirby nodded. More metal meant more scraps, which meant more things to ferret away.

Picking up a fresh piece to work with, she brought it over to her bench and picked up her shears. She risked a glance at the doorway. Three of the same guards idly chatted, watching some slaves pass. None looked at her, at the moment. The guards were complacent in their duty. Not only that, but they were assured in their power. They lived in a city where most would rather walk in the other direction than confront them. They lived in a city where most were afraid to whisper.

Hopefully, that complacency would cost their lives.

Shearing off a long strip of metal, Kirby curved inward, making an angled cut. She left a shank-sized scrap at the end, cutting it off separately and placing it on the table. She repeated the action. With two pieces set aside, Kirby glanced at the guards. One of the guards, a dark-haired man, watched her, foiling her immediate plans.

Averting her eyes, she picked up all three scraps and walked them to the bin.

Dammit.

The shank in her boot moved slightly with each step, reminding her of the danger she was in by carrying the contraband. Rosita smiled as she passed, working her way through a large, stained piece of metal. Finishing her cut, she joined Kirby and dumped some scraps.

The guards stepped out of sight.

"I'll be glad when this project is over," Rosita said, tossing a few pieces of metal in the bin. "Too many days of cutting the same thing have me longing for something else to do."

Kirby nodded, removing one of her plugs.

Rosita clapped a gloved hand on her shoulder. "Some who start here struggle. You have taken to the task."

"Thank you," Kirby said, returning her smile.

"We will finish the project in a shorter time than I planned," Rosita said, walking away from the bin and toward her workstation.

Replacing the plug in her ear, Kirby turned and took a step.

She rammed into a thick, meaty stomach.

A blubbery body shoved her backward, cornering her against the bin.

"Where are you going?" Ollie boomed, pinning her.

The three guards from the door stood behind him, laughing.

"I told you I'd be checking up on you," Ollie said. With

a regretful frown, he said, "It seems as if you've been doing a little too much talking."

He looked sideways at Rosita, who stood by her workbench, watching with fear.

Kirby's eyes flicked to her boot, but Ollie had her pressed tightly. She couldn't bend down more than an inch. She frantically checked her surroundings, looking past Ollie and his guards, toward the rest of the machine shop. The whir of a few last machines stopped, as a few people set down their hand tools or pieces of metal, or held them in the air in surprise.

She had no clear path.

Even if she could make it around an obese man, the guards trapped her.

Ollie made sure all eyes were on him as he leaned in close, making a show of his authority.

"Remember what I told you about making me happy?"

His eyes narrowed.

Kirby had no room to throw a punch.

She had no room to do *anything*.

Ollie raised a hand, as if to caress her. Kirby leaned back, recoiling as far as she could against a bin that wouldn't bend, or move. She could barely get back a knee. But she had to. She wouldn't let him touch her.

Ollie surprised her with a punch from his other hand.

The unexpected blow landed hard, catching Kirby in the face, knocking her sideways as Ollie stepped back and let her fall. And then she was face down on the ground, between the bin and his fat, enormous boots. A delayed pain hit her as blood rushed to her swollen eye. Ollie kicked her ribs, rolling her against the bin.

She blinked, reaching for her boot.

"I told you I'd pay you back for what you did."

The guards laughed.

This was the end.

She reached for her shank, wondering if she'd have the coordination to stab him in the leg before he stomped her to unconsciousness, or the guards cornered her.

"Stop!" a voice screamed, over the din of laughter and Ollie's thunderous bark.

Kirby looked up to find Rosita wedged between them, her chin upturned in defiance.

"Stop, I said!"

Ollie's face twisted with surprise as he gauged an unexpected threat. "You want a beating, too?"

One of the guards cut in. "She seems a little too chatty, as well. Maybe she needs a reminder to focus on her work."

Rosita stood her ground, staring at Ollie through the fear on her face. Kirby's fingers grazed the end of her shiv. She paused as she thought through an unintended consequence.

Rosita might die, if she fought.

"We have work to do," Rosita said, with a voice she was trying to control. Jabbing a finger in the direction of the sheet metal, she added, "Rudyard will be angry if we don't finish this pile."

A thought greater than Ollie's amusement crossed his face as he heard the name. Looking over his shoulder at the guards, a smile crossed his face. "I think she just threatened me with Rudyard."

"You think Rudyard gives a shit what any of you slaves say?" one of the guards taunted.

"I know that he wants these done for The Learning Building," Rosita said. "Leave us be, so we can finish. We won't talk again."

Ollie looked from Rosita to Kirby, contemplating something. Kirby held his gaze in defiant hatred, afraid to make a move for the shiv, or any move, lest Rosita be punished.

Kirby fought the screaming blood rushing to her face, and the adrenaline that told her to move, to fight, to stab.

Rosita stood her ground, keeping her face even, even though her legs shook.

"Please go," Rosita said.

Ollie eyed her for a long moment, looking as if he was torn between choices.

With a snort, he lumbered away, under the chuckles of his guards.

Kirby's breath heaved as she recovered her wind, getting to her feet. She clapped her hand over her puffy, swollen face.

"Your eye," Rosita said, with a regret in her face that showed she blamed herself.

"I'm fine," Kirby swore, anger overtaking her pain.

As soon as she got home, she would make sure her shiv was sharp.

Later, when dinner was done and darkness set in, she would find Ollie and plunge it into his neck.

Chapter 39: Kirby

"By the gods," Esmeralda exclaimed, clutching Fiona in fright as she surveyed Kirby's face. "What happened?"

Kirby looked behind her, through the doorway, as if Ollie might be there. But Ollie was long gone, probably shucking off his boots and waiting for his wife to cook his meal. He would be out of the house at some point, though. After feeding the demons and having dinner, the guards strolled the streets, sipping their flasks and chatting with their friends. She would find him, and shove her shank through his neck.

Realizing Esmeralda waited for an answer, Kirby couldn't help the anger in her voice, as she said, "It is nothing."

"You were beaten," Esmeralda said, crossing the room to study Kirby's swollen, painful eye.

Kirby looked away. She didn't need to confirm the obvious.

"Who did this?" Esmeralda said.

"Does it matter?" Kirby spat, with more venom than she intended.

"I am sorry. I just—" Esmeralda stepped back, clutching Fiona.

Kirby regretted her misdirected emotion. "It was Ollie."

"I knew it," Esmeralda said, as if she might have prevented something. "I knew when he came looking for you..." Esmeralda couldn't speak the words.

"He hit me," Kirby clarified. "That is all he did. And all he will do."

She clamped down on more threats.

Instead of dragging Kirby through a painful memory, or more questions, Esmeralda moved to the hearth. "What do you need? Let me get you something. A wash bucket, some water..."

"I'm fine," Kirby said, hating the lie.

Of course, she wasn't.

Her stinging, sore eye screamed her story to anyone who saw it. Her injury would be another violent incident to talk about around the bonfires, or over meager bowls of supper, until a new, fresh event took its place. But it would never end—not for Kirby. Ollie would keep after her until she died, or worse—at least in her opinion—she wound up like Esmeralda.

Kirby couldn't think of dinner. She couldn't think of washing up.

All she thought about was revenge.

Forcing herself to sit and collect her violent thoughts, she watched Esmeralda scurry around the hearth. Kirby felt guilty for lashing out at Esmeralda, who bore the guilt of her attack, without reason.

Fiona stared at Kirby over her mother's shoulder. Someday, she would be subjected to the same torment— things even a mother's warnings couldn't stop.

Everyone in New City would suffer, until the day something changed.

Kirby couldn't guarantee the success of a revolt.

But she could guarantee one man's life would end.

Reaching under her bedroll, she found the stone she'd used to sharpen the blade, tucking it into her pocket while Esmeralda's back was turned. A moment later, Esmeralda brought her a flask.

"Here you go," she said, lingering nearby as Kirby drank.

The lukewarm water felt strange as it went down Kirby's throat. It felt as if she were living her last moments.

"Maybe he is done with you," Esmeralda said, unable to sell those words to herself.

Kirby nodded, her thoughts focused on the man she wanted to kill.

"Some food in your stomach and some rest will do you good," Esmeralda said. "They will help take your mind off what happened."

Kirby couldn't stay put any longer.

"I'm going for a walk," Kirby said, trying to hide the bitterness in her voice.

"A walk?" Esmeralda seemed surprised.

"I need to get out," Kirby said, standing.

"But The Plagued Ones will come through soon," Esmeralda worried. "The guards do not like us out of our houses until after they eat."

"I'll be back in time for dinner," Kirby said, feeling sorry for another lie.

She was sorry for a lot of things.

But Ollie would be sorry, too.

Kirby walked from the house, her shank jabbing into the side of her boot. She kept down the alleyway, passing houses full of chattering children, filthy parents, and workers washing up. She looked over her shoulder once, feeling another wave of guilt as she saw Esmeralda at the threshold with Fiona, watching her disappear into the crowd.

Chapter 40: Bray

Bells rang in the courtyard.

A couple of worried slaves jogged back to their front-row homes, just ahead of the feeding. The clangs increased in volume as the snarls grew over the wall, and the guards prepared to open the gate. Bray looked over at Teddy, who stood next to him at the doorway, along with a slew of other people staring from their houses across the dirt courtyard.

"I heard about your meeting," Teddy said softly, under the din of the demons and the guards.

"The leaders are worried," Bray said. "It is hard to tell if they will commit. The twisted men concern them."

Teddy nodded. Of course, he understood.

The front gate creaked as the guards opened it, allowing the first batch of filthy demons into the courtyard. The slobbering, wart-covered creatures paraded across the dirt, streaming toward the open gate at the other end, where guards rang the bells and shouted orders, luring them into the Feeding Pen as if they were a herd of cattle. A few demons looked sideways at Bray, obviously preferring a man's flesh to a pile of corn, but none deviated.

Watching the hungry, twisted men, Bray asked, "If a revolt starts, what do you think The Gifted will do?"

Teddy mulled it over. "The Gifted view us as replaceable. They value our work, but they do not value us. I saw it on their faces when they killed those slaves. If it comes to it, they might send The Plagued Ones in to kill all of us." Fear lingered in Teddy's eyes. "It is probably the reason for the hesitation you heard in the voices of The Shadow People's leaders."

"They certainly raised that concern," Bray said.

"Our people will fight, but I'm not sure what the rest of the slaves will do. If we are overrun and people flee, a revolt will quickly become an individual battle for survival."

"What if we barricade the gate?" Bray asked.

Teddy looked over at the gate, and the twelve-foot-high wall to which it connected. "Rudyard has mostly kept up the wall through the toil of the slaves, but there are places where the wall has crumbled—especially in the back of the city. I fear The Plagued Ones could get over, as a few did that time with my daughter. If not, The Gifted have weapons that can surely break parts of the wall down. Or, at least, I suspect they do."

Bray nodded. With as many devices as The Gifted had, he didn't doubt they could figure out a way to let the demons inside.

He watched the batch of demons finish traipsing through the gate and into the pen. The guards stopped ringing the bells and quickly swung the Feeding Pen door closed. From over those high, wooden walls, Bray heard the gnashing of teeth and the cries of hungry demons.

The guards relaxed.

Looking among their faces, Bray noticed, "It seems as if the guards rotate their duties."

"They do," Teddy confirmed.

"Do they have a single set of commands for The Plagued Ones?"

"Not really. Mostly, they just urge The Plagued Ones from gate to gate. I think the words are secondary to the bells," Teddy said with a shrug, looking at a few of the guards. "The Plagued Ones line up before the guards even let them inside. You can hear them over the wall, preparing for dinner. They are trained."

"That's what I've seen, too," Bray observed, watching the guards herd the first batch of demons out of the Feeding Pen.

"Rudyard directs them from the other side of the entrance, of course, but I think they would line up, even without him," Teddy added. Noticing the expression on Bray's face, he said, "Have you thought of something?"

An idea gelled into a hope as Bray said, "I think I might have another plan."

**

Bray walked through the alley. Pots and pans clanked through the open doorways as people started dinner. A few children peered cautiously from their homes, as if the demons might be waiting to pounce, even though they had already gone. Bray kept developing his idea in his mind as he walked down a few more paths, reaching the row where Kirby's house was. Passing the squalid, stone hovel, he saw Esmeralda—her roommate—inside, preparing supper. No Kirby. Esmeralda met his eyes, but he looked away. He didn't need to draw any more attention to himself by asking questions.

Frowning, he turned past the house, headed toward the nearest well. Perhaps Kirby was fetching water. He reached it to find a line of waiting slaves, holding empty buckets as they chatted. Kirby wasn't there, either. Worry overtook him as he scoured a few more alleys, without luck.

Perhaps Ollie had snatched her away to a dank, putrid hole.

Bray's fear intensified as he walked in the direction of Ollie's house. Approaching carefully, he saw the door closed. Numerous voices, including Ollie's loud, raucous voice, came from inside. It sounded like his family was home. Assumedly, Kirby wasn't there. Fruitless alley turned to fruitless alley, as the last rays of light left the sky and everything turned dark. Every time he heard a laugh, he spun, as if he might find Kirby at the center of a circle of guards, but he couldn't find her.

He was heading back to Kirby's home when he thought of something. Taking a shortcut, he headed to the end of her alley.

Deep shadows surrounded the cracked, flooded house where they had met before. He approached carefully, looking over his shoulder. A thin scrape from inside echoed and died. Ducking, he made it through the threshold to find a silhouette inside, kneeling on the floor. The person turned in his direction.

"Kirby?" Bray identified her silhouette in the moonlight. "What are you doing?"

Ambient light struck Kirby's face as she stood and backed away, as if she were hiding something.

"We weren't supposed to meet here anymore," Bray warned.

"You need to go," Kirby said, with a quiver in her voice that told him more than words.

Putting two things together, he whispered, "Ollie."

Kirby turned away, but not before he caught a glimpse of her face through the moonlight. He couldn't see the details, but he saw enough. Bray clenched his fists.

"What did he do?" he asked.

Kirby stuck her face in a spear of moonlight, jabbing a finger at her swollen, bruised eye. "There. Do you see? Now leave, before you are discovered and killed."

Bray fought against his rage. He wanted to march to Ollie's house, pull him from inside, and kill him in front of the other guards. He wanted to unleash a pent-up anger that had been building since the first beating he'd received in New City.

"When did he do that?" he asked.

"Earlier, in the machine shop. He did it before I could defend myself. Someone in the machine shop stepped in. Otherwise, I would've killed him." Kirby's voice trembled with anger.

"I walked by his house looking for you."

"He is there," Kirby said, with enough certainty for Bray to know that she had been there, too. "He is eating with his family, with the door closed."

Bray looked down, catching a glint of the piece of metal in her hand. Even a dim-witted guard could see what she planned. "You will die, if you go after him," he said, trying to contain his own rage. "You will die for a moment of revenge."

"I will die regardless," Kirby said. "I would rather it be after I put a shiv in his neck."

"It will be a last choice," Bray warned.

"Perhaps so, perhaps not," Kirby said. "Maybe I will get lucky and kill him without others around. But I will not let that stop me. Whatever it takes, he dies tonight."

"It won't be hard to figure out it was you, after what happened today in the machine shop," Bray protested. "Even if they don't put two things together, others will pay for your actions. When the guards find Ollie dead, they will penalize the other slaves. Some might lose rations. Some might even be killed."

"I will give myself up, then."

Bray threw up his hands. "You will die for a single moment?"

"What would you have me do? Wait for a revolt that might never come? Spend my nights planning, while Ollie takes my dignity during the day, or whenever else he decides?" Kirby's voice was laced with venom he seldom heard. "I haven't, and I won't." Kirby drew a deep breath. "Ollie will act before Drew and the others do. And then none of our planning will matter. Perhaps my actions will save women like Esmeralda from his abuse."

"For every Ollie, there are many more guards like him, ready to touch women with their filthy hands," Bray said. "And then what will your death be for?"

Kirby smeared tears from her eye. "For me."

Her words hit Bray like a punch to his stomach. He opened and closed his mouth, robbed of words. He wished he could take away all the things that haunted her.

Of course, he couldn't.

Bray looked over his shoulder, as if someone might be there to back up his argument. He needed to find a way to reach her. "A while ago, you told me you worried for the people who had no voice, who were beaten down and unable to make a decision. You regretted leaving those people behind. Do not leave them behind now."

Kirby fell silent.

"Your death—your life—is worth more than a pig-headed man's blood. If you are going to die, make your death matter."

"When we were first in those cells, all those weeks ago, you asked me to give you some time," Kirby whispered. "I did that."

"I know," Bray said. "And I am sorry we are still in this situation. This is my fault."

Shaking her head, laboring through a weighty sigh, Kirby said, "No, it isn't."

Bray stepped toward her, embracing her in the moonlight. She trembled with rage as he squeezed her gently, hoping to defuse some of her anger. In a voice strong with a resolution he had every intention of keeping, Bray said, "If you go after him, I'm coming."

"Foolish man," Kirby said, but he could hear her admiration.

They stood quietly in the dark room, until some of the raw, fresh emotions of her attack passed, and Kirby stopped trembling.

"I came to find you for a reason," Bray said, as he held on to her. "At least let me explain it, before we both run out to our deaths."

Kirby laughed through the silent tears on her face. "Another plan?"

"This plan might be different," Bray said, his original purpose for finding her resurfacing. "Let me convince you that a revolt might work."

Kirby stepped back, but he could see her hesitation in her stance.

"It is worth discussing, before we throw our lives away," Bray said.

Kirby nodded silently in the dark, waiting for him. She was obviously thinking about other things. But he had to get through.

Putting his thoughts into words, he said, "Teddy and I spoke about the demons tonight."

He relayed he and Teddy's concern that The Gifted would command the horde to kill the slaves.

"It is something all The Shadow People fear, of course," Kirby said. "And it is certainly stopping them from acting."

"What if we could eliminate the threat of the demons? Then we would only have to deal with the guards and The Gifted."

Kirby laughed softly, but he could tell she was intrigued. "I don't see how, without slaying them."

"The guards have ingrained a routine that might help us," Bray suggested. "They use their words, and their bells, to herd the demons into the Feeding Pen. What if we could do the same?"

"I do not understand," Kirby said.

"The demons react to the bell, not the people," Bray guessed. "At least, that is what I think. If we can keep close enough to the same ritual, we might be able to get the twisted men inside the Feeding Pen, away from the commands of The Gifted. We might be able to contain them before they can harm us."

"Why would we let them in?" Kirby seemed dubious.

"Outside the city, the demons are an uncertain threat. The Gifted have control of them. Even if we barricade the front gate, The Gifted will find a way to let them in. Teddy mentioned that some parts of the wall are crumbled. The Gifted might know that, and order them over in the unstable areas, or they might use Tech Magic to break down the walls. We will not know which points to defend, or when. We will have no visibility." Bray watched her a second, more of his idea solidifying. "If we trap the demons in the Feeding Pen, they will be contained in a much smaller area than outside the walls of a whole city. And they will be away from their owners. We will not have to worry about The Gifted commanding a swarming mob to kill us. Even if the demons get over the wooden Feeding Pen walls, we can station our people by the walls and take them a few at a time. Or we can feed them corn and keep them subdued while we enact the next part of our plan."

"Which is?"

"We storm the building," Bray said, with a firm nod. "We will have the keys. Hundreds of us slaves can certainly take down ten Gifted. We might suffer some losses, but once we kill them, we will have the power of their Tech Magic to fight the demons. And we can rescue William. The shimmering tower will be ours. We can use it as a base, a place of refuge, or however we see fit."

"It is a brave idea, but it is risky," Kirby said. "And you are forgetting about Rudyard. He helps control the mutants during the feeding. Assuming we kill the guards before the feeding, once we open the gate, he will command the mutants to kill us."

"We do this in the morning, before he wakes," Bray clarified. "Rudyard does not come down to New City until just before the count of the Field Hands. If we do this before daybreak, he will not hear much, from so high up in the tower. At least, that is my hope. We kill the guards in the morning, after first light, as we planned. We take their bells and weapons. And then we head to the main gate, before Rudyard is outside. If we time it right, we lure the demons into the pen before he catches on to what's happening. By the time he or anyone else in the tower hears the bells, it will be too late. The demons will be confined."

"Do you think the mutants will listen to the bells in the morning? That is outside their routine."

"No animal I've seen in the wild will refuse an easy meal," Bray said. "They will follow the bells because they mean food. We can feed them in one large shift, herding them all in at once, instead of in two shifts. I was inside the Feeding Pen. It is large enough to hold all of them. I do not think any of them will stop moving, once they see corn on the other side."

"You hope," Kirby reminded him.

"If something goes wrong, we will have the escape route we talked about," Bray finished.

Kirby was silent a moment.

Finally, she admitted, "It is a bold idea."

"It is worth taking to The Shadow People. It is worth waiting on our deaths. What do you think?"

Kirby looked around the dark house. She didn't agree. But she didn't rush past him, either.

"If we are going to die, let it matter," Bray said, pushing his words into a final argument. "Let us spend our last moments fighting, instead of facing death at the hands of a few cowardly guards. Let us find that golden palace in the clouds."

Kirby sighed again. She said, "I will have Drew set up a meeting, as soon as he is able. It won't be tonight."

"The soonest we can meet, then," Bray said. Feeling the weight of her anger and pain, he said, "We will get revenge for what they have done, Kirby. I promise you. Just hang in a while longer."

Chapter 41: William

William's breath heaved as he pressed his ear against the door of his quarters. He'd waited several days before risking another escapade. In that time, Amelia had only come by once or twice, but his cough had scared her away. She didn't want to risk her own health, or the wellbeing of the others. Instead, she had sent two of the scrawny, stone-faced guards to bring his food and take his empty trays. He already had the ammunition for the old, sentimental gun.

The next time he saw The Gifted, he hoped to have the Tech Magic gun in his possession.

Letting that thought drive him, William opened the door to a darkened hallway, peering out onto a stairwell he couldn't see. He slowly made his way to the landing, clung to the rail, and climbed upward, counting the stairs. He passed the sixteenth floor without incident. Quiet conversation made his heart beat loudly as he passed the seventeenth level, where the guards watched. He imagined they had a dull task, waiting and looking out the windows. Occasionally, he had heard laughter coming from behind that door, when he passed it going to The Library Room, but he seldom saw them.

Still, at any moment, they might step out and find him.

He kept going.

Reaching The Library Room, he picked the lock.

He left the door open to a crack, just in case he had to depart quickly.

The odor of succulent meats and vegetables—smells he recognized from his tray earlier, which he'd taken in his room—wafted into his nose. The moon shone enough light to illuminate the outlines of the grand table and chairs. Operating on muscle memory, William skirted around the furniture, past the bookshelves and the looming, metal devices called fans, heading for Amelia's desk. Looking at the shadowy shelves on the walls filled with books, he recalled the many lessons he'd received.

If his plan went correctly, he would never have a lesson again.

Reaching Amelia's desk, he slid open the drawer and searched for the gun. The panicked thought hit him that Amelia might've moved it, but he found it, sitting idly, as if it had been waiting for him. William felt the power of Tech Magic as he picked up the heavy weapon and held it. The long, metal barrel gleamed in the moonlight shining through the windows.

The gun was freedom and power.

Tears he hadn't expected stung William's eyes as he ran his hands over the gun's smooth surface, thinking he might have the answer to his predicament. Perhaps he'd even see his friends soon.

But not if he wasn't careful.

Returning the way he came, William cautiously made his way past the furniture. He couldn't allow his excitement to make room for a mistake. He'd left the caps, balls, and the flask of black powder in his room. He didn't want the clanking, small pieces of metal making noise and giving him away. Nor was he foolish enough to think he'd have the time to figure out how to load them in the dark Library Room.

He would do it when he got back.

With his eyes adjusted to the moonlight, he moved at a quicker pace, ready to get back to the relative safety of his room. Reaching the door, he eased it open.

The light of a lantern splashed on the stairs.

The person holding it took a step.

Barron.

Barron stopped moving as he saw William.

A moment of uncertainty passed as two people processed an unexpected meeting. William's mouth opened and closed as he thought of an excuse that would save him. Before William could speak, Barron's eyes roamed from William's face to the gun in his hand.

Barron's wart-covered lips twisted to anger.

He lunged up the stairs.

Barron grabbed for William, but William leapt backward and turned. Barron reached again, catching hold of the back of William's robe and pulling. William fought for balance, grabbing for the doorway to avoid being tugged back onto the stairwell. He found a handhold, jerking free.

A pained cry rose from Barron's direction as he lost his balance, falling.

Loud thuds reverberated through the building.

The lantern bounced and shattered.

A small flame erupted as the oil from the lamp caught fire, creating a glow of light on the stairs.

A cold panic coursed through William as he saw Barron's silhouette, lying on the seventeenth-floor landing near the smashed lantern. He wasn't moving. William glanced frantically behind him into The Library Room, about to flee and find refuge there, but the image of that last, frantic standoff panicked him. He wasn't ready to die.

In his terror, all he could think was to get to his room.

William darted down the stairs, rushing as quickly and quietly as he could. He jumped over the small fire and kept to the wall as he reached the landing, skirting around Barron's body, certain that his greasy, infected hands would clamp his ankles and trip him. He didn't. Loud voices emanated from some of the floors above and below. William had just reached his room when doors on the other levels crashed open and shouting filled the stairwell.

He shut his door and sprang for the bureau.

The rounds, the rounds!

He managed to get the supplies and sink to the floor behind the bed as more voices echoed from the stairwell just beyond his room. He fumbled fruitlessly with the gun, the rounds, and the flask.

Even if he knew how to load the gun, he couldn't see what he was doing.

It was over. All of it.

Once Barron awoke, he would expose what he saw. Or he was dead, and The Gifted would connect it to William.

"What's going on?" Tolstoy shouted in the stairwell, to the exclamations of the guards.

Electric lights winked on, illuminating the crack beneath William's door. His nervous hands slid over the gun. More voices echoed as more of The Gifted joined Tolstoy. William heard Amelia's voice, intertwined with the sounds of the guards. Confusion bled through animated voices as people put out the fire and tried to determine what happened. The Gifted and the guards spoke loudly enough that William could hear the words, echoing down the two flights of stairs and to the landing just past his door.

A pronouncement froze William's frantic hands.

"Barron's dead."

William felt a small relief through his icy chills.

"Dead?" Amelia said from the stairwell, in disbelief.

"His neck is snapped," Tolstoy announced, to the grumbles and murmurs of the others. A few of The Gifted talked at once, inspecting the body, or making sense of what must be a gruesome scene.

Footsteps pounded up and down the stairs as they continued inspecting the stairwell, and William stayed put in his room. People answered over one another, trying to explain, or make sense of what they were seeing. Eventually, one of the voices won out.

"What happened?" Tolstoy demanded.

"I'm not sure," said a nervous guard. "We were at the windows when we heard the noise. It took us a moment to retrieve our weapons and come out. We thought it was The Plagued Ones. When we arrived, we found him like that."

"The Library Room door is open," the first guard said, stating the obvious. "I didn't see anyone else upstairs."

"Check the bottom floor," Tolstoy ordered another guard.

Footsteps clapped down the stairs, passing William's floor, continuing to the building's bowels. After a few moments, more guards returned. It sounded as if the guards downstairs had joined the others. "We didn't see anything from the bottom level," said one of them, presumably stationed below. "The Plagued Ones outside are quiet."

"I told Barron to stop going to the Library at night," Amelia said, with a crack of pain in her voice. "I told him he might get hurt."

"It must've been an accident," Leonard proclaimed, repeating her assessment.

An accident.

William's heart hammered in his chest.

He hoped everyone would believe it.

Tolstoy cleared his throat, clearly unnerved. "See if you can move him," he ordered the guards.

Grunts and grumbles echoed through the stairwell as the guards tried moving Barron. Footsteps beat the stairs as someone came up or down. It was only a matter of moments until someone remembered William and thought to question him, coming to his door. His panic heightened as he looked across the room toward the crack of light, making another realization.

He'd left his door unlocked.

In his haste, he'd left a clue that might connect him. Stuffing the gun and the ammunition back in the drawer, William padded across the room, reaching the door handle. He dug for the pin, stuck it in the door, and worked on the lock as The Gifted's chatter grew louder, and they fought with the body, getting it down what sounded like a flight of stairs.

"Where are we going?" asked one of them.

"To Barron's room," said Leonard, in a grave tone. "We'll put him in bed until we can figure out what to do with him."

"Be careful," Tolstoy ordered. "We don't need someone else falling."

Heaves and groans got closer as people carried the body. William knelt on the ground, fiddling with the lock. He had just managed to re-lock it when the people outside reached his landing. Raising a fist, he banged hard on the door. The voices on the other side stopped as they heard a new source of commotion.

Someone unlocked and opened his door.

Rubbing fake sleep from his eyes and putting on the most confused face he could muster, William peered out into the hallway and into the staring faces of The Gifted.

"What's going on?" he asked.

Chapter 42: William

A circle of grave, stony faces stood in a circle around Barron's bed, staring at the lifeless, prone man. Barron's eyes were wide. His mouth was gaped open in an expression of pain and surprise. Several of his warts had broken open, leaving bloody, puss-covered holes in their wake.

Death wasn't pretty.

But then, it never was.

Standing in the far corner of the room, kept away due to his supposed sickness, William watched The Gifted hover around the dead man. They had propped Barron's head up on his pillow, but even then, his neck bent at an unnatural angle, weighed down by his bulbous head. Despite the size of his skull, he seemed to sink into his robe, as if the gods had already claimed him. Amelia, in particular, stared at the body, as if Barron might sit up and speak, even though he would never talk again. A lump in William's throat reminded him that he was the last person to see Barron alive.

William wiped away his fake tears. He was a sickly boy, woken from sleep by a tragedy. Or, that was how he'd played it.

"Three hundred years of life," Tolstoy said with reverie, as he shook his head. "Over in an eye's blink."

"It is a reminder of our fragility," Amelia said in a somber tone.

The other Gifted folded their arms, staring at the scene, as if they hadn't yet processed it.

"We are the most intelligent beings on the planet, but we have our perils." Herman sighed. "If only our bodies were as strong as our minds."

William surveyed Barron's body on the bed. His victim. Any remorse he might've felt was buried by the memory of his friends, rotting away in the city below. Looking around at all the wart-covered figures in the room, he couldn't help but picture them alongside Barron.

"Shall we have a service for him?" asked Leonard, cocking his wart-covered head.

"Perhaps those in the city will mourn," Amelia suggested.

"Mourn?" Tolstoy scoffed, as if he had stepped in a putrid puddle. "They will not mourn. They will blow their pale noses and smear their watery eyes, but they will welcome our end, because they think it means something better. They would rejoice in Barron's loss."

"It is true," Rudyard said, shaking his head. "They are misinformed. We should not speak of Barron's death to the humans."

"They do not deserve it," Tolstoy spat emphatically. "We will honor him in a private service." Turning to the handful of guards hovering by the door, who awaited his orders, he said, "Sneak his body to the Glass Houses and cremate him privately. When you are finished, bring his ashes to me."

Chapter 43: Kirby

Shrill screaming ripped Kirby awake.

She sat up quickly, looking around her small hovel in the morning light. Blinking through the pain of her swollen eye, she saw several guards in the room, arguing with Esmeralda.

Fiona screamed from Esmeralda's arms.

"Please!" Esmeralda cried, to the uncaring faces of the guards.

Kirby tossed aside her bedroll. A guard stopped her before she stood.

"Stay down," he ordered, standing near her to make sure she complied. "You don't want to get involved."

"Tomorrow, you'll bring her to Isabella's," another guard told Esmeralda. "Those were the orders."

"I just need a little more time," Esmeralda pleaded.

"If you're not at the shop for count, you'll be punished," the guard threatened. "You know how it goes."

Esmeralda pleaded with a few guards, but they barely listened. They waved their hands, as if she were a circling gnat. One or two smiled in a way that showed they were used to the commotion and the tears.

"Not all of the new mothers want to go back to work," the guard next to Kirby explained. "Sometimes they need a little coaxing."

Kirby watched the guard, keeping expressionless.

"This time, it is a friendly visit," the guard said. "Next time..." His warning hung in the air.

Esmeralda's pleas turned to tears as the guards left. She hugged Fiona tightly, sniffling. Kirby watched the guards disappear down the alley, swallowed by a few slaves who had emerged from their homes to watch. After a few moments, the slaves lost interest and left.

"I prepared for this moment," Esmeralda explained, wiping away her tears. "But when the guards came to remind me, I lost control of my emotions. I am sorry."

Kirby nodded. Even without children, she knew the strength of a mother's love.

Esmeralda consoled Fiona with gentle words and caresses, as if it might be the last time she saw her.

"They said you are to leave her with Isabella?" Kirby asked.

"One of the caretakers," Esmeralda explained. "A while ago, Isabella lost a finger in one of the machines in the shops. She couldn't work as fast, so they pulled her from the shops and tasked her with taking care of the children. Isabella has a challenging job. She will do her best to handle Fiona, but it will be hard to give her specialized attention."

Kirby nodded. Turning her sympathy into a suggestion, she said, "I am sorry to hear about your trouble. Perhaps you can visit her at lunch?"

"Perhaps, but the guards mostly discourage it." Esmeralda sighed. "We have so little time, as you know."

Kirby nodded. Too many rules.

Wiping the sleep from her eyes, she inadvertently touched her swollen eye.

Guilt passed through Esmeralda's face as she said, "I am sorry to wake you like that. You might've had a few more moments to sleep."

"It is okay. I needed to be up for work anyway." Kirby looked around, surprised she had slept as long as she had. But it made sense, after the physical and emotional pain she'd endured the day before.

"I find that some cold water works best in the first few days, to reduce the swelling of a black eye," Esmeralda said. "Let me get a washcloth for you."

Kirby nodded. Too many previous injuries told her that what Esmeralda said was true. She accepted the washcloth and held it to her eye.

Esmeralda bent down, getting a better look. "I don't see any blood in it. Can you see all right?"

Kirby nodded. In another scenario, she might've considered herself lucky. Not now.

"Thank you," Kirby said, thinking to add, "I'm sorry about Fiona."

"It is fine." Esmeralda looked back at Fiona, perhaps finding some new guilt, or a reason to obey, as she considered Kirby's injury. "I will prepare her things. When the time comes, I will leave with the others."

**

Kirby kept a steady, inconspicuous gait as she walked past the last few houses in her row, approaching the path near the shop buildings. Slaves mingled, or parted ways as they broke from the homes around her, heading for various buildings in time for work to avoid a beating, or a scolding.

She kept her head down, trying to hide her bruised face and her swollen eye. Her injury felt like a beacon to those around her, drawing curiosity or sympathy. More than once, she hurried away from someone whose stare made her uncomfortable.

At the edge of that path, a caravan of wagons and carts trundled up the pathway. Kirby hesitated, watching a line of slaves pull or push the goods inside. Most were covered by cloth, or secured in boxes. One slave fought with a tipsy wagon, loaded with sheets of metal that he continually readjusted, probably headed for one of the many metal shops. Another slave rolled a cart filled with carefully tied bags, about the size of a man's head. She couldn't see what was in them.

Like with most shipments she'd seen, the guards were careful, moving the goods from the gate to the eastern side of the city with haste. None of the slaves faltered or delayed.

Farther back, toward the end, Kirby saw a few guards helping to wheel a wagon covered by a tarp, pulling a heavy load as they headed for the Glass Houses.

Probably some material for the massive building's windows, Kirby thought.

She continued in the direction of her shop, grateful for the distraction that gave the slaves and the guards something to look at, other than her. She spotted Drew. Pushing faster, she caught up, getting his attention long enough for a careful word.

Concern crossed his face as he spotted her injury. "What happened to you?"

"I'm fine," she said, with no desire to explain any more. Drew could read her tone. He didn't ask any more questions.

"Can we meet tonight?"

Drew said, "I will make it happen."

Chapter 44: William

William lay in his bed under the covers, listening to the sounds of footsteps on the stairs. After allowing him out for those few moments to see Barron, Amelia had returned him to his room.

All morning, the guards had either occupied the stair-well, carrying Barron's body down and out of the building, or making preparations. A few times, he'd caught snippets of conversation from The Gifted, speaking about Barron's death. His passing was a sobering reminder of their mortality.

Good, William thought. *Let them think about it.*

William had seen the end of The Gifted in Barron's lifeless eyes as he lay on that bed, staring at nothing. More than that, he'd seen an end to the violence and enslavement.

He had the gun, and the ammunition to go with it.

Looking under the covers, he studied the smooth, antiquated weapon he'd managed to acquire, at the cost of Barron's life. In those quiet moments when The Gifted were in their rooms instead of the stairwell, he'd figured out how to load it. The old weapon wasn't as simple as the guns he'd used in the forest.

The balls and the small, cap-like pieces he'd found in Amelia's tin were easily paired, though he'd had to figure out where to put them. The powder had taken more time. After unlocking the long, metal piece under the gun's barrel, he'd swiveled open the chamber, smelling and seeing some of the black powder's residue inside the holes. That had given him direction.

Studying the flask, he had figured out how to portion out what he needed, using a mechanism that placed some of the powder in the tube.

A few times, he had spilled some of the black substance, stopping to scoop the precious powder. Once he had the hang of it, he'd put some in each of the gun's six chambers, along with a ball, and carefully put each of the caps in the back of the cylinder, using intuition to figure it out. It seemed as if he had loaded it right.

He wasn't sure.

He wouldn't know, until he fired a first shot.

Or the gun failed.

William was unnerved.

The uncertainty of the gun wasn't the only problem. The gun only had places for six balls, making the seventh ball and cap useless. Once he started firing, those rounds would go quickly. The Gifted wouldn't stop and wait for him to ready a last ball.

That meant he had six rounds to kill nine Gifted.

The gun wasn't the solution he'd hoped.

He couldn't stop recalling Barron's grasping hands as they'd struggled. The Gifted were centuries old, but they had adult bodies, and more strength than he did. Taking on all of them at once seemed impossible. He might kill a handful, but not before the others got to him.

Frustrations.

William thought about an individual attack. Maybe he could enter each of The Gifted's rooms at night and take them down singly with his gun, as he had done with Barron. But a single gunshot would rouse attention. He'd kill no more than one or two before the guards and the rest of The Gifted determined that there was a threat and cornered him. A bludgeoning might work, and would be quieter, but he might only kill a few in that manner before he created noise, or a struggle that forced him to use the gun, and then he would blow his cover that way.

He needed a quiet method to dispose of them.

Perhaps smothering them?

Thinking of Tolstoy's large, imposing figure, William couldn't envision taking the man out with his bare hands. Most of The Gifted had similar statures, or were at least bigger than him. He needed to kill all of them at once. Another death would cause too much suspicion, and he'd certainly be questioned, or caught. He felt just as frustrated with the gun as he did without it.

The gun was power.

But it was power he couldn't use.

Even if he could get past the guards downstairs, the demons would eat him before he took a few steps. There was a possibility he could threaten the guards into showing him more weapons, but he didn't know for sure where they were kept. William might raise enough noise in the process to be caught.

William felt as if he had only one chance.

He needed a better way — a more probable way — to use that chance.

The gun was part of the answer, but not all of it.

Chapter 45: Esmeralda

Esmeralda looked out the doorway, holding Fiona in her arms. Hot, mid-morning sun beat down over the stone roofs of the neighboring dwellings. Most of the slaves, including Kirby, were hard at work in the shops, toiling on machines, or sewing clothes in the eastern side of the city. Others worked in the fields in the hot sun.

Holding Fiona tight, Esmeralda walked out to the path and headed down the row of houses, aiming for the main path.

She took several turns, winding between some houses until she approached the larger buildings on the city's eastern side. She glanced at a tall building with an open doorway, with larger buildings in front and behind, peering inside at the room filled with machines. Slaves slid pieces of fabric through the devices in front of them, stepping on pedals at their feet. Head Guards stood outside the doorways. Others walked the rows.

Esmeralda kept going.

Passing another tall, wide building with a large chimney, she saw three furnaces inside one of the Glass Houses. Esmeralda didn't need to get close to feel the heat coming from that room. A few guards stood near the doorway, overseeing the melting of some product.

She continued.

Esmeralda passed a row of machine shops with similar setups. The slaves sweated through the day's heat as they labored on machines, creating whatever pieces The Gifted had in mind. Tomorrow, Esmeralda would return to one of those buildings, producing angular pieces of metal, helping to power the windmills, or other pieces of equipment that she didn't understand. The slaves were taught the skills to do what The Gifted wanted, but rarely more.

Passing more machine shops, and then some woodworking shops, she finally stopped. Esmeralda kept to the sides of a nearby house as she waited to be noticed.

Across the path, Ollie yelled at some people inside a building used for storage. A few guards stood next to him. Esmeralda knew better than to interrupt. She looked down at Fiona, who smiled at her from beneath the blankets. When she looked up, Ollie was coming across the path and toward her.

He looked at her as if she might be lost. "What do you want?" he asked angrily.

Esmeralda lowered her eyes. "I was hoping I might speak with you a moment."

"What is it?" Ollie's eyes showed disdain, as he looked her up and down. A few guards behind him smirked as they stepped in to take over his duties.

"Can we speak privately?" she asked, gesturing toward a nearby alley.

Fiona cooed, forcing Ollie's eyes to Esmeralda's arms. He quickly looked away. "Only for a moment."

Esmeralda led him down an alley that resembled her own, passing a few empty houses whose inhabitants presumably worked. Finding a quiet place, she stopped.

"What is it?" Ollie demanded again.

"It is about my new roommate, Kirby."

A memory flitted through Ollie's oversized head, followed by a smile. "I know who she is," he grunted.

"I wanted to give you a warning," Esmeralda said.

"A warning?" Some anger flitted through Ollie's eyes

as he looked from Esmeralda to Fiona. She didn't want to know what might happen if she wasn't carrying the infant. "It sounds as if you want something."

"I was hoping I might get another month at home with Fiona, if I gave you information."

"You'd be punished for withholding it," Ollie said, a spark of aggression in his eyes.

"Which is why I came to you," Esmeralda added quickly. "I knew you'd need the information."

Ollie looked around, as if someone might be listening, even though they were the only ones around. "Spill what you know."

"She has been sneaking around lately, mostly with the man she came here with," Esmeralda said. "I think they are planning something."

"Planning?" Ollie asked, as if the word itself was foul.

"I think she is up to no good," Esmeralda explained, making an assumption that even a thickheaded brute like Ollie would understand.

Ollie didn't seem impressed. Looking down at Fiona, Esmeralda felt a pang of failure.

"Tell me something that will make it worth stepping away from my work," Ollie growled, "or I will send you away. Maybe I will take away your rations." Esmeralda felt sick to her stomach. She hated him. Fiona was the reason she did this. Not Ollie, and unfortunately, not Kirby.

"Before The Plagued Ones fed last night, I saw her ducking into the flooded house at the end of our row. She skipped dinner." Esmeralda put on a grave expression worthy of the information she gave. "A while later, I saw her meeting the man with whom she was brought here. They are definitely consorting."

"Probably fraternizing," Ollie said.

"I am not sure," Esmeralda answered. "But it seemed more sinister than that."

Ollie's eyes riveted to hers as he made a promise. "She will regret the day she tries anything, if she lives long enough. We have plenty of hungry Plagued Ones to feed, if she steps out of line." Ollie pronounced the words loudly and looked around, as if some others might hear his threat.

Esmeralda remained quiet, waiting. When it was clear she was done speaking, Ollie wiped some sweat away from his forehead with his large, grubby hands. He looked over Esmeralda, his eyes lingering on the top of her shirt.

"Can I receive another month of time with Fiona?" she asked, hating the fear in her stomach, hating that she had to ask twice.

Ollie nodded. "I'll call in a favor with Rudyard and inform the other guards." With a dismissive wave, he said, "Now get out of my sight."

Chapter 46: William

The wind blew through William's shaggy hair as he stood in a semi-circle with the other Gifted on the rooftop, all wearing their robes and hoods, all standing with their arms folded. Tolstoy stood in the center of the curved group, holding Barron's ashes in an urn that he had received from the guards. Every so often, the wind blew loudly enough that he projected his voice to the other Gifted, who adjusted their hoods to keep them from blowing off.

William sucked in a breath of fresh air. He'd spent most of the morning and lunch confined to his room. After a while, Amelia had come for him. He was instructed to keep his distance, but he was allowed out for the ceremony. His gun and ammunition were safely in his bureau.

He listened to Tolstoy's extolling words.

"We are here to celebrate the life of our brother, Barron," Tolstoy said, pronouncing each word with clarity. "A brother who has walked among us for centuries, a brother who has transcended all of the beings who have walked the earth before, or will walk after. One of ten chosen Gifted, the founders of New City."

The Gifted bowed their heads.

"Most of the world will not know the impact of our dead brother, but we will not forget him. Barron had evolved past a simple human, but he still carried the shell of his former self. His vessel was imperfect, as ours are." Tolstoy met each of their eyes before turning to the rooftop, waving a ceremonial hand over the city. "We bear the scars of our human predecessors, and we are forced to breathe the same air. We are prone to accidents of nature. Barron might be gone, but he has given his life for his work. His life is an inspiration, but also a warning. We must be careful. We must stay alive, to follow his vision."

A few of the Gifted murmured their agreement.

Staring at Tolstoy, listening to his pompous words, William wanted to knock him off the roof.

If they were alone, he probably would have considered it.

Tolstoy gestured off the rooftop, toward the tall and short buildings in the distance. The Gifted turned their heads, following his hand. "It was Barron's planning that led to the creation of the walls around our city. It was his intellect that led to the development of the machines the humans use to prepare our clothes, and the innovations of our windmills. It was his ingeniousness that created the parts for our lathes. Barron has helped our city run at a greater efficiency than most of the cities before The Collapse. In his latest years, he developed a vision that will carry us into the next phase of our existence, a mission to find more of our people, through his study of flight. We honor his accomplishments by remembering our brother, but also by continuing his work. Barron might not have lived to see the end of our great experiment, but he has contributed in lasting ways."

The Gifted nodded their agreement. A few shifted, or held onto their hoods.

"We will mourn his loss, but we will continue. We will follow his ideas until we reach our goal. We will build a grand city of our people, if not in this century, then in the next." Tolstoy's voice grew hard as he held up the urn. "Let us take a moment to honor Barron with a moment of silence."

The Gifted tilted their heads, staring at the roof of

Ancient stone. William followed suit, pretending as if he were mourning, while his thoughts ran dark. He recalled when he'd first met Barron, in The Library Room, and the few conversations he'd had with him before his friends were enslaved.

That first day in New City held a magic he couldn't forget.

But each of those memories was overshadowed by Barron's coldness as he stood next to William on the balcony, gripping his arm and forcing him to watch the snarling, writhing demons, pulling out Cullen's insides in the Feeding Pen. Barron's words from that day came back to him.

"The Plagued Ones fight for food. They are always hungry."

Barron said those words as if they were fact, but they weren't always true.

The Gifted's demons fought each other, but not all demons did.

William knew the demons' instincts better than anyone, because he had lived among them. He had spent long days learning, hunting, and sleeping in their presence. The demons obeyed when he spoke with them, but they also helped each other survive.

The demon army fought for food because their owners starved them.

The Gifted ordered them to keep close to New City, allowing them only meager scraps of corn and the animals they could hunt close by. Most of the animals in the nearby forests, or around the walls, had long been killed and eaten. William had seen the hungry looks in the demons' eyes as they chased the remaining small prey through the cornfields. They yearned for more.

Staring at The Gifted, watching them bow their heads in solemn reflection, he wondered if perhaps there was meaning in Barron's death, after all. Maybe Barron's cold words on that day had given William another answer.

Maybe he could show The Gifteds' demons another way.

"Brothers and sister," Tolstoy said, as he opened the small urn and threw the ashes into the wind. "May Barron's ideas, and his intelligence, live on."

Perhaps the demons had always been the answer.

**

"Come in," William said, responding to a knock at his door.

The same, stony-faced guard entered, balancing a tray of food for his dinner. William remained in bed, tucked under the covers, as he watched the guard enter. Sucking in a breath, William hacked his way through a noisy cough before the guard got within a few feet of him. Reacting to Amelia's warnings, the guard set the tray on one of the bureaus, keeping his distance.

"I'll leave it here," he said.

William nodded and touched his throat, as if he was unable to answer. Out on the stairwell, through the open door, he saw another guard waiting. He'd already heard them bringing The Gifted dinner, followed by dessert a while later. They followed the same schedule as always.

William was an afterthought, or at least it seemed that way, now that he was sick and no longer among them as much.

Without another word, the guards shut and locked the door. William listened to their footsteps recede down the fifteen floors to the bottom, before looking over at the food on the bureau.

Meat, potatoes, and corn.

Fighting the hunger in his stomach, he rose from the bed and walked over to the food, but he didn't eat it.

Chapter 47: William

William crept through the moonlight toward his doorway, holding his full plate of food. When everyone was asleep, he snuck out, made his way to the third floor, and unlocked the door.

Inside the room, William veered toward the northern balcony.

He opened the glass door and looked out, searching for guards on the floors above and below before stepping through it. More than likely, they scanned beyond the building's perimeter, or behind the wall. Or perhaps they weren't looking at all. It was a risk he had to take.

The fresh air felt good on his face as he stepped to the railing and peered over.

Something skittered in the shadows, near the building's base three floors down.

Sucking in a nervous breath, William hissed, "It's okay. I'm here to help."

He heard rustling through the cornfields as more shadows emerged to investigate. A handful of demons congregated underneath the moonlight, looking up at him.

"I know you're hungry. I brought food."

An anticipatory hiss echoed from below him as William picked a piece of meat from his plate, aimed, and tossed it. More hissing came as the demons scrambled for it. Teeth tore and chewed noisily. William looked up and down the face of the building, but he heard nothing other than the demons.

Picking up another piece of meat, he reared back and threw it. More shadows came to join the others, hissing with a new sound. Pleasure. They wanted meat, not corn.

Of course, they did.

And he gave it to them.

"Have some more," he said, making sure the demons heard his voice as he threw down the rest of his meat and potatoes, feeding them.

Chapter 48: Bray

"I've been thinking about your idea with the Feeding Pen, and storming the tower," Kirby said to Bray, as they snuck along the alley, heading out of the inhabited part of the city under the moonlight. "I think it might work."

Bray reached over, squeezing her arm. "Hopefully The Shadow People will feel the same."

They fell in step together, looking over their shoulders, as the lights behind them receded and they traveled into deeper shadow. The dirt path on which they walked was littered with stone and debris. All around, a few hooting owls reminded them that animals roamed the dark alongside them, walls or not. More than once since they had that first meeting, Bray considered that a brave demon might skirt over the wall and run out screeching from the shadows, like those few had years ago when they ate Teddy's daughter.

"I had a dream about William the other night," Kirby whispered, when they were far enough away that most of the lights behind them had disappeared. Nostalgia crept into her throat, as she said, "We were riding on the horses, in that valley past the canyon, where the grass rose really high. Do you remember stopping there?"

"We had lunch there," Bray whispered back. "There were so many rabbits, William said we could live there forever. He said that we'd die before we ran out of them."

Kirby laughed softly at the memory. "Perhaps we should have stayed."

"There is no way to know where our choices lead," Bray reminded her.

"Still, it is nice to dream," Kirby said, voicing a rare, sentimental thought.

Bray nodded. "Perhaps one day we can return there."

A noise in the dark made them halt.

They waited, looking in all directions. They'd reached an intersecting alley running east and west. A rat skittered through the darkness somewhere in front of them, finding a nearby hole and hiding. A bat fluttered its wings, leaving its perch.

A light appeared in the distance.

"Is that Drew?" Bray hissed, peering past too many shadows.

"The people we are meeting do not use torches," Kirby warned.

Bray swallowed as he looked behind them. Before they could make a move, two more torches sprang into view, forty feet behind and closing.

"More lights," he said under his breath, as Kirby spun and looked.

"And down there, too," Kirby noticed, pointing west down the intersecting alley.

With no choice but to go east, they headed that way, down the only clear path.

They skirted through the alley, their breath heaving as they ran out of sight of several of the torches. The bobbing torch behind, however, was still in view, and pounding footsteps in other directions told them the other people were converging. Dark, foul-smelling buildings surrounded them. The moon illuminated part of the pathway, but too many objects remained hidden in long, dark shadows. More rodents scurried from harm's way.

They picked up as much speed as they could. The dark doorways and windows around them looked like pits of inky blackness, ready to suck them in and hold onto them. Bray's leg scraped against a jagged piece of stone, hard enough to draw blood. He bit back his pain as the footsteps behind grew louder.

"Over here!" a close voice yelled.

More shouts echoed from other directions.

"Guards!" Kirby hissed.

"If they see our faces, it won't matter if we escape," Bray warned. "They will drag us from our houses as soon as we return."

They took another alley, keeping ahead of the shouts and the lights. Tall buildings loomed above them. Bray wondered if they could come up with a story that would save them from death. The gods knew he had told enough tales. But he doubted the guards would listen.

Everyone knew this area was forbidden.

He couldn't stop thinking of the warning The Shadow People had given them about those who had tried escaping.

They fed them to The Plagued Ones, while the rest of the city watched.

A shout drew his attention to an intersecting alley, where a guard careened around a corner, pointing his finger.

"I've got them!"

Bray tripped over another piece of stone he didn't see.

He fell.

He hit the ground hard, losing his breath. His hands scraped gravel. Jagged rocks scraped his palms as he pushed off, trying to regain his feet, but not before the guard caught up. Bray cried out as the man reached down for him, latching on to his boot.

"We've got one of 'em!"

Bray lashed out, kicking the guard backwards and knocking the torch from his hand. The man grunted and fell.

"Come on!" Kirby urged, reaching Bray's side and pulling him up and away.

More guards caught up to the first, cursing as they turned a nearby corner and fell in line behind him. Bray could see the glow of their torches in his peripheral vision. He scanned the distance for the interior of the city — proof that they were headed the right way.

"We need to get back around other people," he hissed. "We need to blend in."

They raced down a dark, shadowy path between broken monoliths, until another group of lights blocked their path.

Shit.

They were cornered.

Bray thought back to what Clara and the others had told him about Ashville. The guards stayed away, unless they chased someone. Bray and Kirby had been vigilant about sneaking out, but they must've been followed.

There was no time to contemplate how it happened.

Reaching out, he tugged Kirby's shoulder as they darted down a skinny alley branching off from the alley down which they ran. They skirted around a few hunks of broken, ancient stone. With no other choice, they headed to a doorway to hide.

Something clattered to the ground near Kirby.

"Dammit!" she hissed, as she lost something.

"What was that?"

"My shank!" she replied.

"Leave it!" Bray said, as the shouts behind them grew louder.

They ducked inside the building.

Footsteps echoed closer.

Bray clutched Kirby's sleeve, holding her close as they found a spot in the rubble and crouched.

Shouting men slowed their footsteps, passing within a few steps of the place into which they'd ducked, moments ago. Torchlight penetrated the fringes of the doorway. Bray smelled the stink of the men's clothing, heard their ragged breaths as they slowed down.

"They're around here somewhere," a voice said, with certainty.

Ollie.

More guards' thundering footsteps beat the alley.

"Check the buildings," Ollie barked. "They must've hid."

Bray glanced behind him, looking for a break in the darkness that would signify a place to run, or hide. The room was pitch black. A single kicked stone would give away their position. Bray listened as the men started entering doorways. His clenched fists wouldn't go far against so many men with knives.

They had to move.

He tugged Kirby's arm, leading her further into the darkness as they padded gently over a floor they couldn't see. They got only a few steps before a torch splashed light through the doorway.

Bray only had a moment to look around before a greasy-faced man stuck his head through the doorway, holding his torch and his long knife.

Spotting Bray and Kirby, he yelled, "In here!"

Bray and Kirby moved a few more steps, but the room was full of large chunks of cracked stone, and a set of stairs that led nowhere. The windows were caved in. They were trapped.

A group of eight men poured through the entrance, holding their torches high and shouting in triumph, cornering Bray and Kirby against a wall.

Cutting a path through the menacing guards, Ollie approached Bray and Kirby with his knife drawn, getting in their faces. "What are you doing here, forest-dwellers?"

Quiet pervaded the room as all eyes turned to them.

Reaching for a lie he doubted would help, Bray said, "We were taking a walk."

A few soldiers chuckled.

"I think they were kissing in the night." A blonde-haired guard snickered.

Bray and Kirby didn't dispute the claim.

"There are plenty of places to do that in the city," Ollie grunted. "And people with nothing to hide don't run."

A few of the soldiers nodded their agreement.

"Who else is here?" Ollie barked.

Bray wondered if the other Shadow People had been caught, but he heard nothing to give him that impression. Hopefully, they were back in their houses. Further evidence of a consortium would certainly crucify them.

"We are alone," Kirby said simply.

The guards awaited an order, looking at Ollie.

"We only saw them leaving the city," said a guard with a ruddy face. "Maybe Arnie was right. Maybe they were kissing."

Bray put on a serious expression. "That's what we were doing."

Ollie's face twisted into a malevolent smile. "Whatever you were doing, it won't matter much longer." To the guards, he said, "Bring them back to the city. Drag them through the alleys. Make sure everyone sees and hears."

Ollie stepped back, allowing his soldiers to get by him.

Five guards approached Bray, invigorated by the chase that led to this moment. Bray looked sideways at Kirby. If this were the end, neither would give up easily.

Bray swung at the first guard to approach him, catching him in the face. He punched another guard in the stomach, but the three other guards backed him farther against the wall, quickly overwhelming him and pinning his hands.

"Let me go, you dirt-scratchers!" he yelled.

"This is the end!" one of the guards screamed.

Nearby, he heard Kirby fighting back, but three guards surrounded her, too.

"You filthy bastards!" Kirby spat, as she was overpowered.

"Take them out of here!" Ollie thundered.

Kirby's cries echoed through the room as the guards obeyed Ollie's orders. Bray dug his heels into the ground, unable to stop his captors from pulling him into the night.

Chapter 49: Bray

Bray sat with his back against the hard, stone wall of the cell. They'd taken Kirby into a room somewhere at the end of the long building, away from him. She might as well be back in the alleys through which they'd been kicked, beaten, and dragged, to the terrified expressions of the watching slaves. Many slaves had shown shock or sympathy, but no one had helped.

Who would volunteer for death?

Kirby and Bray had struggled, but their efforts were fruitless.

Bray didn't see any of the other Shadow People. It seemed as if he and Kirby were the only ones caught.

It was over.

Staring at the cracks of moonlight, Bray hit a hopeless fist against the ground. The reality Kirby had spoken in the flooded house held more wisdom than his fantasy-fueled revolt. They had no chance of overrunning this filthy prison. They never had.

Kirby had been right, all those days ago.

His fingertips and nails bled from scratching at a locked door that wouldn't budge. His voice was hoarse from shouting. All he could do now was wait for a last chance to prove his bravery. Whatever torture they planned for him, he would die with his fists swinging.

He stared at the walls, shifting positions, occasionally finding the strength to shout through the door at the guards outside. Occasionally, he heard them snickering, or telling loud stories.

Eventually, a long, hopeless night turned to morning.

The light under his door brightened.

Bray smeared some of the sweat and dried blood from his eyes as new sounds filled the courtyard.

Lots of sounds.

The clank of a key in the lock filled Bray's heart with a last sensation of dread, before the door swung open, allowing the morning light to spill in.

The guards entered the room, yanking him several steps out into the dirt.

Through the bright, blinding sun, Bray saw the fringes of an enormous, gathered crowd, the hundreds of slaves that comprised New City, all waiting, watching in a circle in the center of the courtyard. Most of their heads were turned toward Bray and the guards that pulled him toward the side of that crowd, who had left an opening to admit them.

Pulled past the throngs of nervous, waiting people, Bray saw Kirby standing in the courtyard's center.

Ollie stood behind her, grinning with an expression he recognized, as he looked between Kirby and Bray, and the crowd filled in behind Bray and the guards.

He knew what this was.

A horrid feeling took root in Bray's stomach as a chant took hold.

"Come to the center!" Ollie boomed across the courtyard. "Come and fight!"

Avery raised his arms, walking along the edges of the hesitant crowd and riling them up.

"Fight! Fight!"

"Keep walking, or I'll gut this spineless wench!" Ollie said, keeping Bray's attention as he stuck his knife against Kirby's back, making a demonstration of his threat.

Kirby stood rigid in front of him, her face painted in defiance.

The crowd was a single, faceless mass, cheering, screaming, and wailing. Children hid behind their mother's skirts. Some of the slaves with bloodlust stepped forward. The guards stood on the fringes of the circle with their knives out, ready to gut Bray if he didn't comply.

They had learned from Jonah's attack.

Bray took a compliant few steps forward, but he didn't go any farther. He hoped that a few seconds of time would buy his way out of a hopeless situation. Of course, there was no way out. He might as well be standing in a pit of snarling demons.

He scanned the crowd for Drew, but he couldn't find him or the other Shadow People. They had prepared for a meeting, not a revolt.

"Keep walking!" Ollie snarled again.

He nudged Kirby, ready to stab. Bray and Kirby traded a look of resolve. Neither she nor Bray would fight. They would meet their ends in the sharp ends of the guards' blades before they killed each other.

A new voice entered the fray.

"Step aside!"

The crowd parted as several women and children moved to admit a familiar, robed figure. Some of the chanting quieted. Rudyard tilted his misshapen head as he appraised Kirby, Ollie, and Bray. He walked until he was level with Ollie. A smile played across his lips.

"You came," Ollie grunted.

"I heard how much fun you were having," Rudyard said. "I didn't want to miss it."

Bray looked through the crowd past which Rudyard had walked, as if he might find a cluster of demons, ready to enforce Ollie's edict. But it seemed as if Rudyard was alone.

Bray steadied himself in the dirt as he stared across the courtyard at Rudyard. "No beasts to do your work?"

Rudyard's smile was glued to his face. "Not today."

"Perhaps you'd like to fight, yourself, then," Bray said, raising a dirty fist.

A few in the back of the crowd cried out in support, before quickly growing silent.

"You speak bravely, for a slave who is about to kill his friend," Rudyard said, with a confident nod.

"If you believe that, you should have brought your demons." Bray spat in Rudyard's direction.

"They don't want to fight," Ollie grunted, making a fake show of disappointment.

Rudyard looked between Kirby and Bray. "Perhaps I can persuade them." Motioning up at the tower, he said, "Perhaps I will bring William down to spur them on."

Kirby spun, making no effort to hide her fury as she asked, "Where is he?"

"Sleeping," Rudyard said. "But it would be easy to wake him up." Rudyard's nod brought a sick feeling to Bray's stomach as more hopelessness set in.

"You heard him," Ollie bellowed, waving at the building. "Fight, or he brings the Plagued kid down here."

Bray looked from the threatening faces up to the glimmering tower, as if he might find a cluster of robed figures with William on the balcony. The balcony was empty.

They wouldn't harm William.

Would they?

Advancing toward Rudyard, Bray said, "I'll kill you before you take a step toward that tower."

A few guards matched his steps, moving in position to protect Rudyard.

"I am not attached to William, as the others are." Rudyard shrugged as he glanced at the guards, who were eager for blood. "William does not belong down here in the city, but I will have no problem hurting him. Or perhaps, I will ensure that he has many long, miserable years after you are dead."

Bray looked for a bluff beneath Rudyard's threat, but he saw only malice in his eyes. Kirby turned over her shoulder, contemplating a last move, until Ollie raised a boot and kicked her forward.

"Get to fighting!"

Kirby stopped from falling, regained her balance, and watched Bray. Her face was bruised and dirty.

They shared a look of hopelessness. Angry tears spilled down Kirby's cheeks as several of the guards went to the edges of the crowd and riled the slaves up again.

"Fight! Fight!"

"Do I need to explain the rules again?" Ollie called, over the growing cries of the men and women.

A few men and women in the front rows shook their heads.

Bray looked at Kirby, sharing a look both knew would be one of their last.

He balled his fists.

He took a step.

Chapter 50: Kirby

Kirby blinked as cheers and shouts grew louder around her. All at once, she was back in the arena in her homeland, listening to the shouts and cries of another bloodthirsty mob. Spittle flew from people's mouths as they shouted more loudly. Each moment of inaction bred impatience. Only blood would sate their cries.

Fight! Fight!

Finding clarity, she looked over her shoulder at Ollie, who led the crowd with a noisy bellow. Avery stood next to Rudyard, watching with a complacent grin. She felt the surge of adrenaline that always accompanied her in the fights when she was forced against another, unwilling infected. Sometimes they begged, sometimes they groveled, but it only prolonged the pain.

Death was inevitable.

Killing the other infected in the arena had filled her empty stomach, but it had hollowed her soul.

She'd sworn she'd never do it again.

Kirby readied her fists, looking at Bray as he took a step forward. Rudyard's words echoed in her head as she thought about William, alone in the tower with the intelligent monsters who might harm him. For all she knew, Rudyard had lied, and he was dead already. And she would be soon, when the spore claimed her.

She was a walking corpse, waiting for the infection to take her mind.

If only she had deteriorated already, so that she could forget what she was about to do.

Bray stood a few feet away, looking at Kirby with pain in his eyes. Through the dried dirt and blood on his face, she saw the man in the forest with whom she'd shared those meals, conversations, and even her bed. Somehow, she'd seen through the misery of her existence to allow herself a feeling, but that feeling would become a weapon that would hurt her worse than the infection ever could. Or maybe Bray would find the strength to see that he had a future, while she didn't.

Maybe he would kill her, and it would all be over.

She allowed Bray's face to blur. It was the only way she could see past the horror of what they were forced to do.

"Get to it!" Ollie screamed.

"Come on!" Bray urged her, his face contorting with pain. "We have to do this. If we don't, they'll hurt William."

Fight! Fight!

Kirby cocked back a fist. A flurry of faces whipped through her mind as she saw some of the others whom she had fought. She had killed more than she wanted to remember — people with whom she was forced to live before she fought. She'd never forget their names, and she recalled each of those bloodied faces in her sleep. *Terry. Marshall. Angela. Patrick.*

Kirby swung.

Bray threw up a deflective arm, blocking.

Marcus. David. Roger.

People cheered as the unwilling opponents circled, and Kirby prepared another swing.

Kirby struck again, catching Bray in the side. He grunted and circled. Their stalling wouldn't last long.

Jerry. Ben. Josephine.

The hard feeling in Kirby's stomach became a pit she remembered too well.

Bray swung a fist that she easily avoided. Dodging out of the way, Kirby stopped herself before throwing a counter-blow. Watching Bray's hesitant face, she allowed it to blur again, recalling another memory from the arena, all those years ago.

All at once, the faces and the names faded, replaced by a single person.

Edward.

The first man she'd fought.

She remembered Edward's screams as he flung his fists at her, fighting a battle that neither of them wanted, a battle that had lasted too long until one of them had finally succumbed. She recalled the punch that had knocked him from his feet and stopped him from getting up. A few punches in either direction, and Edward might've been the one standing over her at the end.

Edward hadn't died, though, at least not that day.

She had caught him in a manner that had knocked him out, rather than killing him. They had declared her the winner, but they hadn't given her a meal.

Still, Edward had lived past that fight.

There was only one way out of the arena.

One way out, unless…

Moving toward Bray, under the instigating screams of the guards, and the chant of the crowd, Kirby muttered, "When I hit you, stay down."

A look of confusion crossed Bray's face.

Before he could process her words, Kirby charged. She summoned her anger into a fist, recalling the beatings of the guards and Ollie's sneering, pig-headed face. Putting that anger into a swing and a ferocious cry, she aimed between Bray's left temple and ear, as she had done to Edward that day.

Bray's hands came up to block, too late. The blow landed hard and true.

Too hard.

Kirby had a second to wonder if she'd made a mistake before Bray dropped, and stayed down.

He landed on his back, unmoving.

The crowd whooped into frenzy. Kirby regained her fighting stance, as the last of her cry died in the air. Surprised shouts came from the guards, as they approached with their weapons and Bray didn't move. The crowd leaned forward expectantly.

"Get up, forest-dweller!" a guard cried.

"To your feet, you weak-kneed bastard!" another goaded.

Receiving no response, the guards got closer, bending down to look at the fallen combatant. A few circled behind Kirby, guarding her, while others formed a half-circle around Bray. They kept their knives in front of them, as though he might spring up and surprise them.

"What's going on?" Ollie called impatiently from behind them.

Kirby turned to find Ollie, Avery, and Rudyard watching.

Gaining confidence, one of the guards put an ear to Bray's lips.

"He's dead," the guard pronounced, with an unbelieving smile.

Despair filled Kirby's stomach. Whispers swept across the crowd.

I've killed him.

Kirby clenched and unclenched her sore fist as she stared at the body on the ground, images of too many others flooding her memory.

Terry. Marshall. Angela.

Marcus. David. Roger.

Bray.

She'd killed the closest person in her life.

"Not dead," said another, leaning over and pressing a grubby hand against Bray's neck. "He's knocked out."

"Knocked out?" Ollie looked around, as if someone played a trick.

Kirby's despair rose to hope.

A few more guards bent down, verifying the first's findings. A ripple went through the crowd as the news spread. Surprised men, women, and children watched Ollie's reaction, and Rudyard's.

Turning to Rudyard, Ollie guffawed, "Knocked out, by a simple wench!"

A long, hearty laugh came from his throat.

Waving a robed hand, Rudyard said, "Perhaps I should have sent in The Plagued Ones, after all."

A few of the guards chuckled. Kirby kept her eyes down as she waited for that order.

Rudyard cleared his throat as he looked from the crowd to the front gate.

"What should we do?" Ollie asked.

"The slaves need to line up," Rudyard said, losing interest. "Do what you want with them, but the harvest waits for no man."

Rudyard turned and walked away.

The crowd parted to let him through.

Ollie looked around. Watching Rudyard go, perhaps feeling the weight of his orders, Ollie said, "Throw them back in the cells. When they're done recovering, put them back to work."

Kirby stood stock-still, as if she misheard.

Appraising her with a smile, Ollie said, "Keep the weak-kneed man in there longer than the wench. Let him stew in his shame."

Chapter 51: William

"Your food," said the same guard William had seen for days, as he walked into his room.

William sat up, rubbing the bleariness from his tired eyes. Too many nights of sneaking around, thinking, and planning had worn him down. Mistaking his exhaustion for sickness, the guard set the tray down on William's bureau. He retrieved William's empty dinner tray and walked to the doorway, joining the other guard.

They exchanged a sly smile.

"You missed the show," one said.

William frowned. Before he could ask a clarifying question, the guards left, leaving him with the smell of fresh breakfast in his nose and a worry in his heart. William threw aside the covers and hurried to the window, looking out over New City. Below, he saw slaves weaving in between the houses. Of course, he couldn't see Bray or Kirby. Crossing the room and looking north, he saw nothing out of the ordinary.

William couldn't help but feel as if time was slipping away. He might be devising a plan to help two dead friends. He needed to act soon.

Walking back to his tray, he nibbled at some of the fruit, sticking the meat and bread in one of his bureau drawers. Ignoring the hunger in his stomach, he set the tray where the guards left it, keeping the rest of his food hidden.

Chapter 52: Kirby

Five days after the fight, after spending three days in the cell, and the last two days in the metal shop, Kirby wiped the sweat of the mid-day sun from her face. She headed down the long, dirt pathway toward her house. Ever since she'd been let out, she'd spent long days working while Bray spent long days confined. She couldn't get the last glimpse of him out of her mind — his lifeless body lying on the ground.

She knew he wasn't dead.

Late in the evening, after the mutants were fed, she'd crept close to the courtyard, watching with anger as guards stood near the doorway to his cell. Too many snide remarks accompanied those visits. Days after the fight, Bray's loss was still a source of entertainment.

Not much longer.

Kirby looked to her left down an alley, finding someone near the back of a house where they'd agreed to meet, walking slowly enough that she could catch up. Anger laced her words as she stopped close to Drew.

"We need to act," Kirby whispered, no room for arguments.

Drew's face was a mask of seriousness. "I spoke with the others about you and Bray's plan."

"And?" Kirby watched him, prepared to unleash more than a day's worth of fury. She would make a plan of her own, if they rejected her argument.

"Your plan for The Plagued Ones is a risk, but no one can argue against it." Drew sighed, unable to contain the guilt she'd seen on his face, ever since she and Bray had fought in the arena. "It won't be much longer until we are all pitted against one another, or perhaps killed in some other, horrible way. I think the fight in the courtyard allowed the other leaders to see that." Drew looked sideways at Kirby, watching her remorsefully. "I feel badly about what happened to you, Kirby. If I could've stopped it…"

"I know you couldn't," Kirby said, letting go of some of her anger.

"In any case, I want to make sure it doesn't happen again." Drew watched her for a long second. "I have convinced the others of your plan. They are committed."

"Committed?" Seeing the look in her friend's eyes, Kirby felt relief. That relief was weighed down by the guilt of what she'd done to Bray. "When will we meet?"

"Tonight," Drew said.

"With Clara and the others," she assumed.

"No," Drew said. "With fifty of us."

Kirby's surprise was written on her face. "Fifty?"

"Two hundred people would easily be missed. We can't all meet at once. But we can pass the information to the others."

Kirby nodded.

Drew watched her intently for a moment. He looked as if he had something else to say. "After what happened in New Hope, I never thought I'd see you again, Kirby. It was a surprise finding you here, but it was bittersweet. I would not wish this life on anyone. Hopefully, we can outlive our enslavement and find our freedom. With luck, what happened to you will never happen again." A look of resolve crossed Drew's face as he appraised her, making a promise. "The rule of the guards — and The Gifted — is coming to an end."

"I hope so, too."

She thought she saw the hint of a smile on Drew's face as he snuck away.

Chapter 53: Kirby

Kirby, Drew, Clara, Giovanni, and James stood tall on a chunk of ancient stone, looking out over a silent, growing crowd that stood in the courtyard behind one of the buildings in Ashville. Shadows formed in rows on the ground as people appeared from the darkness, lining up and waiting for the leaders to speak. A palpable tension surrounded them, as men and women shuffled nervously, making room for others.

The meeting was a risk.

Hopefully, a last risk.

Standing among the revolt leaders on that high perch, looking out over a crowd for which she couldn't help but feel responsible, Kirby's nerves carved a hollow pit in her stomach. She was apprehensive, but she was ready.

When everyone was present, Clara said, "Let us begin."

Clearing his throat, Drew spoke loudly enough that all the shadows could hear. "For too long, we have stayed idle as the guards beat, mistreat, and starve us. We have watched people dragged from the forest and imprisoned next to us, without the means to help. We have watched our brothers and sisters forced to fight or kill one another, for the guards' perverse amusement. We have lost our families to sickness, or intolerable working conditions. As slaves, we have worked for The Gifteds' profit, without reward or gratitude. No more. The time has come to fight back."

An excitement that had built for months — *years* — boiled

to a head as everyone in the crowd nodded. Had this been a rally, or a village gathering, the crowd might've cheered. Even as they stayed silent, Kirby felt an excitement brewing in them that was impossible to ignore. Bodies shifting in the darkness, living out a moment none would soon forget.

Something far more important than a meeting in the dark was coming, and they were prepared.

"Some of you have heard parts of the plan. Some of you have heard little," Clara said. "We will provide you with the details now, so everyone is clear. Your job is to disseminate the information to the others."

Drew spoke up next. "Over the past days, we have greatly supplemented our weapons cache, enough that each of us can fill a hand, or two. Your efforts, and your risks, are appreciated. When we are all free, we will celebrate. For now, we plan."

A few laughed quietly, or nervously.

Clara took back over the conversation. "I, along with the others up here and some extra people, will take care of the guards on watch first, just before dawn. The rest of you will attack those in their homes immediately afterward. You will be assigned a guard's home that is close to where you live. When you have eliminated the guard, you will help the others around you. We will overwhelm and surprise them before they can defend themselves, or warn The Gifted. We will attack them individually, so they cannot help one another."

A few shadows in the darkness nodded.

"An attack before dawn will ensure that the guards are groggy from sleep, or hung over from drink," Giovanni said, parroting Bray's earlier idea.

"What about the guards' families?" asked a shadow in the front row.

"Many of the wives and children do not understand the pain the guards cause, or they benefit too much to see past it," Clara said. "We will do our best to keep the families quiet and contained, but it is possible we will face some situations."

"This is a war. There will be casualties," Drew said simply.

"Perhaps we can lock the families in their houses to protect them," the shadowy figure suggested.

"It is a nice thought, and certainly something to strive for," Drew said. "But the realities of a battle won't match what we plan. It is your job to make sure the other people around you are safe."

Kirby nodded gravely as she thought of Esmeralda, and some of the other quiet victims of the guard's abuse. War had many victims. Hopefully they could minimize the bloodshed of the innocent.

"We have enough among us to outnumber the guards by two to one," Clara continued. "That is not an exact ratio, of course. For those guards who live in pairs, we will assign more of you. We will maximize our odds. Whatever happens, it is imperative that we do not allow the guards anywhere near the gate. We cannot allow them to warn The Gifted."

"Ideally, we take out most of the guards before anyone in The Learning Building is awake," James said. "By keeping the battle away from the gate and the walls, our hope is to eliminate riling up any of The Plagued Ones. As you know, there is a possibility some might scale the walls. We will need to watch for that."

"Once we kill the guards, we will collect their weapons," Clara said. "Their long knives will give us even better odds."

A shadow person adjusted in one of the back rows, speaking over the people in front. "What if The Gifted are alerted as we fight the guards?"

"It is a risk," Drew admitted. "But the cover of darkness will give us some leeway. Most in the building cannot hear what goes on here. It is simply too high."

"I can verify that is true," Kirby agreed.

Another shadowy figure interrupted, following up on the other's question. "What about the other slaves? We do not know what they will do. What if they decide to fight us?"

"Many are our friends, our families, or our acquaintances from the field, or the shops, as you know," Clara said. "I do not think they will throw themselves in harm's way to save the men who beat them. Once they see what we are doing, hopefully they will join us. They will not choose to side with dead men."

"By the time many realize what is happening, hopefully the guards will be dead," Drew added.

"What then?" one of the shadows asked, shifting nervously in the dark.

"That is the next part of our plan," Clara said. "I will defer to Kirby to explain."

All of the shadows, even the inquisitive ones, fell silent as they swiveled to face Kirby. Looking out over the silhouetted crowd, Kirby realized that she was probably a stranger to most. But they had an unspoken bond stronger than casual conversations or handshakes.

"I do not know all of you, but I know your pain," Kirby started. "I felt it the second I was enslaved here, along with the rest of you. This is not the first time I have been the property of another. For too many years, I suffered at the hands of people who treated me like an animal. I was forced into wars that benefited all except me. A life of enslavement is a fate suited for no one. A few days ago, most of you watched me fight against my friend, for the sake of the bloodthirsty guards. I will not allow that to happen again, to any of you."

A ripple of quiet enthusiasm spread across the crowd.

"We have a bond that is stronger than most people who live in the wild. We will fight together, so that we can gain our freedom."

A few hushed, excited whispers permeated the shadows.

"You have heard our plan for the guards. Once we have beaten them, we have a plan for The Plagued Ones." Kirby paused. "As you know, the guards keep the bells for The Plagued Ones, and the keys to the gates, on them. We will take those bells and keys to the courtyard. We will use the bells to lure The Plagued Ones into the Feeding Pen, once the guards are defeated. We will mimic the guard's orders and trap them, before we enact the next part of our plan."

A slight hesitation went through the crowd.

"Only the guards can use the bells," said someone. "The Plagued Ones will not listen. They will kill us!"

"We believe the bells, not the people, drive their instincts," Drew took over. "I think the ritual is so ingrained in them that it will not matter."

"What about Rudyard?" asked the first person to speak up, again. "He controls them. He is the reason they stay in line."

"I do not believe his presence is necessary," Kirby said, making the argument Bray had sold her on all those days ago. "Once they enter the gate, they will head for the Feeding Pen, out of habit. They will obey their instincts for food. Our words might not even be necessary. We will stock the pen full of corn, so they will go inside and feed. We will close the door and contain them."

"They are used to feeding at night," said another shadow. "This plan will be in the morning."

"It will be at a different time, yes. Our hope is to get The Plagued Ones away before Rudyard realizes what is happening. They will follow the bells to their food."

A few more people shifted, unconvinced.

"Most of you have prepared to fight a revolt for months," Kirby said. "Has there ever been a scenario where you did not expect to fight The Plagued Ones?"

A few people conferred with one another, but no one disputed her.

"If we succeed, we will have The Plagued Ones contained," Clara said, reinforcing Kirby's words. "If not, we will be prepared to fight them on our terms. Ideally, we will have many more slaves—*free* men and women—ready to join us. We will have the guard's long knives, and our weapons. We will be in a position that none of us would have ever dreamed, with the guards alive."

More in the crowd agreed as they heard unity in the leaders.

"If we fail with the mutants, we have another option in place," Kirby took back over. "We have found a path that might provide refuge, if we need it, through a mountain pass to the east. As we prepare to enact the plan, a group of us will work on breaking a hole through the eastern wall, large enough to fit several people through at once. We will have a backup strategy, should we need it. If we succeed, we will move on to the final phase."

"Our goal is to take New City as our own," Clara clarified, capping the discussion. "But this gives us another option."

"What is the last part of the strategy?" asked one of the shadows.

"We will storm The Gifted's building," Kirby said resolutely. "We will have hundreds of people at our side—perhaps more, once others join us—to take down the ten of them. My friend, William, the boy most of you have probably heard or whispered about, is inside. We will free him, and take The Gifted's weapons as our own. Once we have the building, we will have a stronghold to defend. We can pick off The Plagued Ones from the balcony, or however we choose. We will have the numbers—and the weapons—to succeed."

More of the initial excitement returned as the crowd envisioned an end to their enslavement.

"The gods know we have suffered enough," Drew told the crowd. "But if our fight is blessed, we will live out our lives in freedom, rather than under the heel of a guard's boot, or under The Gifteds' disdain. We will raise our families and our flasks in a city that is ours."

"Let us fight for our freedom, the way we pledged to each other when we started this group," Clara said, finalizing the plan. "Let us turn New City into a place of which we can be proud."

Murmurs of agreement rippled through the crowd.

Kirby looked out over the crowd of shadows, waiting for an argument, or a dissenter. None spoke out. They were all here for a reason. They knew what had to be done.

"Over the next few days, we will have a group working on the escape route Kirby mentioned," Giovanni said. "We will break a hole in the wall large enough to fit a few of us at a time. When we are finished, we will pass the word among us. We will let you know the night before we are to act. This will be our last meeting in hiding. Hopefully the next time we meet, we will be free."

"To our freedom!" Clara said, in a voice loud enough to inspire, but not to be heard outside of the small, dark courtyard in which they met.

The Shadow People raised their hands in the air, expressing their excitement.

With the meeting concluded, Kirby looked around her at the faces of the leaders in the dark.

"Here," Drew said, beckoning to the pile of weapons they had gotten out before the meeting. "You can help us pass them out. We will give four per person, so they can distribute them among their neighbors."

Reaching down, Kirby passed the weapons into one sweaty hand after another. She was surprised, but probably shouldn't have been, to see Teddy's face in the moonlight as he came up to receive a shank from her. They shared a look of resolve that needed no interpretation. A little later, a shaggy-haired man she had seen only a few times came up to meet her.

Gabe.

Gabe gave her a solemn, haunted nod in the moonlight. Neither had to speak about the battles they had endured in the courtyard. Theirs was a shared pain.

The next time they saw each other, hopefully they would be fighting alongside one another.

Chapter 54: William

William crouched near the balcony railing under the light of the moon. He smiled as he heard hisses and smelled the familiar scent of his brothers.

"Here you go," he whispered, projecting his voice enough so the twisted men below could hear him, as he had the previous handful of nights. They were acclimating nicely.

William dropped a few pieces of meat from the balcony, watching the shadows converge. A few hissed as they fought for the meager scraps of food. Finishing, they clawed at the rocks at the bottom of the building, as if they might scale the tower's bulky barricade. They listened, but they were restless. That gave him a hint of trepidation that he was trying to see past.

"I know this isn't enough," William said, repeating some of his similar mantras. "But we can get more together. I promise. All you have to do is listen to me."

A few upturned, bulbous heads looked up at him. In the moonlight, he saw a few glinting eyes. William reached into his robe, pulling out a few more pieces of meat and dropping it down to eager hands.

He stood, making sure the demons saw his robe as he threw down the last bits of his saved breakfast and lunch. He had eaten only enough to give him strength, saving the rest for his brothers. With each bite he fed them over the past few days, the demons grew to anticipate the sound of his voice, looking up to him, the way they had done so many times in the forest. But still, he hesitated.

He was worried.

The commands of The Gifted were ingrained in them. How well would they respond, when confronted with the voices of their old masters? Six rounds of his gun wouldn't stave off that many sets of biting teeth, if the demons decided they had enough of his placating words.

William looked past the demons, to the empty cornfields, and to the dirt path that was mostly hidden under the cloudy night sky. He remembered that first trip up the path with Rudyard, when he and his friends had entered New City, armed with more guns than he had now.

If only they had kept hold of them.

But even that wouldn't be enough.

A piece of that conversation came drifting back, as William looked out over the crops and the heads of the waiting demons. He remembered Rudyard's concern as he made sure to take their weapons.

"I will not lie. We are bothered by the items you carry, the guns. They upset The Plagued Ones."

Of course, they did.

William perked up, clutching the railing as an idea took root. He might have another piece to his plan.

He might have a use for the gun, after all.

Chapter 55: Kirby

Kirby dipped her hands in the wash bucket, cleaning dirt away from her calloused hands as she looked around her squalid hovel. Since the meeting, she had worked with her head down, neither talking nor looking at anyone, hoping to avoid another dangerous encounter. A new, sharpened shank accompanied her wherever she went. She envisioned all the other Shadow People going about their business, anticipating what they were about to do. Every so often, she met the eyes of some stranger on the dirty paths, wondering if they were one of the people who would fight alongside her. A few she recognized from those moonlit moments on the stones in Ashville, when she'd passed out weapons.

In whispered, passing conversations with Drew, she had learned that the hole in the wall was a few days from completion. In the night's darkest hours, a few of the Shadow People close to the eastern side of New City were loosening enough stones to create a passageway, covering up the hole before leaving each night. When the time came, they would leave it open. Kirby knew the risk of their actions. If someone found that passageway, a plan would turn to a punishment — not only for the involved slaves, but for all of New City. Who knew what the guards and The Gifted might do?

Finished cleaning her hands, Kirby picked up a rag and wiped her face. She blinked through eyes tired from days of constant focus, and a mind exhausted from nights ruminating. Not for the first time, she realized she was alone.

She'd seen little of Esmeralda in the past few days. It seemed as if she had been quiet, ever since Kirby had been caught in the city. Esmeralda kept her distance, perhaps afraid to break any rules. Or maybe she was afraid to get too close to someone who had gotten on the wrong side of the guards.

Kirby didn't blame her.

Looking around the small house, she saw a few dirtied pots and pans, crusted with the remnants of some cornmeal. It seemed as if Esmeralda had already eaten and gone back to work. Kirby hadn't even seen her going to the shops. She had always headed off before they could walk together.

Perhaps she was visiting Fiona at Isabella's.

Kirby stepped toward the doorway of the house and walked out in the bustling alley. Slaves scurried to and from their homes as they tried to make the most of their mid-day break.

Kirby strode over to the laundry, checking a few hanging clothes to see if they were dry before returning inside to cook her lunch. Looking down the adjacent alley, she was surprised to find Esmeralda standing a handful of houses away. Fiona was in her arms. It looked as if she was hiding between a neighbor's hung sheets.

"Esmeralda!" she called.

Esmeralda's face paled as Kirby spotted her.

Kirby looked over her shoulder, expecting a guard sneaking up on her. She saw no one except slaves. Forgetting the laundry, she walked toward Esmeralda.

"Are you all right?" Kirby asked.

"I'm fine," Esmeralda said quickly, coddling Fiona.

Kirby noticed she didn't look all that dirty, for someone who had spent a morning working in a greasy shop.

"I didn't see you at lunch."

"I ate a little while before you got back," Esmeralda said.

"Would you like to join me while I eat?"

Esmeralda looked around again before agreeing. Kirby walked back toward the house, with Esmeralda trailing.

"How is everything?" she asked Esmeralda.

"Good," Esmeralda answered, keeping her eyes on Fiona.

Kirby asked several more questions, receiving short answers. They fell into a strange silence as they returned to the house. Walking through the threshold, Kirby headed for the hearth to cook some lunch.

Esmeralda sat on the bedroll, setting Fiona down and half-heartedly playing with her.

"How has she been adjusting?" Kirby called over her shoulder, as she started some water boiling.

"She's...fine." Esmeralda hesitated as she stopped playing.

"Isabella has been doing well with her, while you are at work?"

Esmeralda murmured something that sounded like agreement.

Once the water boiled, Kirby started some cornmeal. "I am hoping the guards will release Bray soon."

Kirby turned, finding tears rolling down Esmeralda's face.

"What's wrong?" Kirby asked, abandoning the hearth.

Esmeralda kept her gaze down, refusing to meet her eyes. "I saw the guards outside of Bray's cell this morning." Esmeralda wiped the tears from her face. "I saw them taunting him."

"Bastards," Kirby grumbled. "Their treatment is nothing new."

"I am sorry for what you had to do in the courtyard," Esmeralda said. "I am sorry they made you fight."

"It is no matter," Kirby said, looking away as she battled some of the guilt that had plagued her since that day. Bray was alive. It was much better than another scenario.

"It is my fault," Esmeralda said, clutching Fiona tight.

Kirby looked up suddenly as the words surprised her. "What do you mean?"

Esmeralda slowly lifted her eyes. "I told Ollie you snuck out with Bray. It is my fault you were caught with him."

A realization slammed into Kirby as she stood suddenly, backing away from Esmeralda. She clenched her fists and looked to the doorway, as if another betrayal was coming. Perhaps guards were waiting outside for an incriminating statement. Only Esmeralda sat in the room, more tears filling her eyes. Sensing a change in the room, Fiona looked up from her mother's arms, a curious expression on her face.

"Why would you do that?" Kirby demanded, unable to believe the depth of the betrayal.

Esmeralda's tears grew worse, as she watched Kirby with a guilty expression. "I told him you snuck out with Bray so that I might buy more time with Fiona. I haven't been going to work, Kirby. That is why you haven't seen much of me. I've been hiding." Esmeralda looked as if she was waiting for the fist to strike her face. Holding up an apologetic hand, she said, "I did it for my own, selfish reasons. I'm sorry."

Kirby's eyes blazed with anger as she recalled the strange conversations she and Esmeralda had in the past few days. She remembered the suddenness of their capture, when they'd been on the way to Ashville. It made sense now. The pain they'd endured that night—and the torment Bray still received—overtook any sympathy she felt for Esmeralda.

"You did this to us," Kirby said, venom lacing her words.

"I'm sorry." Esmeralda didn't argue, or excuse her actions. "I saw you sneaking out a few times, meeting him in the dark, in the flooded house. Like I told you, I notice things when I am home. I figured it was something I could use. When I watched you and Bray in the courtyard, I saw the result of my words. It was an awful, selfish thing."

Kirby tried for more anger, as she looked into Esmeralda's despondent eyes, and at the child in her lap, but she couldn't find any. What could she do? Hit the woman? Unleash her anger, and lure in the guards?

Perhaps Esmeralda knew that.

Kirby had seen slaves give each other up for as little as a meal, in her homeland. They were products of their conditions. They lived on empty stomachs, fearing the repercussive beatings of the guards. They did whatever kept them fed, and their families protected.

That didn't excuse Esmeralda's actions, but looking at Fiona, Kirby understood them.

She didn't want to, but she understood them.

Esmeralda clutched Fiona, blotting away more tears. She shook her head, as if she might erase the damage of what she'd done. Surprised at where her legs took her, Kirby crossed the room and sat on the bedroll next to Esmeralda.

"What can I do to make it up to you?" Esmeralda asked her.

"You can tell me what else you told Ollie," Kirby said.

"I told him you were sneaking off," Esmeralda replied, "that is all I said."

Kirby watched her, gauging the sincerity of that response. For all she knew, she might be dragged off before she lived another day. But it seemed as if Esmeralda told the truth.

"I'm sorry," Esmeralda said. She had nothing else to give.

"I forgive you," Kirby said, and she did.

Hopefully soon, Esmeralda's betrayal wouldn't matter. The Shadow People would tear down the system that trapped them in lives of betrayal, hunger, and pain.

In a few days, the guards and The Gifted would pay.

Chapter 56: Bray

Warm sunlight stung Bray's eyes as he made his way across the courtyard, two guards at his side.

"You stink," said one of the guards, holding his nose, as he laughed along with his comrade.

The second guard prodded Bray as he walked through the bright light he wasn't used to seeing.

A few children near the edges of the courtyard ceased their play, as they saw something more interesting than rocks to clap together, or sticks to toss. A few women peered around their hung laundry. Through doorways, Bray saw people breaking from their hearths to watch him. He let the guards lead him as they brought him toward the house he'd thought he'd never see again.

"Make sure you clean up, so you don't bring that stench to the fields with you," said the first guard. "I don't think your buddies will like it."

Despite their words, the guards' taunts were half-hearted. Bray was a plaything they had expended.

Stretching his sore, stiff limbs, he walked the last steps to his open doorway. He looked over at the guards, waiting for an order.

"Make sure you're in the Shucking Room after lunch," a guard said.

Bray nodded as he turned.

An unexpected kick to his back sent him forward.

Bray stumbled, catching himself before he fell through

the threshold. And then the guards were gone. Teddy stood inside, waiting. He looked at Bray as if he were a ghost.

Before Bray could say anything, Teddy crossed the room and embraced him.

Bray bit back a swell of nostalgia he hadn't expected as they clapped each other on the back.

"You made it out," Teddy said. He stepped back and appraised Bray, as if he might disappear, or the guards might pull him away.

"I could use a washcloth," Bray said. "And a drink."

"Of course. I hope water will do," Teddy said with a smile, as he fetched Bray a flask. "I'm surprised to see you out."

"Apparently, I'm good enough for the Shucking Rooms. Another pair of hands to work."

"I thought I wouldn't see you again," Teddy clarified, shaking his head. "I saw the fight from the back row. I wanted to help..." An emotion ran through his face that Bray wasn't used to seeing. "I couldn't...I'm sorry."

"Don't be," Bray said. Voicing the question that he'd been waiting to ask for too many solitary days, he said, "Is Kirby alright?"

"She's fine," Teddy said.

Bray felt a surge of relief. Teddy looked past Bray and into the courtyard, as if he had more to say, and Bray was sure he did.

Keeping his conversation quiet, Teddy said, "I have something for you. But not right now. Let me make you something to eat. You must be starved."

Chapter 57: Kirby

The sun was turning from yellow to amber as Kirby walked up one of the pathways with her water bucket in hand. She turned down a few alleys, passing a few groups of chatting slaves, when she spotted Bray in the distance. He walked with his head bowed, his arms to his sides. Looking around, she spotted no one suspicious nearby as she walked fast enough to overtake him.

Bray looked over carefully. "Kirby," he said, his voice laced with an emotion she had missed.

"How are you?" she asked.

Putting his hand to his head, he said, "If that's how you try to help someone, I'll be sure to never make you angry."

Kirby hid a tearful smile. "I didn't mean to…"

"You kept me alive," Bray said. "I owe you."

"You do not owe me anything," Kirby said, swallowing a tinge of emotion. Looking back and forth to ensure no one heard, she said, "We are almost ready."

"Teddy told me," Bray said, keeping his voice low. "How long until the escape route is finished?"

Kirby felt a pang of nervousness as she spoke the words aloud. "Three days. The people working on it have been taking shifts. They have to work very quietly, of course. A few times, the mutants startled them at night, forcing them to go slower than they would've liked. They have to cover it up afterward, as you know. Drew will pass the word the night before we are to act."

"I'll be ready," Bray said.

A feeling overcame Kirby. Standing in the amber sunlight, she recalled those last moments before she had left her homeland. She remembered the fear behind the resolve in her comrades' eyes, as they prepared for their last fight to freedom.

But her feeling for Bray was stronger.

"Be careful," she said to him.

Bray reached over, gently touching her fingers for a split second, before breaking away, leaving only his familiar smell behind.

Chapter 58: Kirby

Kirby turned back and forth on her bedroll, looking from the ceiling to the dark sky out the open doorway. Long ago, the last, lingering conversations had quieted. The bonfires were doused, leaving a faint smell of smoke that reminded her of the wild. It would take more than a smell to convince her she wasn't living in this hellish place.

Three more days...

Esmeralda quietly snored from her bedroll, getting the few bits of sleep she managed before Fiona roused her for a feeding. Kirby turned, trying to forget her trepidations and the pain of her lumps so she could get comfortable, even though she doubted she'd succeed. Far in the distance, a yowling mutant reminded her of The Shadow People, creeping through the night and finishing the last few bits of the passage, before they committed to a plan that would lead either to salvation or to their deaths.

Forcing her eyes shut, she tried to envision the outcome of their plan.

Before she knew it, she was asleep.

All at once, she was back on that dock in her homeland, running alongside hundreds of sweaty, nervous men and women, as they made for the ships that would lead to their freedom. Kirby looked over her shoulder, glimpsing the silhouette of a city that had provided only torment. The people around her were mere shadows in the moonlight, their breath heaving, their faces indiscernible. Every so often, she recognized one of the people with whom she had shared a cell, a meal, or a conversation. Too many of those discussions had been about this moment.

And now it was here.

Kirby's legs felt as if they might collapse underneath the weight of her nervousness as she forged ahead, reaching the deck of the ship and hissing instructions to the others. The people around her moved with practiced, nervous hands, using their experience in the wars to aid in their freedom. All around her on the docks, she heard the quiet movements of a few hundred others, taking control of similar ships. Any moment, Kirby expected a stream of torches and a litany of shouts to expose them.

"Hurry!" someone next to her exclaimed, as she worked on a rope.

Kirby loosened a knot.

She pulled.

Shouts drew her attention to the docks, where the silhouettes of more people appeared. Not people.

Mutants.

A dream became a nightmare, as more and more mutants appeared, thundering up the dock, snarling and bringing their stench. Kirby panicked as she pulled on the rope on which she worked, only to find another knot, and another. She felt her way along the rope in the moonlight, frantically trying to get the kinks loose, as the mutants closed in. On the boats next to hers, she heard the thud of several mutants getting onto the decks. The screams of her comrades echoed into the night, as the twisted men found hot flesh and tore.

"Come on!" another voice yelled next to Kirby.

Drew's voice wavered in the dark next to her. She heard his fruitless cries as he pulled on the rope on which he worked, only to run into a similar obstacle.

A thudding footstep landed too close.

A shrill cry of terror pierced the air.

"Kirby! Look out!"

Kirby spun, abandoning the rope to find mutants everywhere, clawing, biting, and tackling her comrades. Her friends fought and kicked, but more and more fell, landing on the deck and screaming their death throes, or falling off the side of the boat and splashing into the water.

Kirby spun to find Drew battling a handful of mutants, screaming her name.

She tried to help, but a demon knocked her backward and away.

With a cry, she watched Drew fall next to her, succumbing to hungry mouths and digging fingers. Kirby pushed aside the lunging mutant and punched another, knocking it back. But more surrounded her. Too many. Somewhere above her, she heard her comrades bellowing in agony, or falling silent and succumbing to the monsters' tearing teeth.

Kirby shot upright, awake.

She looked around the small hovel she shared with Esmeralda, gasping for breath.

She reached for her shank, as if the mutants might be everywhere and closing, but she was alone, except for Esmeralda and Fiona.

A nightmare. That's all it was.

Wiping the sweat from her brow, she calmed her breathing and left her bad dream behind.

A nightmare.

Three more days...

Chapter 59: William

William sat on the edge of his unmade bed as he waited for the morning sun to rise. His belly felt as empty as the trays he had been handing back to the guards.

He steeled his heart. Months of searching in the woods, looking for Kirby's golden palace, had culminated in this. It was time to break free. What would happen on the other side, he didn't know.

Looking out the window at the sky, dark for a little longer, he recalled that first night he'd spent in the wild, after leaving Brighton. The stars had never felt as bright, nor the moon as full, as when he looked up at them from that first, tall building. He'd stood next to his mother, high above any place either of them had ever been. The wild had called to him in a way he had never known when he was a young boy in Brighton, with the only things he knew from stories, or the few glimpses he got through the front gate, when the soldiers returned from war. He'd known in his heart he was never going back.

It seemed as if William's life had stemmed from that moment.

He'd traveled farther and done more things than he'd ever thought possible, with Bray and Kirby. But it would end here, if he didn't break free.

When mid-day came, he would do what he planned.

The gods help him if he failed.

Chapter 60: William

Sweat poured down William's cheeks as he crept down the stairs, the heavy gun in his hands. Far below, on the stairwell, he heard the last footsteps of the guards as they returned to the bottom floor, heading to the city to get more food for The Gifteds' lunch. He paused, waiting until the door opened and slammed closed before he moved again.

Silence filled the air, save his nervous breathing and the soft pad of his footsteps. He traveled the flights of stairs, past the floors where The Gifted lived, past the windows that revealed the empty cornfields where the workers had been that morning. Only demons lurked there now. Reaching the last flight of stairs, he dug out his hairpin, listened, and heard nothing from the other side of the thick door. Not a whisper, not a laugh.

He had to work quickly.

Tucking his gun in his robe, he started on the lock, fearful that someone would pull the door from the other side and he would meet resistance. A complication might ruin his plan before it started. The door took a while to unlock, but it opened easily.

William's heart pounded furiously as he peered into a room he hadn't seen since those first days, when he'd taken the guided tour of the building with his friends. He scanned around the dimly lit area. A few pouches of the guards' food sat on the floor, along with their flasks. To his right, he saw the secured box where he and his friends had stashed their weapons on that first day.

He headed for it, hoping their weapons would still be there. Or maybe he'd get lucky, and find even more.

The box was unlocked. Swinging the top open, he found it empty.

To the left side of the box, he saw the thick door leading to the only other room on the floor. Pulling the doorknob, he confirmed that it was locked. Choices.

He might have a few moments before the guards returned with more food.

He could either spend the time getting through a door to an uncertain room, or he could do what he came here to do.

Tiptoeing to the opposite wall, he unlocked the entrance, inched it open, and revealed a sliver of daylight. Through the glare of the sun, he saw the dirt paths leading north to the corn stalks, the first rows of the shorter crops preceding them, and the compost heaps. William opened the door wider, drawing his gun.

No guards.

He scanned the wall that extended from the building, noticing the closed gate that led to a city he had never seen up close. He wanted to run into the sunlight, down the paths between the crops, and take solace in the trees and the comforts of the wild.

But he wouldn't do it without his friends.

Hisses drew his attention to several rows of lettuce, where a few demons appeared, aware of him. A few scratched themselves as they crept down the path and toward him.

More demons joined them as they saw something out of the ordinary. They approached in a cluster, getting within twenty feet of the doorway, trampling some of the crops. William's heart pounded as he realized he might've made a mistake. He gripped his gun tightly. Instinct told him to slam the door, run back inside, and head for his room. Instead, he reached into his pocket and pulled out a few pieces of meat.

"Here you go," he said, holding out his uneaten breakfast.

William mimicked the same tone he'd used on the balcony.

A few of the demons cocked their heads as they heard his familiar voice.

"I know you're hungry," William urged. "Take it."

He flung a piece of meat in the direction of the demons, about halfway between the doorway and where they crept. The first of the curious demons ran over and snatched it, chewing. William broke up the remnants of his meager portion, casting it out over the dirt path and toward the demons. They scampered and grabbed, shoving food into their hungry mouths, getting close enough that he could smell their unwashed skin and the blood of their previous night's kills.

They watched William with red, hungry eyes.

"I told you I'd come for you," William said.

He fed them the remaining food in his pocket as he spoke with them, until he'd exhausted the last of his paltry scraps.

With the food gone, the demons stood, waiting.

William looked toward the gate. Still no guards.

Finding courage in his voice that he hadn't used in too long, his confidence rose as he told the demons, "I know you're still hungry. But I know where you can get more food. Plenty more. Follow me!"

Chapter 61: Tolstoy

Tolstoy sat among his Gifted, passing plates around the table. A few grumbled, or cracked their necks, stretching from a long morning of reading and studying. Picking up a plate of succulent, fresh-killed boar, Tolstoy speared a slice and passed the remainder over to Herman.

"Thank you," Herman said politely, before passing it on to Leonard.

"I am looking forward to the change of seasons," Tolstoy said, to the agreeable nods around him. "The cooler temperatures should yield some nice arugula and celery."

"Hopefully, we will avoid the sicknesses of those below," Amelia said.

Doling out some berries, Tolstoy said, "Rudyard says we have lost a few of our elderly slaves who sorted crops. He will be talking to the Semposi about getting more workers."

"We need to make sure production is steady," Herman agreed.

Finished passing out the food, The Gifted prepared to eat.

Tolstoy looked around at his people, his Gifted. Tapping the table, he startled a few of his companions into setting down their forks. Clearing his throat, ensuring that everyone knew he had something to say, he started, "Too often we take these meals for granted, but perhaps it is time I spoke a few words."

"Like the old traditions." Herman nodded knowingly, adjusting his napkin.

Tolstoy set down his utensil, gazing from the window to the faces of his people. "Long ago, I stopped believing in any of our old faiths. I believe we have forged our own paths, through our intellect and hard work. But perhaps we should take a moment to appreciate what we have, what we have built."

The wart-covered people around him murmured their agreement as they raised their full cups.

"To New City," he said, catching Amelia's gaze.

Smiling, she clinked his glass and repeated, "To New City."

The Gifted tilted back their cups, drank several large gulps, and set them down, starting in on their food.

A knock came at the door.

Making no effort to hide his annoyance, Tolstoy said to Herman, "Dessert is early." To the guards on the other side of the door, he said, "Come in."

He started back in on his plate, chewing a bite of meat.

The knock came again. Louder.

A few of The Gifted looked over, but most kept eating. With an annoyed sigh, Tolstoy rose and crossed the room. Reaching the door, he put his hand on the knob and turned, prepared to scold the ignorant guards on the other side.

The door caved inward.

Tolstoy jolted back.

Shock overtook him as he saw a sight that didn't make sense, in his surroundings. Plagued Ones poured from the hallway, pushing him back into the room. They wove around him, heading toward the table, hissing and salivating.

The Plagued Ones screeched as they stomped into the room, surveying the full plates of steaming, odorous food and the people sitting behind them. A few reached for the plates at the table's edges, unable to control their hunger. The Gifted pushed back their chairs with panic-stricken faces, attempting to stand.

"Get out!" Tolstoy screamed, causing a few of The Plagued Ones to look sideways at him.

"No!" yelled an authoritative voice from the doorway, ripping Tolstoy's attention back to the threshold. His mouth hung agape as he saw a familiar, robed figure in the threshold of the room, fifteen feet away. Determination flickered in William's eyes as he pointed a gun at Tolstoy's chest.

"What are you doing?" Tolstoy managed.

Before Tolstoy could utter another word, loud cracks filled the air. Pain lanced through his chest as a bullet from William's gun thudded in his stomach. His shoulder ripped backward as another round found its mark. He struggled to find words, emitting only a gurgle.

"Kill them!" William shouted to The Plagued Ones. "Kill them all!"

Giving up on the food on the table, The Plagued Ones leapt onto the surprised, terrified Gifted. Plates fell from the table and shattered. Food smashed underneath crazed demons' feet. William's commands — and the gunshots — had whipped them into frenzy.

None of The Plagued Ones listened to the struggling cries of The Gifted, as they fought for their lives.

Seeing the blood leaking from Tolstoy's wounds, one of the infected latched on to his shoulder. Sharp teeth sunk into Tolstoy's skin as he screamed.

"Kill them! Kill them all!" William kept shouting, his voice growing louder.

Leonard cried out as a demon clawed his arm and he fell backward.

Savagely, The Plagued One pulled off a chunk of Tolstoy's wart-covered skin, leaning in for another bite. Tolstoy flailed and staggered, beating the creature's dirty hide as it knocked him backward in a blind stumble. More creatures stampeded into the room, edging past William and leaping onto the table to join their brethren, letting out hungry hisses. A few gorged on the plates of food on the table, knocking over glasses, sending more dishes shattering. Others twisted The Gifteds' arms and sank teeth into their flesh. In his peripheral vision, Tolstoy saw Alfred and Herman ripped from the table, while The Plagued Ones latched onto whatever warm bits of skin their mouths could find. Amelia screamed as two creatures caught hold of her hair, tugging her from her seat and onto the floor, ripping at her clothes and skin. The world became a messy blur of spilled blood and screaming, terrified Gifted as Tolstoy stumbled.

Two more Plagued Ones leapt onto him. He screamed as The Plagued Ones—his Plagued Ones—bit off more of his flesh.

Through his haze of pain, he saw William standing in the doorway, calm amidst the chaos.

Tolstoy's screams found no words as he took a few more unbalanced steps backward, groped the air, and found enough clarity to know he was headed toward the window.

Chapter 62: Kirby

Kirby clutched a bucket as she stood in line for water. The slaves in front of her talked nonchalantly, speaking of the late summer heat, or their children at home. A few impatiently peered around the others, annoyed by the holdup.

"Come on," an elderly man behind her grumbled. "I need my water."

Kirby barely heard him. Her thoughts were consumed by the plan. Every bite of food she took, every step, was accompanied by thoughts of impending doom, or success. Many more than two hundred lives would be affected by whispered discussions in the dark. What would happen when order turned to madness?

All she could do was prepare for Drew's order.

Shifting in the line, she felt the pressure of the shank against the inside of her boot as she walked a few feet with the moving line. She couldn't see past a throng of people, waiting their turns. With nothing to pass the time, she turned and faced the houses on the city's northern side.

And stopped.

A loud crash and a scream echoed through the air.

The people in line spun.

All eyes in the line turned toward the shimmering building.

A robed figure fell from the top floor, shrieking and kicking, the person's long garment billowing around him. Fragments of glass dropped behind. The screaming stopped as the person thudded somewhere below.

A few in the line dropped their buckets. Others stared wordlessly.

"What's going on?" the elderly man behind Kirby shouted.

"I don't know!" someone answered.

The line broke as people scattered, heading toward the source of the commotion. Slaves streamed from their houses with worried or confused faces, talking in excited shouts, trying to decipher what was happening. Frightened mothers pulled their children indoors. A few guards raced past the well, pulling their long knives.

Kirby raced after them.

Her heart slammed in her chest as she stared at the building while she ran. Another robed figure crashed through the windows, kicking and flailing, leaving another shattered hole in the top floor of the building. The person's scream echoed over the roofs of the houses as whomever it was disappeared from view and landed somewhere below. Screams and screeches rang through the air as a few naked, squirming bodies plummeted after.

Mutants.

Kirby kept running as more people flowed past her, bumping shoulders and crowding the alleyways. Mothers held babies tightly as they hovered in doorways, screaming questions without answers. No one knew what was happening. Weaving through several alleyways, Kirby reached the edge of the courtyard.

People clustered near the base of the building. Through gaps in the crowd, Kirby saw a string of guards hovering around two robed bodies. A guess became a certainty as she saw a wart-covered arm sticking from a robe. The Gifteds' bodies were splayed at ugly angles. Their bulbous heads were turned sideways; their mouths open to display lolling tongues.

Dead.

More guards joined a growing circle, shouting frantically and looking upward, where more mutants fell.

"Get back! Get back!" the guards shouted.

Looking left and right, Kirby saw more people streaming from the houses to the courtyard, keeping their distance as they saw what was happening. Looking through the blur of faces, she found Drew twenty feet away. Drew's eyes widened as he looked up at the building. A few of the guards shouted back and forth, already taking steps toward the front gate. Others spun in circles, shocked into inaction.

Drew and Kirby exchanged frantic glances, as an unexpected opportunity arose.

Whatever was happening might never be repeated.

It was time.

Trading a glance with Drew that she hoped wasn't the last, Kirby reached down, tugged the hidden shank from her boot, and screamed as loudly as she could, "Revolt!"

Chapter 63: Kirby

"Revolt!" Kirby screamed, louder.

Kirby looked behind her, spotting a few faces she recognized from the moonlit meeting the night before. Defiance flickered through their eyes as they realized the same things she and Drew had.

"Revolt!"

Twenty feet away, Drew echoed the shout.

More Shadow People took up the mantra, pulling shanks or sharp weapons from their pants or boots, screaming loudly enough to be heard over the commotion. Some of the frightened, uninvolved slaves raced away, shouting for their relatives. Others simply fled for their lives.

Kirby lunged toward the first guard she saw, a red-haired man with a long knife in his hand.

Pouring the hatred of too many beatings into her hand, she plunged her shank into his gut, doubling him over. The guard sputtered and stumbled, clutching his stomach, groping blindly. Kirby struck him in the face, knocking him to the ground. Straddling him, she ripped out her shiv and stuck it in his neck. The guard went still. Retrieving the long knife from his hand, she spun to find another guard coming toward her, a war cry on his lips.

The guard lunged, missing her. Catching him off balance, she stabbed below the ribs. Blood exploded from his mouth as she pulled the long knife out and stabbed him again.

"Revolt! Revolt!"

The cries got louder as more people took action, and more of the guards fell to the revolting slaves, who were spurred to action. The guards were simple men, inured to the power of their privilege. They knew violence.

But they didn't know war.

Many of The Shadow People had lived in the wild. They knew what it took to fight and defend themselves.

In the distance, she saw Drew fighting off a portly, dark-haired guard, swiftly getting an advantage. A few other slaves fought guards who looked as if they were caught in a situation from which they wanted to retreat.

A handful of indecisive, weaponless people stood near Kirby, torn between fleeing and fighting.

Catching their attention, Kirby put her rage into an argument. "Do you want your freedom? Fight now and take it! Get revenge on the guards who have enslaved you! Fight and be free!"

She pointed at one of the guards she'd killed, whose knife was still stuck in his scabbard. One of the men she addressed hesitantly crept over and touched the handle. A buried hope became a reality as he slid the knife out.

"Go and fight!" Kirby said, spurring him on.

The slave raced in another direction, toward a surprised guard. Some of his comrades followed suit, finding other dead guards and claiming their weapons. Others decided to flee.

All around her, the courtyard was a frenzy of madness — slaves versus guards. Gurgling screams bit the air as people on both sides fell. Some of the guards were caught in a state of shock, realizing a truth they had denied for too long: fear might have permitted them to rule, but they were outnumbered. Other guards regained their wits and used their knives to their advantage.

Kirby felt another burst of rage as she saw a guard stab a Shadow Person wielding a sharp hand tool, sending the man to the ground, dead. Kirby ran over and slashed the guard's throat before he could pick a new target.

Nearby, a group of slaves surrounded a frantic guard, who swung his blade in all directions. The men and women were weaponless, but they were testing their numbers. No sooner had the guard swung than a slave struck him from behind. The guard grunted and doubled over.

"Get away, you filthy scum!" he spat.

Pounding fists hit his back as the slaves found a weakness, beating him until he hit the ground. Groping, repressed fingers freed the knife from his hands, ripping it away. The guard flailed and kicked as he tried to get up, but the slaves' stomping boots kept him down. A slave stood triumphantly above him, to the attention of all, before burying the blade in the back of the guard's neck. A triumphant roar emanated from the slaves as the guard went still.

The mob was growing in number.

A shout ripped Kirby's attention thirty feet away.

"Kirby!" Drew yelled.

Blood streaked his face and his shirt as he came toward her. Lifting the weapon he had claimed from a guard, he pointed past several fighting groups toward the gate. Kirby followed his gaze. Most of the field was engaged in battle, but through the pandemonium, a cluster of guards ran toward the gate.

"We can't let them get out!" Drew yelled. "Who knows who is alive in the tower?"

Alarm coursed through Kirby. Drew was right. They couldn't let the guards escape. They might have the upper hand now, but that would quickly change if the mutants got in.

"Come on!" she shouted, running behind Drew and heading for the guards.

They skirted around several grunting people engaged in hand-to-hand combat, desperately trying to get the upper hand. In the distance, a few more groups of slaves headed up the pathways, chasing more guards who fled for safety. She scanned quickly for Bray, but couldn't find him.

Finishing their skirmishes, a few Shadow People watched Kirby and Drew.

"Come with us! We have to protect the gate!" Kirby shouted at them, pointing to the northwest side of the courtyard.

A few hesitated only long enough to glimpse the scenario in the distance. The guards were almost at the entrance. And if they made it, who knew what might happen?

Chapter 64: Bray

Unholy shrieks echoed over the din. Bray looked around the narrow, dirty alley, watching clusters of men and women battling the guards for their freedom. He didn't know where Kirby had gone.

He didn't have time to find her.

The revolt was on.

Clutching the bloody knife that he had ferreted away from the first guard he killed, he charged another enemy, plunging the weapon into the man's gut. The guard reacted in surprise, staggering backward and clawing at the embedded blade. Bray kicked the man in the legs, sending him tumbling and retrieving his weapon.

A shout echoed further up the alley.

A young male slave fought a Head Guard. The young slave lunged fruitlessly with his small weapon, avoiding a parry from the guard's sharp blade. Bray ran to help.

He managed to get a few steps from the scene when the guard stabbed the slave in the gut. Blood soaked the young slave's belly as he dropped his shiv and stepped back, clutching the open wound.

Bray's rage turned into a battle cry as he plowed into the guard, toppling him sideways. Screaming with the anger of all his scars and bruises, and too many days toiling in the fields, Bray reared back and plunged his knife into the side of the man's head, pulling it out. He returned to the young slave, who had shrunk down against the wall of the house, obviously in pain, but trying to keep a strong composure.

"He stabbed me," the slave whispered, as if Bray might reverse the awful action.

"Hold on to your stomach," Bray instructed, grabbing the young man's bloodied hands and placing them more firmly on the wound.

The man nodded, as if the simple act might cure him. The injury was clearly fatal. Of course, no healers could help.

"Bray!" a voice shouted.

Bray looked from the wounded slave to an intersecting pathway, watching a familiar man run in his direction. Teddy's face was smeared with blood as he said, "Some of the guards are going to their houses! They are locking themselves inside!"

Bray nodded as he looked from Teddy's hardened, determined face to the fallen slave. The young man's head had already rolled to the side; his eyes looked skyward. New fury drove Bray to his feet as he followed Teddy's bloody finger.

"This way!" Teddy instructed.

Bray ran next to him, heading up the path toward the frenzied mob.

Two frightened guards veered toward a home with a door, managing to get inside and slam it shut. The slaves pounded with furious fists, bashing the door, or clanging their weapons against it. After a while of pounding, they managed to crash the door inward, rushing inside and finishing off the cowardly guards.

A loud shout drew Bray's attention to a nearby house, which a guard had managed to reach, but not in time to unlock the closed door. His keys fell from his hands. Three slaves ripped him away. He spun and lashed out, catching one of the slaves in the leg with his blade. The man cried out and fell back, clutching his bloody wound. The others lunged, grabbing the guard's hands and confiscating the weapon before he could injure anyone else. They pulled him further from the threshold, throwing him to the ground and pummeling him with angry fists.

"I hear someone inside!" one of the slaves yelled, retrieving the keys.

He unlocked the door and pushed.

He met resistance.

Grunting, he tried harder. Bray and Teddy joined a few other tenacious slaves, fighting until the door gave way. A surprised, scared woman with two children leapt back, holding up a sword that was much too big for her.

"Leave us alone!" she screamed, waving her oversized weapon.

Bray looked from the woman, to the children, to the hovel in which they lived, which was larger than any the slaves occupied. An angry handful of slaves pushed past Bray and Teddy. A look of malice spread over their faces as they saw an outlet to their repressed anger.

"Kill them!" a slave shouted, rage in his voice.

"Death to the guards and their families!" shouted another.

The woman and the children backed into a corner. The woman's sword wouldn't last long against an angry mob, once an attack started. A few slaves took offensive steps into the room. Before they could get further, Bray shouted, "Stop!"

There was enough power in his voice to make even this bloodthirsty group pause.

The slaves in front turned to face him, surprised.

"They are not responsible for our slavery," Bray yelled. "They did not beat us, as the others did."

He traded a look with Teddy.

"Let them live," Teddy said sternly.

A few slaves stuck out their chins in defiance. One or two looked at Bray and Teddy angrily.

"They live their lives with more food in their stomachs than we receive all week," one man argued.

"They did not ask for it," Bray said. "If you kill or touch them, deal with me."

The slaves looked at him with intensity. Seeing the combative look in both Bray's and Teddy's eyes, they backed down and left the house. The frightened, shaking woman and her children remained in the corner, watching Bray and Teddy, as if they still planned something awful.

Bray plucked the keys from the door, throwing them toward the woman's feet.

Motioning toward her heavy sword, he said, "My knife will fit your hand better. You can barely hold that sword. Trade me for it."

"The sword is my husband's," the woman said, with tears in her eyes.

Losing some of his patient tone, Bray said, "Hurry. I won't ask again."

With hesitant steps, the woman crossed the room and traded the sword for Bray's knife. Bray hefted it. The sword was old and didn't feel as good in his grasp as his old one, but it was better than a shorter weapon in a fight like this.

"Lock the door when we leave. Don't come out until this is over," he instructed.

Together, he and Teddy departed.

Behind them, they heard the woman frantically locking the door.

Chapter 65: William

William stood at the threshold of The Library Room, unable to pry his eyes from the gory scene. A few of The Gifted — the first to be attacked — were reduced to mangled carcasses, bloody bits of flesh hanging around arms and legs. Others kicked weakly as the demons took the last of their life from them.

Those who hadn't been knocked through the windows probably wished they had. Their misshapen, bulbous heads bled from various bite wounds. Their robes hung in tatters. One or two pleaded to William as the demons ate them, but he ignored them. None had listened to Cullen's cries, when the demons ate him alive.

Fifteen feet from where William stood, Amelia lay on her back as demons gnawed on her legs and torso. To his surprise, her eyes were still open and looking at him.

"William," she whispered, her voice shaking with pain. "Help me."

Looking at her, all William saw was his friends being beaten and pulled into that city all those weeks ago. Any sympathy he might've had was stripped away because of her lies.

Soon, she would be a ghost, just like Cullen, or the people trapped in her glass windows, now scattered over the bottom of New City.

Spitting a mouthful of blood, her eyes left his face and turned toward the window. "You could have been one of us."

William shook his head. "Never."

He listened as her last, gurgling whisper went quiet.

Loud commotion drew his attention from the feeding demons to the windows, where shouts floated up from the city. Something was going on outside.

He needed to get down and help his friends.

He turned, ready to head down the stairs.

And stopped.

Two staring, frightened guards stood on the landing, looking from William to the gun in his hand. The blades in their hands were wholly inadequate for a roomful of demons and a boy with Tech Magic. William pointed his gun. Neither advanced.

Finding a moment of mercy, he said, "Go!"

He nodded to the stairs below them.

A vengeful thought passed through one man's eyes.

"Come on!" urged his friend, shutting down the man's suicidal fantasy.

They took a last look before darting down the stairs, their footsteps echoing down several flights. William was surprised, but probably shouldn't have been, to hear them screaming a moment later.

The demons in the room weren't the only ones in the building.

He'd left the door open.

**

William headed down the stairs, away from the gnashing of flesh in The Library Room. With each flight he descended, the cries from the city outside grew louder.

It sounded like a war.

The actions he'd taken up here had sparked something below. Or maybe something else was happening.

His friends were in danger. And staying in a lofty tower would do nothing to help them.

Heading fast down the stairs, he tensed as a few snarling demons came up and toward him. Building off of the power he'd reclaimed with the demons in The Library Room, William said, "The food up there is all gone. Come with me!"

The demons watched him with red eyes.

They listened.

Blowing a breath of relief, William continued down the stairs with his new brothers. Some of the twisted men had bashed down the doors on the other levels, searching for more food, exploring a place in which they'd never been allowed. They dug through the bureaus and tore up the bed sheets, turning a place of luxury into a place of ruin.

The Gifted would never occupy those rooms again.

Commotion from the next landing startled him. Holding up his gun, William approached slowly as a cluster of demons feasted on more human bodies. He recognized the stone-faced guard who had given him meals, and his comrade. Demons gnawed on their skin, pulling out their entrails. Next to one of their bodies, William saw a set of keys.

"It's okay," William said to the demons, using a soothing tone. "Keep feasting, my brothers."

He skirted around the bloody scene, carefully retrieving the keys without disturbing the twisted men.

On the bottom floor again, William paused. The noise from over the city walls had become a vicious roar. Shouts and pained screams wafted through the open doorway and to where he stood.

He looked down at the gun in his hand, which only contained four rounds. He needed more weapons, along with the demons he'd collected.

One chance to save his friends.

He spun, facing the locked door he hadn't had a chance to go through earlier. Finding the right key from the guard's key ring, he unlocked it.

Chapter 66: Kirby

"Hurry!" Kirby screamed to the running slaves next to her, as they chased the guards toward the front gate, cutting through the bonfire area. Up ahead, Drew managed to tackle one guard to the ground.

"Help!" someone screamed, pulling Kirby's attention away.

She looked over to find a woman struggling with a guard. The woman swung her bloody shiv with weak arms as the guard overpowered her. Momentarily diverted, Kirby raced over to assist.

"Keep going!" she yelled to the other slaves, who kept bounding to the gate.

She surprised the guard, plunging her knife into his back, sending him sprawling. Looking over at the woman, she found her on the ground, clutching a severe, bloody wound.

"It's over," the woman whispered, opening and closing her eyes as she held her chest.

Someone slammed into Kirby.

Losing her balance, Kirby hit the dirt and rolled. Her weapon flew from her grasp. Warm blood trickled down her face as she stopped on her belly, robbed of breath.

In the distance, she heard the cries and shouts of Drew and the others, clashing with the guards by the gate.

Kirby blinked and found the strength to turn her head sideways.

A shadow loomed over her.

Ollie.

Ollie smiled through the blood on his face. In his hands was his bloodied blade. Reaching down, he grabbed hold of her shirt, pulled her up, and slammed her back to the ground.

"Filthy forest-dweller!" he sneered.

Pain shocked through Kirby as he booted her in the ribs. She rolled with the blow and kept going.

Ollie stomped after her as if she was a bug he might squash underfoot. "You aren't going anywhere," he snorted.

A dam of violence seemed to have broken loose inside him.

Perhaps he realized the same thing as Kirby: whether they lived or died, New City no longer belonged to him.

Kirby pushed herself up on her hands, but another kick from Ollie's thick boots sent her back down. Her eyes watered with pain. Grunting, she lifted her head, noticing a few slaves who had fallen at the start of the battle, their expressions pale in death. Far in the distance, she saw the stomping boots of slaves and guards as they battled the guards by the gate. Screams and shouts penetrated the air. Slaves fell. Others cried out in pain.

Her life was a barrage of those images, because of the people in her homeland.

Because of people like Ollie.

Kirby rolled and jumped to her feet, avoiding Ollie's swiping knife. She backed off a few steps and caught her breath.

Ollie faced her with a snarl.

The expression on his face was clear: she was the obstinate slave he had beaten all those weeks ago outside the cell and pulled through the alleys of Ashville. She represented the death of a system that had provided Ollie the power to punch, kick, and rule.

And she would never forgive his beatings.

Kirby rushed past Ollie, trying to reach her dropped weapon, which had skittered to the other side of him.

Realizing her intention, Ollie slashed at her, hitting nothing but air.

Kirby leapt back.

"You want your weapon, forest-dweller?" Ollie spat, his eyes lit with rage. He kept between her and the knife as he jabbed in her direction with bulky, fat arms. "Come get it."

She scanned the ground for something else that might give her more advantage. Slaves had scavenged most of the available weapons from fallen bodies. Of course, they had.

She wasn't fleeing.

Kirby clenched her fists as Ollie came closer. She felt as if a courtyard of people watched her, cheering for blood. But the shouts she heard now were from the other slaves, fighting for their freedom by the gate. No one was in a position to help.

Forcing logic through her anger, she recalled the battles she'd fought as a soldier. Ollie had a weapon. She didn't.

She needed to get it from his hands.

"Come on, forest-dweller!" he roared again, losing his patience.

Ollie lumbered toward her on thick, meaty legs. She waited until he got close, turned sideways, and darted next to the blade, getting into the zone where he couldn't stab, as she had done so many times in battle. Kirby dropped a closed fist on his knife hand, knocking the weapon from his fingers. Rearing back, she punched him in the gut. Ollie grunted, but managed to plow forward, pushing his blubbery body against her and knocking her backward.

Kirby landed in the dirt on her face. A crack and a flash of pain told her she'd broken her nose. Blood dripped from her nostrils into the dirt. She looked for something— *anything*—to help her.

The fire pits.

Kirby crawled, spitting dripping blood from her mouth as she made for the charred remains of the previous night's blaze.

"Get back here, bitch!"

Ollie recovered from her punch, found his weapon, and went after her. Kirby's breath heaved as she crawled fast. Her fingers stung from the blows she'd landed. The blood from her nose felt as if it was choking her. A fat hand grabbed hold of her boot, but she kicked it off, buying enough time to heave herself over the circle of stones and into the fire pit's center.

She got hold of a handful of ashes and spun, throwing them into Ollie's face. Ollie cursed and staggered backward, clutching his eyes.

Kirby pushed herself upright.

She grabbed one of the more intact logs from the middle of the fire, turned, and faced him.

To relent was to die.

Ollie tried to wipe away the soot covering his eyes. She ran toward him, wielding the log in a double-handed grip, and swung. Ollie screamed out as the log bashed his fingers, and he lost his weapon again.

"Filthy bitch!"

Kirby swung again, as Ollie ineffectively tried to block with wounded, ash-covered hands.

"Stupid forest-dweller!"

He blinked through the ash and blood stuck to his face as he fought to see and defend himself. Kirby didn't stop swinging.

She couldn't.

She reared back, throwing her revenge into another swing of the log as she battered his face, knocking Ollie's jaw sideways. Blood erupted from his nostrils as she hit him again, and again, breaking his nose, as he'd done to her. Sharp ends of the log splintered into his face as Ollie screamed, and Kirby kept hitting, until she caved in one of his eye sockets.

Ollie fell.

Holding up his bloodied hands, he muttered curses he would take to his grave.

"Stupid bitch..." He blinked his good eye as he looked at her, venom in his expression.

His spiteful words ended here.

Kirby raised the log high above her head.

She finished him.

Chapter 67: Bray

Bray and Teddy raced through the narrow alleys. Mobs ruled. Everywhere they looked, slaves rampaged the filthy streets, brandishing their weapons. Some fought against the guards foolish enough to still battle them. Others battered at the locked doors of the homes where guards had barricaded themselves inside. Every so often, a door burst inward, ushering in a new string of cries and triumphant cheers as slaves swarmed inside.

Passing a slave's hovel, Bray saw two parents holding their scared children, waiting for the violence to end. More than one house contained the slaves who had chosen not to fight. In others, he saw bodies strewn about the floors, sprawled over bedrolls or amongst pots and pans, presumably victims of the guards who had slaughtered them. No one — not even those who didn't fight — were safe.

"Too many people are hiding in their homes," Teddy said.

"I do not blame them," said Bray.

"At least most of the guards in this area have been killed."

Bray and Teddy looked toward some guards running in the direction of the shops. Close behind, a group of revolting men and women ran that way to cut them off.

Bray felt a tug of trepidation as he looked north, in the direction where he suspected Kirby might be. "I hear a lot of commotion from the courtyard. We should get back."

Teddy agreed.

They headed north, stepping over bodies. A few wounded people stared at them from the surrounding houses, tending injuries, or receiving help from comrades. Children huddled close to each other, waiting for an end to the bloody battle.

They had just turned a corner when a group of slaves ran down an adjacent alleyway, screaming and obviously in pursuit of someone. Thinking they might need help, Bray and Teddy raced after them, passing between several dingy houses with cracks in the walls. The path smelled of blood and vomit. Catching up to a winded, dirty man who had paused for breath, Bray asked, "What's going on?"

"The bastard killed an unarmed woman and child," the slave said. "They weren't even fighting. They were in his way."

The man pointed further down the alley, where a boy lay on his back, unmoving, a sharpened piece of metal sticking from his chest. Past him, a woman lay on her side, fresh puncture wounds beneath her ribs. Both were obviously dead.

"Who killed them?"

"Avery." The slave swallowed as he spoke the Head Guard's name. "He ran that way. The others are chasing him."

Bray and Teddy resumed their pursuit. Veering around a corner, they discovered a mob of people gathered around a house. The bulk of the commotion came from the doorway, where a determined man smashed against the door. The people around him stepped away, allowing him a clear path.

"Face me, you coward!" the man yelled. "Face us! Face what you've done!"

Bray got close enough to recognize the angry slave.

Gabe.

Gabe's face still bore some of the bruises from the

beating he'd received after his fight in the courtyard, when he'd killed his friend Jonah. His eyes blazed as he battered the door with his shoulder. The other slaves stepped back, afraid to get in the way of a man clearly on a path for vengeance. Bray couldn't blame them. Gabe's eyes were lit with the same anger Bray saw the day he'd been forced to kill his friend. Blood covered his knuckles as he pounded the door.

"You are a coward!" Gabe shouted. "I heard how you laughed as you and the other guards pulled Jonah to the Glass Houses. I will laugh as you draw your last breaths!"

After some more pounding, and no response, Gabe hesitated. A few slaves disappeared around a corner, returning a few moments later with torches.

"Why don't we allow the gods to reap their vengeance?" a man proposed, sympathy in his eyes as he passed one of the torches to Gabe.

Gabe nodded as he accepted the torch. "If he wants to die a coward, let him. He will die in the place where he slept soundlessly, after he made me kill my friend."

Angry tears flowed down Gabe's face as he held the torch to the door, watching the wood lick the flames. The other slaves threw torches through the windows, guarding them. Slowly, angry, licking fire engulfed the front door, and the interior filled with smoke. Gabe and the other slaves waited until the door had deteriorated before they kicked it in, tossing more torches inside.

"Let me out!" Avery screamed, as if the angry mob might allow him to escape his fiery prison.

Of course, no one moved.

Avery knew better than to pass.

The room filled with more smoke and fire, licking some of the furniture and spreading uncontrollably, finding new things to burn, eventually finding a man's flesh.

From inside the dwelling, Bray heard the agonizing screams of a man who would rather die in the flames than let the forest-dwellers reap their vengeance.

But they already had.

Chapter 68: William

William's eyes widened as he unlocked the door on the first floor. Weapons filled the room, organized neatly on wooden shelves, hanging on pegs, or stacked on tables.

"Tech Magic," he whispered.

Guns of various sizes lay next to their ammunition, packed away in special cases he'd never seen. A few were slipped in pieces of leather that he knew were holsters. Many of the guns looked stranger than the ones Kirby had given him. Some were older, or constructed in a cruder fashion.

A few he recognized.

William took an excited step as he identified the guns that had been taken from them.

The demons behind William shifted, looking curiously over his shoulder. Others stood just beyond the doorway, waiting.

William needed to bring as many weapons as he could, to help Bray and Kirby.

Death or not, this was the end of his time in captivity.

Stepping toward the shelf, he grabbed the long gun Kirby had showed him how to use, all those months ago. The weapon felt natural in his hands as he slipped the strap over his shoulder and tucked Amelia's gun in his robe. He grabbed hold of the other pistol and a holster he had carried in the woods, placing them where they rightfully belonged.

A footstep echoed across the room.

Too late, William turned to find a swishing robe coming toward him.

Before he could react, someone slammed a fist on the side of his head, knocking him to the floor.

Chapter 69: Kirby

Kirby ran across the courtyard, leaving Ollie's body behind. She pushed away the stinging pain in her nose as she joined the embittered battle by the gate.

Running into the fray, Kirby slashed at a Head Guard with a thick beard and a thicker neck, cutting his throat. He keeled over and fell. She gritted her teeth and swung at another guard, hacking his weapon from his hand. He cried out in surprise as she plunged her knife beneath his ribs, sending him reeling.

Someone struck her with a surprise blow. She spun, facing a square-jawed guard with empty hands. Blood soaked his shirt and pants. It appeared he was making a final attempt at survival.

He wanted her knife.

Before Kirby could swing at him, he dove, knocking her to the ground. Pinned, she fought to keep hold of her weapon as he pawed her fingers with bloody, frantic hands. He released his hold on her weapon, striking her in the face. Kirby spat fresh blood from her mouth.

"I've got him!" a voice cried.

Strong hands ripped the man off her, throwing him aside. An ally she couldn't see lifted his blade high, jabbing it through the guard's back, and stopping his attack for good. The guard fell flat, emitting a final gasp. She looked up to find Drew reaching down and helping her up.

"Come on," Drew said.

Kirby smiled through her pain. "Thanks."

They looked around, assessing the scene.

For every guard, more than one of the repressed residents of New City attacked.

"I think we've beaten them," Drew said with a smile.

Together, they leapt into the smaller battles, assisting in finishing off the guards. When the last guard had cried his death throes, an eerie calm hung over the scene. The surviving people huddled together, assessing the condition of the wounded, or checking on their comrades.

Noises from beyond the courtyard drew their attention.

Not war cries.

Shouts of triumph.

A stampede of a hundred men and women raced across the courtyard, coming fast. A smile crossed Kirby's face as she saw Bray, Teddy, Clara, Giovanni, and James, and Gabe among them.

Wiping the blood from her face, Kirby crossed the courtyard to Bray and embraced him. Both were hurt, stained and bedraggled, but neither had suffered any injuries that wouldn't heal.

"Where did you come from?" Kirby asked, recovering her breath.

"Farther back in the city," Bray said, cranking a thumb over his shoulder.

"You have a sword," she noticed.

Bray's smile covered most of his face. Pride overtook his expression, as he hoisted it up.

"Are the rest of the guards dead?" Kirby asked.

"Those that are alive in the city will be dead soon," Bray said. "A mob about the size of this one is banging down the doors of one of the shops, where some of them holed up. They are ferreting the others out of their hiding places." His smile remained as he added, "The guards are finished."

Kirby nodded.

The guards might be defeated.

But she wasn't foolish enough to believe it was over.

Chapter 70: Kirby

Kirby looked around at the two hundred men and women in the courtyard, standing side by side around her. Their gaunt, dirty faces were stained and bruised from the fighting. Next to her, Bray, Teddy, Gabe, Drew, Clara, James, and Giovanni looked from the courtyard littered with bodies to the gate and the surrounding walls. They had only a moment to catch their breaths.

"What's that noise?" asked one of the slaves, taking a step backward as more noises filled the void of the fighting.

Snarls wafted from the other side of the gate.

Mutants.

Twisted men scratched at the walls, rattling the trinkets strung to the other side to keep the inhabitants inside. Anything with a brain and a hungry stomach could tell that things had changed in New City. The battle cries and bloodshed had alerted any demon within the range of hearing.

The guards were gone, and Kirby suspected The Gifted might be, too.

All that was left were the unmanaged demons.

The noise of hundreds of scratching, clawing demons was enough to put fear in the heart of any slave, especially those with only shivs, knives, and pieces of metal to protect them. Kirby looked around at the people around her.

"What happened to the others?" Kirby looked over at Bray, expecting more people to join them.

"Most of those with families ran when the fighting started," Bray said. "They hid in the houses further back in the city. Others hid, too."

With a grim expression on his face, Drew said, "We hoped they would join us, but the commotion from The Gifted's building scared them. They feared for their lives."

Kirby nodded as she looked over at the two dead Gifted. She still wasn't certain what had happened. But there was no time to figure it out.

"We gained some people, but we lost some, too," Clara said, as she shook her head. "Others are still in the city, chasing guards. More are dead."

"We never had time to finish the escape route," James reminded them, his expression grim. "The parts we removed are covered up."

A particularly loud snarl echoed over the walls, making the two hundred slaves tense.

"Should we try the bells?" Drew asked, looking over at Bray, Kirby, and the other Shadow People leaders. His face showed he knew the answer.

"I think we're past the bells," said Bray with a grunt.

"The demons are too riled," Kirby agreed, thinking better of an earlier plan. "If we let them in that gate, we might be overrun and eaten before we lift our weapons. It is too much of a risk."

"Then we'll fight them when they come over." Drew's eyes blazed with determination. "Certainly not all of them can get inside."

"I'm not so sure about that," Teddy said beside them, with a regretful look of certainty. "They will find a way. They have before."

Kirby looked again at the people around her—two hundred men and women with fear in their eyes, and weapons in their hands that were foreign to some of them, until today. When the mutants came over, fear would drive

---

some of these people from the courtyard to the nearest house they could find. Even well-trained soldiers fled when the realities of a tough battle hit them.

The people around her were tired from a long fight with the guards. More than a few were injured.

A scratching noise ripped her attention to the western end of the gate, where the scratching grew louder. The tone of the snarls changed. A filthy, dirty hand found the top of the wall, pulling and grasping. Its other hand slapped its way into view.

"They're coming!" Bray warned.

More than a few in the crowd gasped as a nightmare of which they had dreamed for years became a reality, and a beast pulled its ugly head over the top of the wall, snarling and looking from the wall to the crowd. It angled a leg over. The crowd swiveled as one, as the demon got the rest of its body to the top of the wall, dropped, and fell into the courtyard. It rose, taking a staggering step.

Hunger blazed in its eyes.

It ran towards them.

"Stand your ground!" Kirby yelled, hoping her words would inspire.

The people tensed. Men and women clutched their knives and shivs. Drew stepped forward in front of the crowd. With a war cry that echoed from his lungs to the approaching demon, he rushed to meet the creature, planting his long knife in its chest and pulling it back out. One of the creature's hands flew to the wound, but it took another step, its free hand thrashing and groping. Drew kicked it, sending it toppling. Standing above it, he thrust his weapon into its face. The creature writhed once and was still.

More dirty hands slapped the top of the wall. Three more bulbous heads appeared.

A handful of dirty beasts dragged their way over the wall, oblivious to the death of their brother. They kicked and clawed, swinging over the wall and falling to the ground, finding their feet and immediately running. Inspired by Drew, a few people took courageous steps forward, wielding their weapons. The brave people hacked and slashed, cutting the demons' bodies and fighting them back until they convulsed on the ground and grew still.

"That's what we have to do!" Kirby yelled. "Slay them as soon as they arrive!"

The people cleaned their dirty weapons on the ground, inspired by an easy win.

A hope became a plan. Taken a few at a time, the mutants weren't much of a threat. The two hundred men and women could pick them off as they came over, whittling them down until the last mutant was killed. Looking over at a few others, she saw victory flicker through their eyes. They had the numbers, and the advantage of a protecting wall. Their weapons weren't ideal, but they were good enough.

"Pick them off as they come over!" she yelled, to some more encouraging cries.

"Destroy the filthy beasts!" yelled a woman, bolstered with courage.

The snarls on the other side of the wall ceased.

The scampering of the demons died down.

"What's going on?" Drew asked, looking between Bray and Kirby.

"Maybe they realize they are coming in to death," said another man, hopefully. "Perhaps they have given up on the wall."

"Or maybe they are fleeing," said the woman, her knife shaking in her hands.

The crowd grew quiet as they listened. A few shifted impatiently, clutching their weapons with trepidation in their eyes. A few looked around the courtyard, as if an attack might come from another direction. Peering over her shoulder, Kirby saw only rows of dirty houses, scattered flasks and clothing in the alleys, and dead bodies.

Nodding toward the wall, Bray said, "They're still there. I can hear them."

Kirby tensed. It was true. The scampering and hisses were still audible, even though the beasts had stopped trying to get over the wall. The trinkets stopped rattling.

A scraping noise sounded from the gate's middle.

The gate creaked and swung slowly open.

Rudyard stood at the threshold, holding a battered, bloodied William, pressing a heavy gun against the boy's head. A mob of demons hissed behind him. Several Tech Magic guns were slung across his back.

"Stupid, wretched humans," he spat. "Now you will all die."

Chapter 71: Bray

Bray didn't need to inspect William up close to understand the beating he'd taken. Red drool dripped from William's cracked lips. His cheeks were swollen and bruised. He raised a swollen eye to the crowd, looking as if he was barely conscious. Rudyard choked him with a robed arm, pressing the barrel of the gun tight against his skull.

Rudyard's eyes roamed from the crowd, to the battered hovels, to the bodies of the slaves and guards. They stopped at the corpses of The Gifted.

"Stupid humans," he repeated, as if someone might agree.

His attention returned to the front row of slaves, stopping at Bray and Kirby, who had stepped to the head of the crowd. The demons snapped and snarled from behind him, clearly fighting an instinct to run, to feast. William mumbled something no one could hear. Rudyard tightened his arm around William's throat.

"You have earned your deaths," Rudyard spat. "All of you!"

Unable to tamp his anger any longer, Bray yelled, "Let the boy go!"

Rudyard shook his head as he returned a shout. "He will watch The Plagued Ones suck the marrow from your bones before he goes to his gods."

Behind Rudyard, the mutants grew more agitated. A few tripped over each other's feet, anticipating a meal that would sate them for days. Bray clenched his sword. He wanted to race to Rudyard, plunge his sharp blade past his sneering lips and out of the back of his head. He wanted to take his pathetic life and rip William away and to safety. But a few hundred demons would chew his flesh before he made it that far.

"Let him die among us, then."

"Among you?" Rudyard scoffed.

"We are his people," Bray shouted, angrily.

"His people?" Rudyard's voice was incredulous. "He killed his people, only to watch a pack of foolish slaves die. He has no people." He shook his head, as if he described a tragedy. "He could have lived among us as a god. Now he will die at my hands. But only after he has seen the last of you ripped apart."

Bray exchanged a frantic, hopeless glance with Kirby. A truth that had been only a guess was proven. William had killed The Gifted. He had done what no other slave could.

But that didn't matter now.

William wriggled weakly against Rudyard's firm grasp. Anxiety tightened Bray's chest. Somehow, he had protected William through the forest, the Ancient City, and outside of Brighton, keeping him from the hands of demons and men, only to have him die now.

Bray wouldn't break his promise.

Putting his thoughts into a battle cry, Bray ran.

Surprise leapt across Rudyard's face as he saw a single, darting man coming across the courtyard, ready to face demons and certain death. A few bloodthirsty demons, unable to tamp their hunger any longer, broke from behind Rudyard. Their dirty feet kicked up dust as they narrowed the gap to Bray. Bray tore open the first beast's stomach with his sword, heaving with the wind of battle. Swinging again, he slashed another's face before it opened its bloodstained maw. He knocked back a few more, killing them before they sank their teeth into his flesh. His rage was a furious cry, echoing across the courtyard.

Behind him, Bray heard the shouts and cries of his fellow slaves, joining him and running forward, but he didn't break from his fight. He focused on the demons in front of him, on Rudyard and William. Once Rudyard spirited the boy away, he would never see him alive again.

Everyone knew it.

A few more twisted men fell as they met Bray's sharp sword.

Barreling down a few more twisted men, he managed to find a break in the screeching mob, enough to see Rudyard and William heading through the gate.

Rudyard was leaving, and taking William with him.

"William!" Bray screamed.

He raced through a few more demons, avoiding them instead of fighting, making a last, frantic dash toward the gate, getting close enough to see Rudyard's sneering face and his tilted, wart-covered head.

Bray raised his sword and yelled.

Rudyard raised his gun.

A crack of thunder split the air.

An invisible punch struck Bray in the stomach.

Pain sent flashes of light through his eyes as Bray's sword slipped from his hand and he fell. A horde of demon footsteps beat the ground around him. But Bray didn't see any of that. The last image he recalled was William, writhing and screaming as Rudyard pulled him away.

Chapter 72: Kirby

"Bray!" Kirby screamed. A hollow, gutted feeling filled her stomach as she watched him fall. She'd only lost a few steps before she chased after him, but by then the demons were coming. She slashed aside a mutant, fighting for a better view.

Tears she didn't realize fell from her eyes as a mob of demons swamped the area of Bray's body, and the courtyard became a frenzied charge of them. Yowls and battle cries filled the air. Kirby sliced at a mutant, spilling its entrails, but not before another took its place. She slashed and hacked, trying to make it to her fallen friend, even though she knew it was too late.

That final, fatal gunshot echoed in her ears.

Rudyard and William were gone. The rest of them were trapped in what was probably the last, bitter battle they'd wage.

Kirby kept fighting, trying to get to Bray, as if she might somehow reverse what had happened when she reached him.

All around her, slaves battled mutants: hacking, stabbing, or falling under their pawing hands. A few punched with their fists, having lost their weapons, or unable to retrieve them from a monster's bleeding throat. Too many weapons were only good for one use, before they fell with a dying monster. The courtyard was a graveyard for mutants and men.

To her right, she saw Drew ramming a shiv into a beast's bony, wart-covered neck.

He paused only long enough to scream: "Keep fighting! We will win against them!"

Slaves gave frenzied war cries.

Pulling her knife from the groin of a staggering creature, Kirby plunged it in higher, turning a slow, fatal wound into instant death. Beasts and slaves fell around her as she fought to the place where her friend had disappeared. Four mutants hovered on the ground, feasting over a bloodied corpse. Kirby cried out in anger, ripping the first off, stabbing it in the back. Entrails dripped from its cracked teeth. She lunged for the other, pulling it off as she fought to preserve the last bit of Bray's dignity. Stabbing the demon in the head, she toppled it over. She killed the other two with jabs from her knife. With the demons gone, she stared into the face of a blonde-haired man, his mouth hung open in a last expression of death.

Not Bray.

Confusion hit her for a moment, until she realized Bray lay underneath. The man must've died and fallen on top of him.

Or perhaps Bray had crawled under.

Kirby managed to pull the man's body sideways and off. Blood covered Bray's abdomen. His hair stuck in all directions.

Surprise hit Kirby as his eyes rolled from the sky to her face.

"Am I alive?" he asked.

Kirby couldn't hide her shock. "You're alive," she repeated, glancing around her as mutants and people fought.

"Where's William?" he asked, through the obvious pain on his face.

"Rudyard has him." Kirby glanced around, as if the boy might reappear, even though she'd seen Rudyard dragging him through the gate and closing it. She couldn't think about that now. She couldn't even allow herself any relief. Swallowing a breath, she told Bray, "You need to get to the houses, before another demon finishes what Rudyard started."

"The demons are still alive," Bray said adamantly.

"That doesn't matter. You will die, if you don't get out of here," Kirby warned.

"Help me up."

Bray's groan turned into a grunt as she helped him to his feet. All around, demons and men clashed. Grabbing hold of Bray's shoulder, she steadied him. He found his balance, sweat running down his face.

"You need to get to the houses," she repeated. "Let's go."

"My sword," he said, with a stubborn expression she'd seen too many times.

"Forget the sword," Kirby said vehemently.

"We'll never kill them, without all of us to fight," Bray insisted, scanning the ground until he found the weapon a few feet away.

He made a move for it, until the pain in his abdomen forced him to stop. Helping him, Kirby bent to retrieve it for him, putting it into his bloodied hand.

"Thanks," he said, with the same smile he'd given her that first day in the forest, and all the days since. Bray's face hardened into a determination she knew almost as well as his smile. They both knew he wasn't leaving the battlefield. Bray watched her as he raised his sword, and some demons snarled behind them. He took another step, finding his balance.

With a grim smile, he said, "We can't leave, until these filthy pig scratchers are dead."

Kirby nodded.

Together, they turned against the advancing mutants.

Chapter 73: William

Rudyard choked William, pressing Amelia's heavy pistol against his skull as he pulled him back toward the building. William knew how this worked. One small squeeze from that Tech Magic gun would turn his body into a useless lump of flesh. He would fall and never get up. He would see, once and for all, if the gods accepted a frightened, infected boy. Perhaps the afterworld was a wave of endless torment, too.

He couldn't imagine a life without Bray.

William had lost one of his only friends in the world.

He had seen that final look in Bray's eyes as he made a frantic lunge toward the gate. *He was coming for me,* he thought. *None of that matters anymore. Rudyard will kill me, like he already killed Bray.*

"Come on," Rudyard growled, squeezing William tighter.

William couldn't answer. Tears rolled down his cheeks as he wriggled unsuccessfully.

"Dead boys don't need legs," Rudyard said. "I can shoot off a foot and drag you. Don't make me waste a bullet."

Fear made William cooperate as Rudyard pulled him through the entrance of the shimmering building. On the other side of the doorway, Rudyard let William go, pointing the pistol at the side of his head as he locked the door.

"Don't move," he said menacingly, as he kept an eye on William.

Rudyard's threat was meaningless. He was going to shoot him anyway. William's eyes roamed the room. For a moment, he considered fleeing and trying to get through one of the other closed doors, but the gun would punch a hole in him before he got far. His eyes were bleary from the beating Rudyard had given him. His legs were wobbly.

The sounds of the battlefield were loud enough that he still heard wailing and death cries through the walls. For all William knew, Kirby had died, too, and he had lost two friends in the span of moments.

Rudyard gestured toward the door leading to the stairwell.

He stuck the gun at William's back, forced him to open the door, and prompted him up the first flight of stairs.

William's hatred ran strong. He wished he could've watched Rudyard torn apart and screaming, the way the other robed men and woman had met their demise. Every one of them deserved it, for the pain and suffering they had caused. But Rudyard deserved it more than the others, for what he'd done to Bray.

If only he had been at that table with the others…

Rudyard's heavy gun kept him moving. They passed a floor before stopping on the third level. Rudyard ushered William through the open door, into the room in which he had spent too many of his nights sneaking around and plotting.

The demons had overturned the drafting table, scattering the plans of the plane that would never exist. Now they were in the city, feasting on the slaves.

William didn't even need Rudyard to speak the words to know where he was dragging him. He had heard what he said in the courtyard.

He's bringing me to the balcony, so I can watch.

Chapter 74: Kirby

With a ferocious cry, Kirby slammed her knife into a mutant's jaw, watching the stinking beast fall backward. For every mutant she killed, it felt as if two more appeared.

The demons fought with a recklessness the people hadn't seen in the guards. They flailed and squirmed, driven by their single-minded purpose. They valued their lives less than the people they attacked, or at least it seemed that way, as they flung themselves at their prey.

The men and women with the tenacity to keep battling were rewarded with more confidence. Each demon they slayed pushed them on to the next. The wounded stuck in groups where they could defend themselves more easily. A few of the severely injured limped off, huddling in the first houses on the edge of the courtyard, where they could recover.

More than half of the ugly demons were dead. But too many people had turned into meals.

Next to Kirby, Bray roared with anger as he slayed a demon.

It seemed as if Bray had received a second wind. Kirby had seen a few miraculous recoveries by soldiers in battle — men and women in the arena who had been counted dead. There was no question Bray needed a healer. But she held out hope that he would recover.

A scream drew their attention to a frightened, weapon-less man, encircled by three demons.

"Over there!" Bray cried, pointing his sword.

They raced toward the overwhelmed man. Kirby stabbed one of the demons, severing its spine. Bray thrust his sword in a mutant's shoulder, pulling it out and goring the third in the chest. They finished the staggering demons with killing blows while the grateful man darted off to find another weapon.

They had only taken a step when four more demons raced toward them. A shiv hung from the socket of one mutant's protuberant eye. Another had deep slashes on its arm. Behind them, Kirby saw the remains of a bloody gorging.

Anger drove her as she stuck her long knife in the face of the eye-demon, halting its progress for good. Pulling her knife out, she cut open another demon's bowels, sending it reeling. Bray lopped off a third's head with a heavy swing of his sword, while she finished the fourth. A feral cry made her spin.

"Bray, watch out!" she yelled, as another mutant latched onto his back and sank its nasty teeth between his neck and shoulder.

Bray cursed loudly and spun, sending the mutant flailing. It landed hard on its back. He stood over it, thrust his blade between its eyes, and twisted.

"Filthy beasts," he spat, removing the blade with a sickening squelch.

With a moment to breathe, he clamped a palm on his fresh wound.

A splotch of blood soaked his shirt. It looked as if the creature had torn off a good chunk of his skin. But Kirby was more worried about the bullet wound to his gut, which seemed to worsen with every step he took.

Before Kirby could ask Bray a question, he said, "I'm fine."

Loud shrieks drew their attention toward the northern wall of the courtyard.

About fifty feet west of the gate, a horde of monsters converged on a group of yelling slaves, pinning them against a wall. Kirby tensed as she saw what must be forty monsters. A few of the slaves seemed as if they had lost their weapons. More than one fought with their hands as they struggled to keep the beasts away.

"Clara and Giovanni!" she shouted to Bray, as she recognized a few of the punching, shouting revolters. "We need to help them!"

With fierce battle cries, Bray and Kirby leapt into the fray.

Chapter 75: William

Rudyard booted William across the balcony with a vicious kick to his back. William flew forward, catching himself on the railing before he fell. Thirty feet below, a fierce battle waged in the courtyard.

What looked like a few hundred slaves and mutants remained in various locations — enough that the fighting was impossible to take in at once. Demons lay writhing on the ground, or dead, with sharp weapons protruding from their corpses. Wounded slaves limped from the battlefield, or screamed their death throes. Toward the back of the settlement, a few demons ran through the streets, laying claim to a new wasteland.

William scanned for Bray's body, or for Kirby. His eyes riveted on a large group congregated by the northern wall, which seemed to make up the bulk of the battle.

Before he could find either of his friends, the tip of a gun graced the back of his neck.

"A last lesson," Rudyard snarled, pushing William harder against the railing, making him think he might die from a fall rather than a bullet. "Perhaps the most important. You will watch the rest of the humans die."

William found his hatred as he spat, "You will die, too."

It was a hope, more than a reality. Even if the slaves somehow survived and got the keys to the building, Rudyard would see them coming. He had several powerful Tech Magic weapons slung across his back to easily pick them off. He had enough protection to last him some time, and the knowledge to determine a strategy that might save his life. His death was uncertain.

An idea struck William.

He leaned forward to yell.

Rudyard yanked him hard, poking his gun into William's skin. "If you try calling out to the demons, I will shoot you."

"The slaves will win the battle, and they will come for you," William hissed.

"I will watch the last of this city crumble," Rudyard said confidently. "When it is over, I will decide what to do with the survivors, if anyone lives."

William scanned the battlefield, looking unsuccessfully for Bray. The mutants must have torn his flesh from his bones. They must have reduced him to an unrecognizable corpse.

Food for the worms.

"Tolstoy made a mistake," Rudyard said arrogantly. "Too much time in the tower left him weak. He built a city from which he was disconnected. Things will be different, once this is over. I will make sure of it."

"Your demon army is gone," William retaliated. Taking a hopeful guess, he said, "So are your guards."

"So be it," Rudyard said dismissively. "There are more demons, just as there are more humans. I can get more of both."

William swallowed a useless retort. Rudyard was right. Looking toward the large fight by the wall, and the other, smaller battles, he saw more demons than he could count easily. Scanning from one gory scene to the next, his eyes returned to the wall.

And stopped.

On the outskirts of that frenzied battle, Bray swung his sword, hacking away at a demon. A ghost? William blinked, as if he might be in the midst of a waking dream. But it was no dream. Blood soaked Bray's shirt as he fought valiantly, slashing at the demon with the same skill that William remembered, from their time together in the woods. Nearby, Kirby speared a beast in the head with a knife. It looked as if they were trying to break through a line of demons. All around them, slaves yelled their war cries as they steadily progressed toward some people pinned against the wall.

Hope flickered in William's stomach.

Maybe they would win.

But that wouldn't matter to William.

He would die on this balcony, at the hands of a vengeful monster who never cared if he lived or died in the first place.

William wouldn't let it end that way.

Swallowing what might be his last breath of air, he spun and dove at Rudyard.

Chapter 76: Kirby

Bray and Kirby fought their way through the screeching demons, trying to get to Clara, Giovanni, and the dozen other trapped people by the wall. It seemed as if the large batch of twisted men were the last sizeable group of the demon army, other than a few at the fringes of the courtyard.

But forty monsters were no small force.

Most had survived long enough to taste the blood of an enemy.

They wanted more.

Kirby and Bray killed the demons on the outskirts, as more and more people from other parts of the courtyard finished their individual battles, joining them.

"We need to draw them away!" someone near Kirby shouted.

Looking over, she spotted the source of the voice. *Drew.* Drew shouted instructions as he fought vigorously. Hope filled her stomach.

"Protect the people by the wall!" Kirby joined his rallying cry.

Near Drew, she saw Teddy, Gabe, and James putting up an equally stubborn fight. Bray swung his sword furiously.

They might win this battle, if they persisted.

Catching on to Drew's and Kirby's idea, Bray yelled, "Spread out! Make as much noise as you can to draw them away, before they overwhelm them!"

Bray inspired more people to spread out down the line

of demons, yelling and drawing their attention to siphon them from the larger horde. The trapped people against the wall stood in a tight line, protecting each other as best they could with fists and the last of their weapons.

Together, Kirby's group thinned the layer of twisted men. Some of the mutants fell into confusion, torn between attacking those in front and those behind. Their moment of indecision cost their lives.

Demons shrieked and fell.

Kirby's compatriots cried out triumphantly.

All around her, The Shadow People — and the other slaves who had joined them — made good on their whispered frustrations, fighting with more bravery than she could have hoped.

"Keep going!" Kirby screamed.

A scream ripped her attention to someone by the wall. One of the demons had broken ahead of the others, catching a mouthful of Clara's arm. Clara screamed in agony, pulling instinctively away, leaving a chunk of meat behind. Driven by the sight of blood, some of the confused demons refocused their attack.

"Clara!" Giovanni yelled. "No!"

He broke from the dozen trapped others and rushed to her aid.

Clara shrieked in agony, clutching her wound.

To Kirby's horror, the mutants swarmed. Clara's face was painted crimson as she flailed ineffectually and the demons tugged her down. Moments later Giovanni fell. The demons knelt, showing their naked, wart-covered backs, hunkering down and feeding.

"Giovanni! Clara!" James yelled in shock.

The rest of the dozen people by the wall panicked, making final, fatal attempts at fighting, or running.

With intermittent screams, they fell and were overtaken.

And then they were gone.

Pointless tears fell down Kirby's face as she fought. But there was no one left to save.

Blood dripping from his stomach and his shoulder, Bray found a savage cry in his voice, and yelled, "Kill these dirt-scratchers!"

More and more people joined him with ravenous war cries, pinning the demons against the wall. Hearing the cries of the angry mob, the feeding demons abandoned their meals, facing the oncoming people.

"Keep closing! Do not flee!" Kirby yelled to the others, as she listened to their invigorated cries and the sounds of the dying mutants. "We almost have them!"

They'd lost too many comrades.

But the battle was almost over.

Chapter 77: William

William threw all his weight into a tackle, crashing into Rudyard.

The gun fired.

The ear-splitting blast screamed in William's ears as he knocked Rudyard backward, pinning him against the glass window. Knocked off balance, Rudyard slid sideways against the pane. The world became a blur as William pawed, kicked, and grabbed for the gun.

Finding it, he pushed the barrel up and away as another blast filled the air. Rudyard flung up a knee, but missed.

William twisted the gun again with all the force he could muster, but Rudyard found his footing and his strength, pushing William back a step. William dug in his heels, keeping hold of the gun. A scream of death echoed from somewhere below. That scream would be William's, if his last attempt failed.

With an enraged cry, William put the last of his efforts into wrenching the gun away from him.

The gun went off again. Wet blood sprayed his face. William's breath heaved as he fell backward, pulling the gun away in his slippery hands.

Surprise hit William as Rudyard's eyes widened, and he looked down at a growing splotch of blood in the center of his chest. A realization crossed Rudyard's face. A snarl he could barely muster crossed his lips.

He took a staggering step, groping.

"Stay back!" William warned, thrusting the gun in front of him.

He pulled the trigger.

Nothing happened.

Amelia's old gun was empty.

Of course, it was.

He and Rudyard had expended the last of the rounds.

Rudyard's bulbous head sagged to the side, and his mouth parted open, as if he might issue one final gloat. He took a final step toward William, missing a grab, hitting the rail, pitching over. He made no sound as he fell three stories to his death, into the midst of the battle below.

William stood frozen a moment, waiting for the delayed pain that would let him know one of the gunshots had hit him, but the blood on his shaking fingers belonged to Rudyard. He turned and clutched the railing, looking down to find a few hungry, skittering demons racing from the fringes of the courtyard to Rudyard's unmoving body, slurping greedily.

They tore new holes in Rudyard's robe, burying their faces in his bleeding wound and making new ones, digging at his oversized head and making a meal of it.

Their former master was nothing more than a carcass.

Vengeance.

William had no time to revel in it. He looked from Rudyard's body to Bray and Kirby, who were still furiously fighting. It looked as if they battled the last of the demons.

Cupping his bloody hands around his mouth, William shouted with all the force he could muster, "Stop!"

Not one head — demon or human — turned. The commotion was too thick to make a difference from here. The rest of Rudyard's guns had fallen with him.

William needed to get down to the courtyard. He had to help them.

The guns… The guns…

William took the tower steps two at a time, ignoring the pain of the wounds he had suffered at Rudyard's hands.

Passing the dead guards, he grabbed a set of keys and headed downstairs for the weapons room, unlocking it.

William's breath heaved as he ran inside, pulled several long and short guns from the racks, and verified that they were loaded. He threw the straps over his head, tucking smaller weapons into his robe. Juggling more guns than he could use, he unlocked the main door of the building and raced outside.

He hurried for the front gate.

An eerie silence settled over the air.

For all William knew, he was too late. Finding the correct key took a while, but he managed to unlock the gate Rudyard had locked. Swinging it slowly open, he stuck the guns in front of him, prepared for an onslaught of unruly demons.

No demons came.

In the center of the courtyard, a line of a hundred dirty, war-torn slaves faced him with their weapons. He looked among the strange, bedraggled people. All around them, people lay motionless, with last, fateful cries of rebellion on their tongues. Demons were dead and scattered all around the battlefield, snarls caught on their lips.

The battle was over.

Not over.

Won.

Finding a face that he recognized, William took a staggering step.

"Kirby?" William's voice was cracked with emotional and physical pain.

"William!"

Kirby broke from the front row, crossing the distance to William, scanning over his shoulder, as if someone might come in and surprise her.

"It's okay," he called out. "They're dead."

Kirby squeezed William tightly. He closed his eyes, as if he might awake from a pleasant moment and back into a nightmare. After a moment, he leaned back and opened them. Kirby's face was skinny and speckled in blood, but her eyes lit with the same kindness he used to see every morning in the forests, when she checked on him.

"Are you okay?"

"I'm fine," William said, instinctively wiping some of the blood from his face.

The slaves — *free men and women* — in the distance relaxed.

A gaunt, serious man crossed the battlefield, coming within a few feet of William and Kirby and stopping.

"Is this William?" he asked Kirby.

William frowned, unsure how the man knew his name.

"You are a brave boy, for what you have done," the man said, a grim smile crossing his face. "You have helped us win this rebellion. I'm Drew."

Looking among them again, William directed his next question at Kirby. "Where's Bray?"

Kirby's face changed from relief to concern. "In one of the houses."

"What is he doing there?"

A strange expression crossed Kirby's face as she said, "Let's go. I'll take you to him."

Chapter 78: William

William followed Kirby toward the first row of houses, apprehension in his heart. Behind them, the people dispersed, checking on the wounded or the dead. A few stuck their knives in the last of the demons, ensuring that they wouldn't bother anyone again.

Others secured the gate.

Approaching the open doorways of the houses, William saw small rooms with bedrolls, pots and pans, and hearths — images he only imagined, from up so high in the tower. A few people stared at him while they tended their wounds, seeing for the first time the boy they had whispered about, or perhaps seen on the balcony with The Gifted. Tears spackled a few of their faces. William met their gazes only long enough to nod.

His mind was focused on Bray.

"This way," Kirby said, leading him toward a house in the front row, in the courtyard's western end.

He followed Kirby through a doorway. William's steps hastened as he saw two people inside. Bray lie against the wall, his sword in his lap. Another man knelt next to him, holding a cloth to Bray's stomach.

Bray's pained expression became a smile as he saw William.

"You made it, kid."

William crossed the room, kneeling by his wounded friend. His eyes roamed from Bray's happy expression to the bloody cloth pressed against his stomach, and the man tending it.

"Will he be okay?" William asked the man, a pit growing in his stomach as he saw the mask of buried pain behind Bray's eyes.

Lines etched a grave expression in the man's face, as he said, "He has some serious injuries."

"The healer is coming," Kirby said, as if those words might console William. She looked behind her, as if someone might be waiting to assist, even though everyone else in the courtyard was busy.

"They should be here soon," the kneeling man said.

"Who are you?" William asked.

"I'm Teddy, his roommate," he said.

William's eyes roamed from Bray's face to the cloth Teddy held, which was already soaked through with blood.

"Did the bullet pass through?" William asked, remembering the injury Bray had received all those months ago.

"It's still in there," Teddy said gravely. "It is too dangerous to try pulling it out."

William nodded through his falling tears.

Seeing William's expression, Bray pulled a weakened breath past his smile. "I'll be fine."

Long ago, William had learned to see through Bray's fabrications.

He knew what this was.

The expression in Bray's eyes was the same one William had seen too many times—on Rudyard's face, and on his mother's, when she had breathed her final breaths.

"We won, Bray," William said, forcing a smile through his tears, as if the words might heal Bray's wounds.

"Of course, we did," Bray said. "I knew we would. I knew *you* would."

Setting down his guns, William turned and sat on the other side of his friend, pulling his knees up to his chest.

"You killed them, didn't you?" Bray asked, nodding in the direction of the shimmering tower.

"Yes," William said, nodding through his tears.

Pride filled Bray's face as he said, "And here I was, thinking I was going to rescue you."

William couldn't find any words as he looked at Bray's wound.

"The bullet will leave a nasty scar," Bray said, keeping his smile. "I'm sure Kirby won't be too happy."

William looked from Bray to Kirby, who stood with her hands clenched. She tried to hide her imminent tears as her gaze flicked from Bray to William. For the first time, it seemed as if she had lost her words.

"Can't you help him, like you did in the forest outside of Brighton?" William asked helplessly.

"Taking a bullet out from a stomach is risky," Kirby said, her voice wavering. "It could do more damage than good."

"I'm sorry," William whispered, looking back at Bray.

"Sorry?" Bray laughed through a bloodied cough. "For what?"

"This is my fault. All of it." William's heart sunk in his chest. "It is my fault we left Brighton. It is my fault we wandered through the woods and came here. If we had not done that, you would be in the taverns, telling stories."

"If we had stayed in Brighton, we would be dead," Bray said firmly. "We made the choice together."

William looked around the room as if someone— anyone—might come in and change what he knew was unchangeable. He needed a reason to hope.

"No place has a guarantee of safety," Bray said. "We all know that."

William smeared tears from his eyes.

"I'm going to go help find the healer," Teddy said,

looking at Kirby. "Perhaps I will have better luck than Drew."

"I'll put pressure on the bandage," Kirby said.

Kirby crossed the room, taking over for Teddy. Before leaving, Teddy looked at Bray, emotion in his eyes.

"I never thought I would be free again," he told Bray, swallowing through a lump in his throat. "All these years of hoping, praying to the gods for vengeance for my daughter…"

"It was a brave battle," Bray said, with a smile.

"It was," Teddy agreed.

He squeezed Bray's arm again. And then he was gone.

William and Kirby knelt near Bray for a few moments, listening to Bray's labored breathing.

After a moment or so, trying for anger, Kirby asked, "Where is the healer?"

"Kirby," Bray said, loudly enough that she looked over at him. "Let Teddy worry about the healer. Forget the bandage. Sit with me."

She stared at him, fresh tears welling in her eyes.

"It would mean something to me," Bray told her, softening his voice.

Kirby watched him for a long moment, as if she might not listen. "I won't let go of it, but I'll sit with you," she said. Still holding the bandage, she occupied the wall on one side of Bray, while William sat on the other.

Together, they listened to the sounds of the people outside, cleaning up or stacking the weapons. Every so often, a happy voice cut through the mourning.

"The people are free," Bray said, pride finding its way through the pain on his face as he looked over at William.

William nodded, choking on more words.

Guilt crossed Bray's face. "I wish I could've gotten to you earlier, William. Perhaps I could have spared you some pain." He reached over, touching some of the wounds on William's face.

"You did enough," William said, making no effort to hide his tears. "You did everything. You were always there, since the first day we met. You followed me when you didn't have to. You looked after me, even after my mother died and you had no obligation to me. I never doubted that you were my friend."

"I'm sorry about your mother," Bray said.

"I forgive you," William said, and he meant it, as he gave Bray a sideways hug.

Memories flickered through Bray's eyes as he looked down at William. Neither needed to relive them, because they had experienced them together.

"All of those years in the wild, when I fought demons and men, or nearly froze or starved, I always wondered what dying would be like," Bray said, looking back and forth between Kirby and William. "But I never thought it would be as good as this."

Reaching out, he took hold of each of their hands.

William clutched Bray's bloody fingers. From the other side, Kirby leaned against his shoulder. Together, they listened to the sounds of free men and women outside, until Bray's soft breathing ceased and his head rolled serenely to the side.

Chapter 79: William

William sat against the outside wall of Bray's house, watching the sun set over the city as he picked up pebble after pebble from the ground, tossing them into the courtyard. All around him, men and women pulled away bodies, or used wagons to haul them off. Others tugged sharp weapons from the demons' skin, placing them in piles before dragging the twisted corpses to the Glass Houses. Finished throwing the last pebble from his pile, William pulled the hood of his robe over his face, hiding his ugly warts.

He couldn't cry. He couldn't think.

All he wanted was to disappear.

After spending the rest of the afternoon in Bray's house, he had asked Kirby for some time alone, thinking he might make sense of a situation he couldn't believe. All he had were questions. The more he thought about Bray's death, the more his mind grew numb. He couldn't allow himself to process it.

Eventually, he stood.

William walked over to a scraggly, dead demon that lay next to the house, staring at its cracked teeth and hollow eyes. It had fallen on top of its hands, with its head to the side. It looked as if the creature might push off the ground and find its feet, even though it was dead.

Maybe William should've died, too.

If he had died, perhaps Bray would be alive.

The thought was irrational, and yet, he couldn't help it.

A few chatting people pulled another dead demon corpse past William, pulling him from his dark thoughts. Seeing him lingering over the body, one of them asked, "Do you need help dragging it?"

"I'm fine," William said, after a pause.

Pulling his hood tighter over the sides of his face, he grabbed hold of the demon's arm and started pulling. It took him more than a few tries to get it moving, but eventually he made progress, tugging it toward the pathway on the eastern side of the courtyard, following a line of other people cleaning up the mess of the ugly war.

William kept his gaze straight ahead as he pulled the demon past some more corpses. More people walked past him, discussing the results of a battle none would soon forget. A few mentioned the people they had thought were dead, but found alive. William knew how this went. Eventually, the details of the battle would fade, until all that was left was the next meal, the next sunset, or the next war.

But that wouldn't bring Bray back.

And it wouldn't erase William's guilt.

William's demon stopped short, snagging on one of its dead brother's limbs. William bent to untangle it, inadvertently knocking off his hood.

Loud whispers drew his attention to his right, where two children huddled twenty feet away, pointing.

William let the demon's legs drop. His hands flew to his face.

Unapologetically, the boy said, "It's even worse than I imagined."

William hid his head in shame.

Guilt and fear crossed the little girl's face as she pointed a nervous finger in his direction.

"I've never seen a Plagued One," she said, her eyes wide.

William met her gaze. To his surprise, she wasn't referring to him, but the dead demon.

The boy next to her explained, "We've only ever seen them alive. Even then, we usually only hear them. Our mother keeps us away from the walls and the gates."

With a frightened expression, the little girl asked, "Do you think there are more Plagued Ones waiting to come in?"

William felt some trepidation as the children looked from the body to him. Surely, they must see his warts. Surely, they knew what he was.

Feeling the need to explain his appearance, he uncovered his forehead and pointed at his warts. "I am not like them. I am infected, but I won't hurt you."

"We know that," the girl said with a frown, as if he had told her something obvious. "You aren't a Plagued One. You are like The Gifted, except nice."

"You helped us win the war," the boy added.

A mother's call echoed through a distant alley. Hearing her, the children raced away.

**

"William," Kirby said, a worried expression on her face. "I was looking for you."

William tried to smile as she took up next to him on the pathway, heading back for the courtyard. "I was bringing some bodies to the Glass Houses."

"I know. Teddy told me." Kirby watched him. "How are you holding up?"

William looked over at her. He knew what she meant. "Bray was my best friend. I would do anything to get him back."

"I would, too, of course." Kirby looked down. "He died in the same way he lived — with a sword in his hand. He never gave up, even when death was close."

"I feel as if I was away for so long in the tower. I wish I could've made it to you sooner." William beckoned regretfully toward the glimmering building in the distance. "If only I could've..."

"You did everything you could," Kirby assured him. "Even when we were away from each other, he never stopped speaking of you. He would've fought a thousand demons or men to get back to you."

"I know he would have," William said, swallowing. "He was more like a father than a friend. He came for me when my mother died. He stuck with me when most would have abandoned me."

"He did what a father does," Kirby said with certainty. "He might not have been a father by blood, but he looked after you. He taught you, and made sure you had what you needed to survive."

William nodded through his tears. "And I will never forget him."

A distant look came into Kirby's eyes. It was the same, endearing expression he saw on his mother's face, when she spoke of his deceased father. "Bray had an honor that everyone could see, in the end. I am grateful for every moment we spent together."

William sniffled.

"Are you going to be okay?"

William looked over at her, blinking through a few more tears. Kirby reached over, pulling him into a tight hug. Together, they both cried, watching the sun sink in the horizon.

"You are not the only one who learned from him," Kirby said, blotting her eyes.

"He taught you?" William wiped some of the dried blood from his face.

"When we were imprisoned here, I wanted to give up," Kirby explained. "Bray convinced me to keep going. He lent me hope when I had none." She gestured toward the courtyard, where a man and woman hugged. "I never thought I would see another day of freedom. And most of these people didn't, either. And yet, here we are. Bray's persistence was a large part of that. He was a hero."

"You are right." A smile bled through William's sadness. "Bray always kept his promises."

Kirby nodded as she reached for her back, scratching at something.

"Are you okay?" William asked her.

"I'm fine," Kirby reassured him. "My warts are sore from battle."

"Mine, too." William nodded as he pointed to his knees.

Theirs was a shared pain.

Looking over his shoulder, William let out a shuddering sigh. "What are we going to do?" he asked, watching Kirby as he waited.

"As long as we are alive, there is hope, William," Kirby said. "We will survive together. We will keep breathing, because that is all we can do. Because that is what Bray would've wanted."

Looking at the orange sun setting below the wall, William said, "I think you are right."

Chapter 80: William

William walked under the glow of a new morning's sun, among a crowd of six hundred slaves as they headed along the path just outside the wall, next to the shortest row of crops. All around him, men, women, and children moved in tandem, holding each other for support, or staring up at a sky the youngest had never seen, beyond the walls of New City.

The survivors.

Most carried weapons, just in case any demons came from the forests, even though they hadn't seen any in a few days. To their left and behind, the creaking, spinning windmills turned, oblivious to the changes behind the walls. For the first time in many years — longer than anyone living could remember — the crop fields were empty, absent the sweating slaves and the guards' barking commands.

William turned his attention forward as they passed the western edge of the crops and came alongside the overgrown field Amelia had shown him from high up on the building's roof, all those days ago. Not for the first time, he thought that the square stones looked much bigger when he wasn't looking at them through the device called binoculars.

They kept on the path, walking past the rows of stones to a new area of overturned soil. Wagons and shovels sat near several long rows of plots that had been cleared from the overgrown weeds.

A new graveyard.

Stopping, the hundreds of survivors shuffled sideways, turning their attention toward four people who were already waiting at the graveyard's edge: Drew, Kirby, James, and Gabe.

Clearing his throat, Drew spoke loudly enough that even those in the back could hear. The people bowed their heads as they listened. Kirby, James, and Gabe stood silently next to Drew.

William remained in the front row of spectating people.

"No words can express the depth of our loss," Drew said, looking out over the grieving crowd, "but the people who lie in this new graveyard are among the bravest that New City has seen. They fought, so that the rest of us may have our freedom. They fought to break the bonds of our enslavement. They gave their lives in the hope that we will never have to suffer again. All are heroes."

Gabe, James, and Kirby nodded in agreement. A few women near William wiped away silent tears. Looking over, he spotted Teddy among the crowd, who caught his eye, sharing a tearful nod.

"Every step we take inside the walls of New City, or outside, will remind us of their bravery. Every meal we eat as free men and women will recall their courage. We will celebrate their lives by living ours well, and making the most of our second chance."

A few murmurs went across the crowd as men and women hugged each other, or their children.

Clearing his throat, James said, "All of us have suffered, starved, and lost loved ones, but this is a new beginning for all of us. These markers will forever commemorate our loved ones. Too many have been burned and forgotten. No more."

Heads nodded vigorously.

Beckoning to the graves behind him, Drew said, "We

would like to share the names of a few who have importance to us."

Kirby stepped forward. "Clara, Giovanni, and Bray, may whatever gods you believed in look after you. You deserve peace in death that life could not give you."

William felt a shimmer in his heart as his friend's name was said aloud. A few people cried as they grieved their lost relatives. Others stepped forward, reciting the names of friends or family members. The survivors nodded sympathetically as they bonded in grief.

"We have a lot to figure out in the coming days," Drew said. "But we will make those decisions as free men and women. Together, we will figure out where we go from here. We will live our lives in honor of those we have lost."

Finished speaking, Drew, James, Kirby, and Gabe motioned to the graves behind them.

The crowd dispersed, heading to their loved ones' markers.

**

Walking with purpose, Kirby and William strode to the end of one of the fresh rows of graves, stopping a hundred feet from the forest. William swallowed as he looked out over the vast expanse of strange, long-stemmed trees. A few people strode close by, stopping next to the graves of their loved ones, most of which were marked with crude lines that meant something to them.

"I think he would've liked it here, so close to the wild," Kirby said with a smile. "It was a good choice for his burial."

They knelt down beside a gray, unmarked stone, listening to the call of birds and the chirps and chatter of animals. William looked from the graves to the crop fields, where the demon army used to roam.

"It seems as if even the wildlife is relieved," William said with a sigh.

"I noticed that, too," Kirby replied.

They stood quietly for a moment, listening to the sounds of nature without the bristling commands of the guards, or the looming fear of The Gifted.

After a pause, Kirby asked, "Do you have them?"

William nodded, pulling out the chisel he'd taken from the shops, and the round-ended piece of metal that went with it. Kneeling down next to the square gravestone, he picked a spot on the stone, placed his chisel, and rapped on it, etching letters into the stone's face. Kirby watched with fascination as he slowly moved from one letter to the next.

"I've never done something like this before," William admitted, growing more comfortable with each strike.

"I think you are doing a good job," Kirby said, "though I wouldn't know, for sure."

William smiled as some letters appeared under his guiding hands.

"I'm glad we waited to mark the stone," Kirby said. "You had a good idea."

William nodded.

"It still fascinates me to see words written," Kirby marveled. "The owners in my homeland never taught us our letters. Perhaps you can show me, sometime." She ran her fingers over the first indent in the stone.

"I would like that," said William, as he finished. He paused to inspect the letters he'd carved. He'd had to guess at the word's spelling. Of course, Amelia hadn't taught him Bray's name. Pointing at the letters, he read them off. "B-R-A-Y."

"B-R-A-Y," Kirby repeated, with a smile.

Voices drew their attention to some people nearby. A man and woman walked over to the next grave marker, bending down and uttering some words. Noticing William's strange carvings, they looked over.

"Is that a name?" the woman inquired.

"Yes," William said with a pride tainted by sadness. "It is the name of our friend, Bray."

"I am sorry for your loss," the woman said. "Our son is buried here."

William offered his condolences as the man and woman quietly looked down at the stone in front of them, lost in grief. The stone had some of the same, crude markings as the others.

An idea took root in his mind. "Would you like me to carve your son's name?"

Slowly, hope filled the peoples' faces and they raised their heads. "You would do that for us?"

William looked down the rows of graves, watching the other people kneeling beside them. "Sure. I'd be glad to."

Chapter 81: Kirby

Kirby stood next to Drew in the tower on the eighteenth floor, looking out over the sprawling city, and the people walking between the alleys and houses far below. Over the past week, they had cleaned up the building, replacing whatever books hadn't been torn or destroyed. Most of The Gifted's devices were intact, as were the cases in The Library Room, and the guns and ammunition in the weapons room.

"Plenty of knowledge resides within these walls," Drew said. "Over time, it is sure to be a help to our people."

"You are right," Kirby agreed.

Drew gestured out over the city through the broken windows they had patched. "We have buried our dead. We have cremated The Gifted's bodies. We have guards stationed on more than one floor on the building, who are now trained with their guns. We have plenty of food, and the means to produce more." Drew paused. "Now it is time to start looking forward and putting new systems in place."

Kirby nodded as she listened. Looking out over the city, she wanted to believe in a better future.

"You look unsettled," Drew said, reading her expression.

"I am happy for every person here who has escaped enslavement, or fought for his or her freedom," she clarified. "I am happy for the children who will not have to grow up under the guards' or The Gifteds' oppression. I am happy for the women who will no longer be subjugated."

"Like your roommate," Drew said knowingly.

Kirby nodded.

"How is Esmeralda?" Drew asked.

"She and Fiona are safe. They have taken a larger home that belonged to one of the guards, as many others have done, like a few people I worked with. In time, perhaps we can house some of our people here."

"Or we can continue using the tower as a communal space." Drew thought on it. Noticing her expression, he said, "Something still troubles you."

"Each time I look at the streets below, or walk them, I picture the bodies we pulled through those alleys. Every time I walk through the courtyard, I have memories of what I've done, or memories of the pain the guards inflicted, as most people do."

"In a world as old as the one in which we live, I don't think you can find a place that hasn't been touched by pain," Drew said.

"You are probably right." Kirby sighed.

"You have suffered deep losses, Kirby," Drew said. "They aren't easily forgotten. But this place is much different than our old settlement of New Hope. We have a place we can defend. We have weapons, and a wall. The systems The Gifted built weren't perfect, but we can adapt them to our purposes. Perhaps we can find what we were looking for when we left our homeland."

Kirby nodded, trying to convince herself.

"Give yourself a chance to be happy, Kirby," Drew said. "After so many years of strife, you certainly deserve it."

Chapter 82: William

William looked around his bedroom. Weeks after the battle, he still recalled the times he'd spent huddled under his covers, thinking, planning, or listening for footsteps. Now those footsteps belonged to the free people who had volunteered to keep watch out the windows, or clean up the building.

He looked over at Kirby, who cleaned one of her guns on another bed.

"Without the protection of demons, we need to stay vigilant," Kirby said, turning the pistol she'd reclaimed in her hand. "We'll need to watch out for anyone who might attack us, like The Clickers."

"What will we do, if they come?" William asked.

"We'll be ready," Kirby said resolutely.

William nodded. They had enough people—and Tech Magic weapons—to ensure The Clickers were never a problem again. He sighed, looking past Kirby and out the window, watching the sun setting over the city.

"You seem tired," Kirby said.

"I suppose I am. I spent lots of my nights awake here," William said. "At least toward the end, when The Gifted were alive."

Kirby paused and set down her gun. She could sense William's unease. "You don't just seem tired. You seem restless, too."

William nodded. "I guess that could be true. Every time

I thought about escaping this building and finding you, I pictured things differently."

"How so?"

William thought on it. "I guess I always thought we would return to the wild."

"That's what I thought at first, too, until I met The Shadow People and heard what they planned," Kirby admitted.

"After so many months of travel, the wild seems more like our home than this place does." William shrugged. "Or maybe it is the memories I have here that make it hard to sleep. I know this place is safer than anywhere else we are likely to come across."

"And yet, you think about it," Kirby said with a knowing smile.

"I suppose I do." William's gaze wandered back outside. "But I know it would be foolish. You have a friend here. And we have everything we need."

"It has been nice reuniting with Drew," Kirby said. "I never thought I would see him again."

Kirby fell silent, returning to cleaning her pistol. She let the conversation die. Still, William thought he saw a faraway look in her eyes that he knew too well.

**

William tossed back and forth in his bed. He couldn't sleep. Every so often, he peered through the darkness at the bed beside him, watching Kirby's blanket rise and fall as she breathed. He couldn't stop thinking about their conversation.

The Gifted were dead. The slaves' war for freedom was over.

William should've been comfortable.

But he wasn't.

He peered out the window at a bright sky littered with

stars. The moon hung on the horizon, casting a glow that reminded him of the nights he'd spent creeping around, aching for his freedom.

Now that he had his freedom, it felt tainted.

The shimmering building felt like one of the Ancient's museums, bottling up the ghosts of the people who had walked its floors. Each time he closed his eyes, he heard the screech of feasting demons in The Library Room, or the death cries of The Gifted.

William tried unsuccessfully to sleep, until the first beams of light shone through the windows and he sat upright. He softly got to his feet so as not to disturb Kirby, crossed the room, and looked out the northern windows.

He was surprised — but probably shouldn't have been — to see a small band of travelers approaching from the forests.

"Kirby!" he hissed, startling her from sleep. "Wake up!"

Chapter 83: William

William, Kirby, Drew, and a handful of New City free men and women traveled down the stairs, past the secured doors, and out into the sunny fields, carrying their weapons. On either side of them, the enormous windmills creaked. Noticing them coming, the band of visitors stopped midway up the path.

"Keep your guns ready," Kirby instructed the people around her.

The men and women heeded her instructions. William kept his hand near his holstered gun. As they continued, he noticed the men wore loose white garments, with strange adornments around their necks. The visitors looked like some of the people he'd seen from up high, but never up close. With relief, William noticed they bore only sheathed blades at their sides.

"Good morning," Drew said to the newcomers, as they got within fifteen feet.

The strange men looked around the fields, processing a change from what they were used to. One or two eyed the guns warily, probably second-guessing their decision to approach.

"We are looking for Rudyard," said one man, looking back and forth as if he expected demons to spring out and ambush them.

"Rudyard is dead," Drew said simply. "And so are the rest of The Gifted."

The two groups watched each other warily.

Leaving no room for guesses, Drew added, "We own New City now. We are the new owners of this land, and everything on it."

William swallowed. He knew the importance of staking claim to a piece of land that others might try to take. To his relief, the men didn't seem as if they were in for a fight.

Stepping forward, holding up his hands to show his good intent, the man said, "My name is Xavier. Our people have traded here with The Gifted for many years. We would be willing to trade with you, too, if that is agreeable."

"You are the Yatari," Kirby said.

Xavier nodded. "We are here for a peaceful meeting. Perhaps we can come to a similar agreement as we had with the previous owners."

The men shifted nervously, perhaps wondering whether the people in front of them might take their things forcefully and kill them.

Kirby watched Xavier. After a long moment, she said, "You helped one of our friends, a while ago. A man named Bray."

A flicker of recognition crossed Xavier's face. "I remember."

"Bray is dead," Kirby said, "but we appreciate the help you gave him. Such favors are not easily forgotten."

Putting two things together, Xavier said, "I will admit, I am glad to see you standing here, and not some others."

A few of his men nodded their agreement.

Xavier continued. "It is customary for our people to give a gift as a gesture of good faith. If you are interested in our wares, we would be glad to provide you a sample, like the people with whom we used to trade."

"Are those shells?" Drew asked as he pointed to the bags, seeming as if he already knew the answer.

"Yes, for the glass you produce in the city, as The Gifted

requested," Xavier said. "Along with some other goods from the ocean. They are things you cannot easily get here, as you know."

The men stepped forward politely, placing the bags down for Drew, Kirby, and the others to inspect. Drew opened one of them, revealing an array of colorful shells. William's eyes widened with curiosity as he examined the strange goods.

"If there is anything else we can do for you, let us know," Xavier said kindly.

Kirby exchanged a long glance with William, the same expression flickering in her eyes that he'd seen in their room the night before. Turning to Xavier, she said, "There is something I might want to discuss."

Epilogue

Warm sunlight created a shimmering glare over the ocean as William and Kirby peered across the blue water, off the side of the boat the Yatari had traded them. A few birds swooped and dove, plucking small fish from the rippling water. Others soared on smooth wings, searching for prey beneath the ocean's surface.

"Do you think Drew was upset with our decision to leave?" William asked Kirby.

"No," Kirby said. "Drew is an honorable man, like Bray. He knows that we did what we needed to be happy. He was grateful you spent some time teaching him what you learned about reading and writing. He'll pass that knowledge to others."

"Perhaps we will be back one day," William said wistfully. Turning his attention to the vast expanse of blue around them, his face turned to wonder as he said, "I can't believe we are on the never-ending river."

"The ocean," Kirby clarified, smiling, as a breeze blew through her hair.

"The ocean," William repeated, trying to break his old habits. "I remember seeing it in the Ancient City, and in a few places we traveled, but I've never floated on top of it. The people of Brighton used to say that it goes on forever."

"Not forever," Kirby said, keeping her smile. "Or, at least, that is not what our people think. But a long way. In most directions you sail, you will find land. Or, that is what we've been taught."

"Who knows what sort of people we might find out here?" he asked.

"Other people, perhaps other civilizations," Kirby mused. "We can only speculate what is beyond the large piece of land we left." Holding up the map in her hand, which the Yatari had given her, she said, "For now, we'll keep close to land, looking for these islands. We don't want to run into a storm that will knock us off course, or damage the boat. Who knows? Perhaps we will like one of the islands enough to stay a while."

"We can be the Wardens of the sea," William said. A swell of excitement overtook him as he envisioned hunting, or fishing, in some faraway place.

Kirby smiled.

A soft wind blew from the east, rippling the water and running through William's shaggy hair. Leaning back, he felt a sense of calm he hadn't enjoyed in a long while. He'd never seen so much empty space around him. Kirby had told him about a group of dangerous, sea-faring people, but he couldn't envision anyone bothering them so far from land. He certainly felt safer than when he was back in the townships, or anywhere else they had been—perhaps even safer than New City. And they had plenty of guns from Drew.

Peering over the edge of the large, smooth boat, William stuck a hand against the opposing wind.

"I think Bray would've liked it out here," William said, with certainty.

Kirby fell silent a moment, reflecting, before a gentle smile appeared across her face. "I think he might've been wary about this contraption, but he would've gotten used to it."

William retrieved the flask he'd taken from New City,

which he'd marked with Bray's initials. He took a long sip, looking down at Bray's sword, which still hung by his side. Wherever he went, he would carry his friend with him.

"Did the Yatari have names for these islands?" he asked Kirby.

Kirby shook her head.

"Perhaps we can name them," William said excitedly.

"You'll have to write the names on the map," Kirby reminded him. "Or maybe I can try, with what you showed me."

They sailed for most of a day, under the hot sun, with only the accompaniment of some birds, or the occasional splash of a fish close to the hull. Sometimes, the sun shone too hot, and William and Kirby covered their faces with thin blankets. The water created a glare that made it hard to see occasionally, but was always magnificent.

Around mid-day, they snacked on some dried meat and figs they had taken from New City. William marveled that the goods tasted even fresher over the ocean. Perhaps it was the excitement of the trip, which made every breath, every sight, seem different and unique.

The sun was settling over the horizon when William spotted a small patch of green and brown in the distance, sprouting up as if the gods had dropped it in the middle of the water. He stood, taking out his binoculars.

"Is that the first island?" he asked, unable to stop his excitement as he looked through his device.

"I think so," Kirby said. Frowning, she pulled out the map. "Although it looks a little different than the drawing the Yatari made. Can I see the binoculars?"

He handed them to her, and she surveyed the island in the distance.

"Perhaps we have discovered a new place," she said with wonder.

"Maybe we can add it to our map," William said.

Kirby smiled. Reaching over, she took William's hand, as they watched the shore grow closer.

THE END

Afterword

Writing the last chapter of THE RUINS was bittersweet.

After ten books and three years of living in the heads of these characters, it has been hard parting with them.

Perhaps one of the most important story arcs of The Ruins (and The Last Survivors) has been William's. From his initial experiences as an infected boy escaping his township, to his journey with Bray and Kirby, William evaded death and endured loss. He forged his way through a ruined world with the guidance of his protectors.

In the end, he stood on his own.

Or at least, that is my hope.

As I wrote the last few scenes with Bray, I couldn't help but recall an earlier passage from Book 5 of The Last Survivors.

"The best thing you can do [for your children] is to teach them for when you're not around. They'll need your good sense to fall back on. That's the way to keep them safe. Like my father did for me. Like your parents did for you." – **Bray**

I'd like to think William and Kirby found their golden palace in the clouds. The gods know they have both earned it.

It is possible I'll return to the world of THE RUINS, but for now, the story is concluded.

For those wondering what is coming next, I have several projects on the horizon. The closest to THE RUINS – at least in tone – will be a sci-fi novel called SANDSTORM, set on a desert planet in a post-apocalyptic setting.

If you'd like to be the first to know when SANDSTORM comes out, or other stories similar to THE RUINS, sign up for my email newsletter at **http://eepurl.com/qy_SH**. I usually send emails out about once a month, telling you about new releases or specials on my other books.

From the bottom of my heart, thank you for sticking with THE RUINS. I hope you have enjoyed the series. I'll talk to you soon!

Tyler Piperbrook

-January 2018

P.S. **If you enjoyed THE RUINS books, please leave a review!**

Email & Facebook

If you're interested in getting an email when books like **THE RUINS** come out, sign up for T.W. Piperbrook's newsletter at: **http://eepurl.com/qy_SH**.

You'll periodically get updates on other books but no spam. Unsubscribe at any time.

If you'd like to get a bit more involved, you can find me on **Facebook** at:

http://www.facebook.com/twpiperbrook

Other Things To Read

Haven't read **CONTAMINATION**? It's a fast-paced, action-oriented zombie series with a twist. You can check it out now on all retailers.

Made in the USA
Columbia, SC
31 March 2018